PLIGHT OF THE T(

Published by:

BATFIRE PRESS LLC.

P.O. BOX 30
Mena, Arkansas 71953

(479) 394-5058

Second printing

Artwork by Bill Wells

Graphics: Powell Advertising

ISBN 978-0-615-14665-2

ACKNOWLEDGEMENTS

First and foremost, I'd like to thank everyone who has a sense of humor for selecting this novel. I'm certain you'll have as much fun reading this book as I did writing it.

My editor Doug Patrick, artist Bill Wells, and lifelong friend Key Anderson were steadfast in their commitments to excellence and supportive ideas. Before going to press, local editors Jay Strasner and Andy Philpot offered to review and critique this manuscript. Without everyone's assistance, none of this would have been possible.

Even though she's not a writer, my wife Alicia probably worked the hardest at this project because she was forced to believe in me. Now that takes a special amount of faith, especially when our creditors started calling and I refused to leave my desk.

Mom and dad were skeptical until I proved myself worthy by landing a couple of freelance assignments for some popular sporting publications. Establishing credibility was easy, but convincing family was tough. Now that I'm finished, they're all telling me, "We knew you could do it."

Death…Lurking in the shadows at a friendly neighborhood park

PLIGHT OF THE TOOTHLESS VAMPIRE

By Steve Stillwell

CHAPTER 1, CHRISTMAS PLIGHT

It was a cold December night, colder than usual for Houston, Texas, weather. The weekend forecast predicted freezing rain followed by another cold front. Chester Watkins stepped outside of his modest suburban home and looked at the thermometer on his porch.

"Twenty-four degrees," he mumbled.

Christmas lights flickered throughout the neighborhood as he buttoned his coat and surveyed his surroundings. Things looked unusually quiet that evening, and he liked it that way. The previous week, a group of sneaky, night-stalking vandals wreaked havoc on their street, knocking over trashcans and purposely spilling the contents in the middle of several targeted yards. Chester's mailbox was stolen, and all of the bags of leaves he carefully raked were torn open and littered in his driveway. He considered himself fortunate because the people living next door to him suffered far more damage than anyone.

The 84-year-old man was depressed, and he hated this time of year. His wife Ruby died from lung cancer three years before on Christmas Eve, and when he looked around at all of the decorations he was constantly reminded of her passing. They were happily married for 51 years and now he was alone. Being considerately mindful of his wife's terminal condition while she was still alive, Watkins stopped smoking indoors and began walking as an escape to smoke his expensive cigars and much-needed cigarettes. No matter how hard he tried, he just couldn't break the habit. Nicotine gum, patches and self-help books written by the positive-thinking gurus compelled him to indulge even more, so eventually he gave up.

The voices in his head continued to torment him as he fired up his fat, imported cigar. *"Mr. Watkins, your wife's lung cancer is a result of secondhand smoke."*

Aware of the icy conditions, the old man cautiously felt his way a step at a time down the concrete stairs of his porch. With cane in hand, he puffed his cigar like a slow-moving locomotive and shuffled his way to the end of his sidewalk, never looking back. His walks were pretty routine, taking him to the end of the block past the Thornton place and then over to the next street, which paralleled a drainage ditch. The empty lot next to the neighborhood park was his marker, and from there he would circle back. The property sported a "For Sale" sign in the middle and a bright streetlight was positioned directly in front of the curb illuminating the immediate area.

The trashy park was a pitiful sight. It was dark, eerie and the public buildings were in dire need of painting and repair. Most of the lights didn't work because they had been shot out by the local juvenile delinquents who marauded at night with their pellet guns, and the adjacent sidewalk was littered from the fragments of broken glass. In the old man's opinion, to venture near the playgrounds after dark only invited trouble, so he always steered clear. The walk usually lasted about half an hour if he didn't stop to talk to any neighbors, and tonight he knew this would be the case.

As Watkins rounded the block, he could see a row of lights evenly spaced through the neighborhood extending to the lot at the end of the street. The old-timer pressed forward and noticed a Nativity display in one of the front yards and pondered to himself, *"I thought Mary and Joseph were white."*

Another display caught his attention. This one had a big, plastic red devil with horns clasping a pitchfork and standing in Santa's sleigh. A sign next to the reindeer read: "Satan Claus."

The old man busted out laughing until he began to wheeze and cough, spitting up tobacco phlegm. The purple-faced, oxygen-deprived man grunted loudly, clearing his throat and spit a slime ball at the devil, hitting it in the face.

"This neighborhood has gone to hell."

Chester continued his journey, but when he reached the lot he noticed something lurking in the shadows behind a tree in the dimly lit park. He squinted and adjusted his glasses, but he couldn't make out the figure. An instinctive fear swept over the man as he did an about-face and retreated in the opposite direction. When he turned his head to look back, a shapely girl emerged from the darkness and she looked like a skimpy-dressed harlot.

Watkins thought to himself, *"It's 24 degrees and this kid isn't wearing a coat. She must be on dope."*

Chester made his way to the first house next to the lot, and when he turned his head a second time to look, the girl was only a few feet behind him. The old man whirled around and extended his cane with both hands like he was trained to do in the Marine Corps during bayonet practice.

"One more step you little witch and I'll take out both of your lungs."

The wary man noticed that the girl was deathly white and she was wearing a black miniskirt and matching short sleeve blouse. As he looked into her dark, lifeless eyes, he knew something was seriously wrong. Suddenly, she convulsed and displayed a sinister smile revealing sharp, pearly-white fangs.

He began to reason in his mind, *"I survived World War II. I'm a combat veteran. Tarawa and Guadalcanal, I fought the Japanese and now some punk girl on crack is going to do me in. The boys at the VFW and American Legion would laugh their asses off if they saw me now."*

In an attempt to gain an advantage, Watkins charged with his cane and yelled, "I'm going to knock those stupid-looking teeth out of your head and send your ass to the orthodontist!"

The young girl stepped aside causing the old Marine to flail at the air and she laughed at him saying, "You missed me."

In his next breath, Chester screamed, "Parry Left!" and struck the surprised teenager with a stabbing blow in the stomach. The determined man pulled back, swooping upward as the girl cringed and fell backwards onto the sidewalk. Watkins reassessed his situation and thought he just might have enough wits to win this fight.

With the cigar dangling from his mouth, the cocky man looked down at the dizzy-looking girl and said, "Well, princess, are you ready to give up or do you want me to put this cigar out on your face next?"

Suddenly, the teenager leaped to her feet and snatched the walking stick out of the former Marine's hands, snapping it in two. Watkins stood there with a puzzled look on his face as she politely smiled and handed both pieces back to him.

"You old bastard, you hit me and that hurt. You're in for it now."

With a sweeping kick to his legs, the senior citizen was toppled head first to the ground. When his face hit the sidewalk, his cigar and false teeth were simultaneously spit out. Dazed, Chester opened his eyes just in time to see his chattering dentures roll across the sidewalk and into the street.

The young girl rolled her victim over and hissed as her hands fanned away stagnant cigar smoke. "Nothing personal gramps, I'm just hungry."

When she bit into his neck, the sharp jolt into Chester's jugular caused him to regain consciousness. As the life-giving blood was being sucked from his body, the helpless man emptied his bowels causing the vampire to gag and choke as she fed. Coming up for air, she complained, "You stinky old man, you shit your pants."

Too weak to continue the fight and barely clinging to life, Chester lay motionless as she dragged his body into the shadows toward the drainage ditch to finish him off. In his last breath, the condemned man faintly whispered, "I thought vampires were folklore."

With a malicious smile, the young girl looked into the dying man's eyes. "That's what I thought too."

The next day, Chester's rigid, lifeless corpse was discovered in the polluted, trash-riddled gully. His body floated for several hundred yards in the icy waters and lodged in a connecting pipe, prompting utility workers to respond. In an attempt to unclog the channel, one of the laborers used a large aluminum pole to try and free the clump of leaves, beer bottles and debris he saw blocking the pipeline. When the heavy mass broke loose, a shower of icy water and mud spewed into the man's face causing him to throw his arms up and close his eyes. As he regained his composure, he looked down at his wet feet and let out a shrieking cry when he saw the blank, cross-eyed face staring up at him. The work crew's foreman immediately contacted the authorities and pleaded with them to send an ambulance for his hysterical worker who fainted after seeing a minnow wiggle out of the dead man's mouth.

A hasty police report was filed and the small puncture wounds in the cadaver's neck were noted, but for the most part ignored. After the cops finished their paperwork, the old, blue stiff was pulled from the ditch and loaded into the coroner's van. From there, it would be transported downtown for an autopsy, identification and notification of any family members, if there were any to be located.

Upon arrival at the city morgue, the senior coroner, who was an experienced professional in regards to forensic science, did a quick inspection of the victim. When he observed the bite marks on the man's neck, he quickly recognized them for what they were. Calling for his assistant, who was still in training, the supervisor slapped his hand on the table. "Dennis, get in here quick!"

"What is it?" the trainee replied.

"Vampirism is a guarded secret among morticians and this isn't something that your college professor is allowed to teach you in class. See the symmetrical puncture marks in the cadaver's neck? This is the first thing to look for. The second sign to confirm if there's a threat is to look into the corpse's mouth. See the abnormal, golden-black coloration in the roof of his mouth? This confirms incubation is occurring."

"So you're telling me vampires are real?" Dennis replied with a puzzled look on his face.

"Yes, and if we don't cremate him within the window of opportunity, he'll revive and become what's categorized as the living dead. When this happens, he'll start breathing and this worn out, arthritic-stricken body will become revitalized, possessing supernatural strength. This harmless-looking, old geezer will become extremely bloodthirsty, killing anyone who gets in his way. Fortunately, the cold weather has inhibited his transformation."

The young assistant took a closer look into the dead man's mouth and snickered, "Hey Doc, you missed something else. This old fart doesn't have any teeth."

Together, the pair started laughing and the supervisor rolled his eyes. "Lucky for us, we've got plenty of time. Let's put the toothless vampire on ice for the evening and in the morning we'll send him to the furnace where he belongs."

Working as a team, both of the morticians placed the corpse in an empty, refrigerated box next to the other frozen bodies they had in storage. When their work was finished, they departed for the evening feeling confident they made the right decision. As the sun began to set, the temperature plummeted with the arrival of a second cold front. Inside the metal icebox, strange happenings began taking place, and late that night the newly transformed vampire revived earlier than anticipated to the sound of complete silence.

Watkins slowly opened his eyes and began thinking, "*Death is sure strange. I remember being killed and now I'm awake and conscious. Where am I and what kind of place is this?*" The old man began to probe his surroundings and realized he was in some sort of container. He suddenly noticed he was alive and breathing. Terror and anxiety swept through his body as the thought entered his mind,

"*They must have buried me alive*." The panic-stricken man began screaming as he pounded the sides of the metal box with his fists.

The confused man settled down for a few seconds and began collecting his thoughts when the freezer door swung open and his gurney was pulled out. The intense, florescent lights were momentarily blinding. As his eyes adjusted, he saw a very distinguished-looking man standing over him dressed in a white overcoat with black, slicked-back hair.

"Who are you and where am I?" Chester asked.

The mysterious-looking guy answered with a strong Romanian accent and said, "I am Count Marius, master of all vampires. I will answer your questions shortly, but first we must get you out of here. You are scheduled to be destroyed in a few more hours."

The Count gave the new vampire a set of clean clothes and ordered him to put on another white jacket with a badge that he had stolen from the examiner's office.

"Next," said the dark-haired leader, "we waltz right out of here like we own the place."

The pair made their way out of the morgue basement and proceeded to a stairwell leading upstairs. When they flung the door open on the first floor, they were met by a Mexican janitor who said in broken English, "I just mop floor. Be careful you no slip."

The two passed, not even giving the custodian a second look, and within a few short minutes were out the front doors and walking away from the building. Marius said, "We must keep moving because time is very important. I have two other vampires to visit tonight."

The men kept walking until they came to a dark, secluded alley. The Romanian scanned in all directions. His night vision was far superior to that of a normal human being. Seeing no danger, the pair entered the darkness and took refuge behind a big dumpster and began their conversation.

Chester's first question was, "How did you know who I am

and where to find me?"

"I'm over 700 years old," replied Marius. "I know many things and have eyes and ears in distant places."

The Romanian made a habit of visiting all new converts and explaining to them the rules and principals of vampirism. The Count advised Chester the mortician had miscalculated his incubation period by a couple of hours.

"You're lucky to be alive," he said. "The only thing that saved you was a genetic anomaly which sped up your transformation process. If you were still incubating, I would have had no choice but to abandon your body. Vampirism and our existence is a well-guarded secret among the elect. There are guidelines that all immortals must adhere to. Those who strike out on their own usually do not survive."

Marius handed the new vampire a thick book titled "*Wisdom of the Dead*" and told him that this was the *Vampire's Bible*. He instructed him to read it from cover to cover. Chester thumbed through the book and opened to Chapter 1: Rejuvenation.

Confused, the old guy sighed, "What's this about?"

"There is 'Life Sustaining Force' in the blood and by drinking it, depending on your age, you will progressively grow older, or younger, until you reach a pristine appearance of approximately 40 years old. You will possess superhuman strength, being as strong as four or five men. In your case, it will take a considerable amount of time, probably decades."

As the master vampire spoke to Watkins, he raised his eyebrows and asked him to come closer. "Open your mouth."

The gray vampire did as he was ordered, inquiring, "Is something wrong?"

Immediately, the Count put his hands over his own mouth, hissing like a cagey alley cat. "I can't believe it, you're completely toothless."

Chester scratched his short hair and looked the man directly in the eye, replying, "I haven't had teeth for almost 25 years, so what's the problem?"

"When you grow hungry, you will see."

Marius' conversation turned to the subject of rogue vampires and freelancers who fancied doing their own thing apart from the Dynasty of Immortals in which he was chancellor.

"The young girl who bit you will be severely disciplined. We might even destroy her. She had no business biting an old, toothless man. There is order in our realm and this is critical to our continual existence. Inside the *Vampire's Bible*, you will find a phone number to assist you in finding a safe house. Call it before daybreak or escape to the sewer system below. Beware of the sunrise and the Crusaders of Light."

Watkins was watching a rat scurry under the trash-littered dumpster while Marius was speaking. When he looked up to ask who the Crusaders of Light were, he noticed that the Count had silently vanished. Chester began wondering, *"How in the heck did he do that?"*

With sunrise only a couple of hours away, the old man decided he had better not procrastinate. *"Sewer system or safe house?"* he pondered.

The gray vampire exited the alley still contemplating where to spend the next day. As he began walking, he noticed something unusual. All of the arthritic pain in his arms and legs was gone. His eyesight was also sharp and considerably better than before. He took in a breath of fresh air and exhaled. The feeling was exhilarating. After a few short steps, the old Marine began to slowly jog through downtown Houston.

Most of the night traffic he observed consisted of taxi cabs and a couple of late night trash trucks beginning their early morning routes. Watkins' run took him a couple of blocks and then he turned heading south on San Jacinto Street. After covering about half a mile, the old man was accosted by two homeless men standing in front of a convenience store. The men stepped in the middle of the sidewalk, blocking his path. Chester slowed to a walk, sized the two bums up and stopped 10 feet shy of them.

"What do you fine, outstanding gentlemen want?"

The white man was a large, stupid-looking guy with buckteeth and the short, skinny little black man had a huge, filthy Afro with a cigarette butt hanging from the side. Both vagrants reeked from the smell of cheap wine, and from the looks of their clothes neither had changed or bathed in weeks.

Scratching his dirty hair, the skinny man reached into his pocket and took a couple of steps forward. "Hey pops, can you spot me a couple of bucks? I'm thirsty and the Salvation Army is closed."

Looking out of the corner of his eye, the streetwise Marine noticed the big guy was flanking him, circling to his right.

"Say grandpa, why you wearing that white coat? You some sort of rich doctor or something? What's that book you're holding?"

Chester realized the situation didn't look good, and these idiots' actions were beginning to agitate him. He'd already died once within the past 24 hours and he didn't want any more trouble.

"Listen here punks, I'm broke. Get the hell out of my way before I beat the shit out of both of you and leave your stinky asses balled up on this sidewalk. Now move it!"

Both hobos rushed at the same time trying to tackle the old man, only to collide into one another as he jumped out of the way. The vagrants hit each other so hard that both of them fell backwards and into the street. The stunned men lay squealing on their backs as the cagey vampire jogged across the street. When he reached the opposite side, he heard the unruly white guy lash-out in anger, "You stupid coon, you knocked out one of my teeth. I'm gonna kick your ass."

The short little black man jumped to his feet and pulled up his baggy pants. "Who you callin' coon, you stupid, snaggletooth honky? I'll knock the rest of those green teeth out of your mouth if you don't shut up."

The pair began to fight, screaming indistinguishable obscenities. Several cars slowed down to watch the sideshow as the pair kicked and punched each other.

Laughing to himself, the man slowed to a brisk pace and quickly removed the white coat. It was drawing too much attention. Rolling it up into a tight little ball, the vampire tucked it under his arm for safe-keeping. He might need it later.

Several minutes passed and Chester began looking for an inconspicuous place to hide out and collect his thoughts. Watkins kept searching until he found an obscure alleyway. Located in front of it was a manhole cover. Confident no one was watching, he walked over to the metal object and slid it aside with ease. *"I feel as strong as two men,"* he cheerfully thought. Once inside, Chester replaced the lid, clasped the ladder, and easily descended the 10 feet into the dark, cemented pit.

The vampire began to wander aimlessly through the dimly lit, interconnecting drainage systems. The stagnant smell of mildew and grimy water caused the old Marine to cough as he continued exploring. The only ambient light available came from the street-lights that were shining through the drainage vents. Rats were everywhere, and occasionally he'd step on one, only to hear it screech. *"There's got to be a dry place down here somewhere?"* he pondered.

As time passed, Chester made his way to a ledge and felt his way up to a cement pad that was big enough to accommodate him. He swept a rat's nest off with his left hand and laid the *Vampire's Bible* down with his right. Before he could lift his arm up again, a starving wharf rat latched onto his fingers and chomped down with all its might. Twirling his arm like a cheerleader, Watkins shouted, "Ouch, you stupid little sucker, let go!"

After subduing the pesky rodent, Watkins sat down and tried to sort things out. His attention was drawn to another manhole cover approximately 30 feet away. Faint rays of sunlight were coming through the tiny finger holes. Squinting, an uncontrollable, reactionary hiss came out of his mouth and his head jerked spasmodically. He felt completely drained, almost to the point of death by the sight of the yellow light. He unrolled the white coat and pulled it over his face as he lay down on the cold, cement slab. Instantaneously, he fell into a trance-like state, similar to a reptile reacting to cold weather. His respiratory rate began to slow and within seconds his body took on the waxen appearance of death.

The city of Houston came to life that morning. The hustle and bustle of noisy traffic, delivery drivers, ambulances, police sirens and work crews flooded the air, while unbeknownst to all lay the seemingly lifeless body of Mr. Watkins in the sewer below.

CHAPTER 2, THE AWAKENING

As the sun descended below the horizon, Chester's respiratory system began to speed up. His vital signs and facial color returned to normal. With a loud gasp the vampire inhaled a huge breath of sewer air. Coughing, he opened his eyes and sat straight up with the white coat still draped over his head.

Watkins began to contemplate. *"I don't remember a thing after going to sleep. No dreams, no tossing or turning. I slept like the dead."*

The vampire removed the white coat and rolled it up tightly. There was a terrible gnawing sensation in the pit of his stomach and he had the worst case of cotton mouth he had ever experienced in his life.

He could hear the roar of traffic above him. Horns were honking, diesel engines from busses were humming and the sound of an occasional police whistle echoed below. He picked up his *Vampire's Bible* and headed to the ladder by the manhole cover.

The vampire began his ascent, climbing up until he reached the metal cover. He had to time his exit perfectly so he wouldn't interfere with the traffic flow or draw too much attention to himself. He knew that it was inevitable someone would see him, but he also knew a lot of weird things happen in big cities. If he didn't stay in the same area very long, no one would question him.

Chester could feel the traffic vibrating as it passed overhead. Several minutes passed and then the flow ceased momentarily. This was his chance. He lifted the cover a few inches so he could peek out. In front of him was a line of traffic silhouetted in the twilight waiting at the red light. The old man slid the lid aside and quickly climbed out. Just as he was pushing it back into place, the light turned green and the vehicles began racing toward him. he sprinted to the sidewalk and almost knocked over a homeless bag-woman pushing a shopping cart full of trash and aluminum cans.

"Excuse me," he said.

The filthy hag just ignored him and continued to walk in the opposite direction not even acknowledging him. Several people, including a couple of well-dressed businessmen, stared at him as he made his way down the sidewalk. Within a few seconds, he faded into obscurity and melted into the sea of people making their way down the busy street. The old vampire had no idea where he was because he had become disoriented while wandering underground. As he continued, his bearings came to him and he realized he was on the northwest side of downtown. "*Just where I want to be,*" he thought.

The gnawing sensation in his stomach began to grow worse. He started to feel an overwhelming hunger like he had never experienced in his life. The senior kept heading north and hoped that the feeling would subside, but it only grew in intensity. Chester was becoming more and more aggravated. This uncontrollable sensation was beginning to take over and dominate his personality. As he passed a nicely dressed woman, she spoke up, "Hello sir."

The old man responded with a hiss, "Shut up you pearly-toothed bitch!"

In the distance, about half a block away, the vampire saw a small store. He hadn't eaten since he died and the thought of drinking blood just didn't appeal to him. He was broke, but thinking back he wished he had asked Marius for a few dollars.

Watkins headed straight for the convenience store. He began walking so fast that he passed several people who were ahead of him. When an obese man got in his way, he pushed him aside and growled, "Move it fatso!"

He started grumbling under his breath, "Food. Food."

The twilight faded into darkness as he neared his destination. When he reached the store's parking lot, he ran across it and slowed to a brisk walk as he entered the door. In front of him was a magazine rack with a couple of men thumbing through the girly books. He glanced at the counter on his right at the store's clerk who looked like an Arab wearing a turban. In the second aisle, several things caught his eye—potato chips, candy bars and beef jerky. All of these items looked appealing to the hunger-driven man.

Watkins made his way over to the food racks trying to look as inconspicuous as possible. As he roamed up and down the aisle, he palmed a candy bar, placing it in the small of his back, and pocketed a bag of potato chips.

He slowly looked back at the manager who was shaking his head no and pointing at him. In a commanding tone, the Arab shouted, "Put it back or I call police!"

The vampire was so consumed with hunger that he ignored the clerk's warnings and headed straight for the door.

In an attempt to stop the shoplifter, the manager opened a small partition behind the counter, raced to the entryway and proceeded to lock it. When Chester reached the Arab, he grabbed him by the throat, ripped his turban off and spun him around, tossing him into the magazine rack. With a crash, newspapers, books and magazines were sent flying in different directions. The two guys reading the pornographic materials were caught completely by surprise. "Shit, let's get out of here. The old man's gone crazy."

The furious vampire smashed his fist into the door jam, dislodging it from its hinges. Once outside, he ran behind the store and climbed over a tall, wooden fence bordering the property.

When he reached the other side, he unrolled his white coat and put it on in hopes of disguising himself. He knew that in a matter of minutes the police would be combing the area, but his mind was inundated with confusion. The hunger was turning to rage as he reached for the candy bar, tearing its wrapper off and shoving it into his mouth. Like a toothless, old cow, Watkins began gumming the chocolate bar when he observed a homeless man sleeping in a cardboard box just 15 feet in front of him. The vampire tried to swallow but began to cough violently. The candy tasted like salty mud causing him to spit it out involuntarily. When he tried to eat the chips, he had the same reaction.

Chester quickly opened his vampire's manual and tried to focus his eyes on the pages. There might be something in there that could explain what was happening to him.

Chapter 1: Rejuvenation. *"It is impossible for a vampire to consume anything except for the blood of a human being."*

Chester's attention was immediately turned to the tattooed vagrant sleeping in the box. The vampire charged in a blind rage, screaming like a Marine hitting the beaches of Tarawa. The startled man's eyes popped open as he attempted to sit up, but he was flattened like a football tackling dummy when the advancing warrior pounced on his chest.

The helpless guy began screaming like a little girl and was quickly overpowered by the enraged madman. Chester placed his right hand over the man's mouth and attempted to silence him. "Quiet, there's cops in the area and they're looking for me."

With squinted eyes, the man pleaded, "Please don't hurt me. I'll do anything you want."

With his next breath, the vampire bit into the bum's neck with the force of a famished snapping turtle, but to no avail. The fangless creature was unable to penetrate the man's thick neck muscles. Like an alligator with prey in his mouth, Chester thrashed around, whipping his head back and forth swiftly as he fought to break through the man's skin. Through muffled hand, the homeless man moaned in agony and urinated in his pants.

Frustrated, the vampire jumped to his feet and ran off yelling. When the battered hobo caught his breath, he assumed that the old man was trying to rape him. Feeling that his dignity had been violated, he cried out, "You crazy faggot."

Watkins emerged from behind the fence and slowed down to a steady pace as he headed west. He traveled several blocks before being passed by a squad car. Perceiving him as a harmless senior citizen, the police continued heading in the opposite direction.

Thirty minutes passed and the vampire was far away from the little store and the homeless person whom he had viciously assaulted. As he continued walking westward on Washington Street, he witnessed a terrible accident. A delivery truck ran a red light and crashed into a bus full of nursing home patients. Dozens of concerned citizens came out of their stores and shops to converge on the scene. Two elderly ladies, climbed from the wreckage and began crawling toward the curb. Chester's heart began pounding in his chest as he saw all of the blood coming out of these people.

Without hesitation, he sprinted to the mangled vehicles, hollering, "Get out of the way, I'm a doctor!"

When he reached the overturned van, he ripped the back doors off their hinges with superhuman strength and threw them in the direction of the ducking crowd. Climbing in, he saw a white-bearded man who was knocked unconscious and severely injured. His bleeding arm was barely attached and was dangling below the elbow. The vampire rolled him over on his side, locked his mouth to the man's wound and began licking and sucking like a parasitic leach. Immediately, Chester felt an electrical serge of power shoot through his whole body. The feeling was purely euphoric. His vision began to sharpen and his mind started clearing. In the distance he could hear the high-pitched wailing sounds of approaching sirens.

As the fiasco continued, someone in the crowd cried out, "What's that crazy doctor doing to that man?"

After regaining his senses, he realized that his desire wasn't to kill, but only to feed. He quickly removed his mouth and repositioned the injured man to render first aid. He tore his white jacket at the sleeve and fastened a tourniquet above the elbow to stop the bleeding. As he exited the vehicle, he wiped his mouth. Two blocks away, he could see the flashing lights of an ambulance and fire truck. He quickly made his way into the crowd and tossed his blood-soaked jacket aside virtually unnoticed. Walking briskly, he continued his journey westward never looking back

Now that he was thinking straight, Watkins realized that the *Vampire's Bible* was a very important book and it was essential for his survival. He had to read more. The senior citizen decided to head for Memorial Park and study this strange manuscript and reassess his situation.

As the vampire proceeded down Washington street, a Lincoln Town Car eased to the curb alongside of him. Chester glanced to his left and watched the electric window slowly retract downward. Inside the fancy vehicle, Chester saw an older man behind the wheel.

"Hey old timer, where are you headed?"

"To Memorial Park."

"Need a lift? I'm going that way myself."

"Sure. At this pace, it'll take me another hour to get there. Much obliged."

Watkins climbed inside of the plush car and reached for the seatbelt to buckle himself in.

"I saw you walking and thought to myself, *'It's dangerous for an old man to be out at night.'* We senior citizens have to stick together you know. By the way, what's your name?"

"Chester."

The Lincoln slowly made its way in the direction of the park as the two elders engaged in casual conversation. The curious vampire studied the unusual facial features of the other senior citizen and did a double-take when he saw his eyes. The funny-looking guy had frizzy white hair, a glaring, lazy eye and a voice that made him sound like a high seas pirate. The shiny diamond ring, expensive Rolex watch and neatly tailored suit signaled to the gray vampire that this gentleman had money and lots of it. When they arrived at the park, the two said farewell and Watkins waved goodbye as the vehicle drove away.

The vampire scanned his surroundings and headed for a set of benches adjacent to the restroom facilities. The entire area was illuminated and this was a perfect setting for him to study his manual.

When he reached the seats, he observed a young couple fondling one another in the bushes, an Oriental man walking a dog and a late night jogger running through the park.

A predominant thought raced through the old man's mind as he continued looking around, "*My life depends on me reading this book.*"

When the vampire opened the cover, he noticed it was leather bound and all of the materials were of premium quality. Watkins had considerable knowledge regarding antiques and he knew this book would fetch a substantial price if it were ever sold to a specialized collector. There were 400 pages divided into 20 chapters and every word was printed in gold, except the word blood, which was written in red. He hadn't noticed these details earlier because of his uncontrollable hunger.

He turned to Chapter 2: Wisdom of the Ages.

The first paragraph read, "*Trust no one except for those who have as much to lose as yourself. Money and power will corrupt a weak soul, but the wise will strive to seek immortality, which is far greater than all riches. What will a vampire give in exchange for his life? All of the world's wealth accounts for nothing when your existence is in jeopardy. When you cease to live, nothing matters except for tomorrow. What price would you pay for one thousand years of life? Choose your friends wisely, because fools will cause you to waste many hours. The temporal-minded know nothing except immediate gratification.*

"*Time is precious and so is life. It's worth more than gold. You can spend time to find gold, but you can't spend gold to increase your days on earth.*

"*When a wise man speaks and no one listens, he is in the company of the simple hearted. Depart from such and seek the eternally-minded.*"

Watkins closed the book and took a deep breath. "*A lot of things to consider,*" he pondered.

The vampire opened the manuscript again, this time turning to Chapter 3: Enemies of the Brotherhood. This segment gave a historical account of different factions of enemies who arose throughout the ages and their attempts to vanquish the undead. Several deaths of prominent vampires were recorded, as well as their grisly demises. These gory details made the hair on Chester's neck literally stand up. The final group of dissidents recorded was the Crusaders of Light. These fanatics were vampire hunters and they showed no mercy to their captives. He was familiar with these tactics having faced the Imperial Army in World War II. He was aware of the levels of degradation humanity could stoop to.

The military veteran closed the manual again and wished for the best, *"I hope I never meet up with that bunch,"* but instinctively he knew it was inevitable. Just as he knew he would fight in the Pacific Theater and kill many hardened Japanese defenders in battle, he was certain, he wouldn't see peace until he saw war.

The vampire decided it was time to stretch his legs for a little while, so he stood up and looked around for about five minutes. The park was practically empty and he estimated the time to be around 1 a.m. Watkins had more time to spare so he sat back down and thumbed through the index of his book. He saw a phone number listed with a warning printed next to it: *"All phone lines have the potential to be tapped and monitored. Use discretion when calling this number. Begin the conversation by giving your last name only and answer yes or no to the questions given. Further dialog will cause this phone call to be terminated immediately."*

"This must be a safe house," he mumbled. "I sure as heck don't want to sleep in that rat-infested sewer again."

Without hesitation, Chester sprang to his feet and headed to the public restrooms which had a pay phone mounted on the outside wall. When he reached the building, he picked the receiver up and stuck it to his left ear. Feeling something sticky on the side of his head, he jerked the object away and examined it. Yellow earwax and pink lipstick were caked on both ends.

"Yuck, nasty ass people. I wish I had a cellular phone," he grumbled. Taking his shirtsleeve, he wiped the device clean and proceeded to dial the 800 number.

The phone rang three times and a woman answered. "Nightly deposits and investments, this is Suzie can I help you?"

The old vampire scratched his chin and replied, "Watkins."

"One moment, your call is being transferred."

The phone rang three more times and another voice came on the line, which Chester immediately recognized as Marius.

"Hello, Watkins, I see you've been doing your homework."

"Yes."

"Good, would you like for me to arrange sleeping accommodations?"

"Yes."

"Stay where you are because we know your location. We've been tracking your movements. The same gentleman who dropped you off will return to pick you up. If any other vehicle arrives, avoid contact. If you see anything suspicious, run for your life."

"Yes."

"We will speak again," the Romanian confidently said before ending the conversation.

Chester walked away from the lighted area surrounding the public buildings and headed toward the wooded section of the park where he could observe the rendezvous point from a distance. The gray vampire faded into the shadows as he waited for his ride.

A few minutes passed and a police car made its rounds through the park. Watkins observed from the darkness as the patrol vehicle drove by him totally unaware of his presence. The vampire knew that his altered physical state and heightened senses would only improve with time. *"When you cease to exist, nothing matters except for time. Time is my most precious ally,"* he deliberated, reflecting back on his book. Chester watched the cruiser leave the park as he leaned against a tree.

Ten minutes elapsed and a red Chevrolet Impala low-rider full of Mexicans drove up to the public restrooms. All of the doors flung open at the same time and four motley-dressed men climbed out. A small, skinny man began staggering and fell to the ground spilling his half-empty, 32-ounce bottle of beer. The others looked down at him and started laughing hysterically as he wallowed around on the cement. One of the men extended his hand and helped his drunken friend to his feet.

The small gang made their way to the building and a taller man, who appeared to be the leader, kicked a trash receptacle over sending Coke cans, papers and baby diapers all over the sidewalk. When they reached the facility, the same guy reached into his baggy pants and whipped out an aerosol can of spray paint. In a frenzy, he started cursing in Spanish and writing graffiti and gang symbols all over the walls.

"This is our turf, man. We kick any dude's ass who says different."

The young man that had fallen down a few seconds earlier unzipped his pants and began urinating on the bathroom door. He hollered in a slurred voice, "Knock, knock, mi casa es su casa!" The others started laughing at him as he continued with his antics.

The vampire thought, "*I hope these punks leave before my ride gets here. I don't need any more trouble.*"

A few more minutes passed and the gang members returned to their vehicle. Two of them sat on the hood while the other men stood directly in front of the car facing their friends. The man with the baggy pants reached into his coat pocket, pulled out a hand-rolled cigarette and lit it up with his butane lighter. He took a few puffs and passed it on to the guy standing beside him. Each of the Mexicans took a drag, passing it in a circle until it was finished. When the smoke drifted in the direction of the old vampire, he recognized the familiar smell of marijuana. "*From the way they were acting, it appeared to be some pretty good stuff,"* the vampire intuitively surmised. The young men began to laugh and Watkins struggled to hear their conversations.

As fate would have it, the vampire's ride arrived and drove right past the small gang. The old man emerged from the shadows and stepped into the street to reveal himself.

One of the Mexicans cried out, "Say dude, you spying on us?"

Watkins piped up, "Yes, and I've already called your mothers."

Appreciating his sense of humor, the laughing gang leader ordered his friends to stay put. "He's cool, don't jack with him."

The vampire began to laugh also as he approached the Town Car. The driver's side window retracted and the same funny-looking guy who was behind the wheel a couple of hours ago inquired, "Need another lift?"

Chester quoted from the manual, "Trust no one except for those who have as much to lose as yourself."

The driver responded, "I've dedicated my life so others might live."

The cock-eyed senior extended his hand outside of the window. "I'm Doctor Fabian Rubenstein."

The vampire firmly gripped his hand, "Chester Watkins."

"Get in. We've been here too long."

Watkins briskly walked to the passenger's side, climbed inside the Lincoln and the doctor drove off, heading for Interstate 10.

"Where are we going?"

"Bear Creek."

The pair remained silent for the remainder of the trip until they reached Fabian's neighborhood. The physician took special precautions, making sure they weren't being followed, and detoured an extra block to ensure their safety.

"The Crusaders of Light don't mess around," stated Fabian.

"The group is fanatically insane and they have a deep-seeded hatred for people assisting the living dead. Murder, torture and rape are the rewards for those of us who are caught helping vampires."

"Don't worry, I'll watch your back. I owe you one for the ride."

Rubenstein's estate was surrounded by a tall, wrought iron fence with security cameras strategically mounted on the corner posts. The stately, two-story brick mansion was a striking sight covered with ivy vines and prominent evergreen bushes planted in front. Watkins noticed every window had security bars installed in their frames.

The doctor opened the remote-controlled security gate and quickly drove inside onto a nice, red brick driveway. Chester glanced back and noticed how the gates were already closing. "*Boy, that was quick,*" he thought. When they reached the front of the house, Chester observed a circular driveway that had a beautiful water fountain in the center. The doctor drove around the centerpiece and headed to the four-car garage, which was also electronically operated. Once inside, Fabian exited his car and walked over to a set of security monitors located on the garage wall. None of the cameras revealed anything suspicious-looking.

"You don't take any chances, do you Doc?"

"I've come too far in my research to become careless," replied the frizzy-headed man.

The vampire quickly scanned the interior of the building and saw a blue Porsche and a gray Suburban parked on the far left side of the garage.

"How's that spiffy sports car handle?"

"Nicely. I'll let you drive it in a few weeks after we establish your new identity," replied the doctor. "Let's go inside. I want you to meet my darling wife."

When they entered the mansion, the pair was greeted by a small, frail, sophisticated-looking woman in her late 50s with a crook in her nose and a pair of bifocals dangling from the end.

"Hello Mr. Watkins, we've been expecting you. My name is Doctor Patricia Rubenstein."

"I'm impressed," replied Chester. "You already know my name."

"We've been doing this for awhile."

The three made their way single file through the hallway and into a huge living room. The vampire's head turned from side to side as he admired all of the diplomas, certificates and credentials hanging on the walls. Both of the doctors' names were prominently displayed on these numerous awards of achievement.

On the east wall was a stone fireplace surrounded by leather furniture. An elk's head was mounted over the mantle and its tall antlers were almost touching the ceiling.

"I love grandfather clocks," Watkins said as he walked over to the north wall to take a closer look at the timepiece which displayed 3:25 a.m. "Is this a family heirloom? It's in magnificent condition."

"Sort of," answered the petite lady.

"I bet that thing's over a hundred years old," Chester surmised.

"One hundred and fifty-four to be exact," replied the doctor.

The Rubensteins approached the fireplace and sat down together on one of the couches while Chester continued to study the rare antique.

"I bet this thing comes from the old country. Have you ever had it appraised?"

Fabian leaned forward, responding, "It was handcrafted in Prussia or Germany. I can't sell it because it belonged to a vampire. He was killed by the Crusaders."

"I'm starting to dislike that group." The old vampire walked over next to the fireplace and sat down in a chair across from the cozy couple.

The lazy-eyed doctor expounded on his interests in vampires and why he'd dedicated his life researching them. "DNA abnormalities, hereditary deficiencies, diseases and all cancers could be totally eradicated if we could tap into your genetic secrets."

"Yes, you hold the key to immortality," the crooked-nosed woman added. "Please allow us to do a little research and take some small tissue and blood samples."

Watkins stood up and, waving his arms, said, "You can do some research, but I'm not bending over for anyone. If I hear a rubber glove snap, I'm running for my life. You can take me back to the sewer and I'll spend the next hundred years living down there."

The trio began chuckling and the frizzy-headed man calmly said, "Our research is extensive, but the majority of it takes place under a microscope."

The Rubensteins told Chester not to worry about his meals because they had the authority to access as much blood as they needed from the Texas Medical Research Center.

Having assisted dozens of vampires in the past, the doctors were confident they could trust their new guest. Watkins had a way of putting people at ease when he spoke to them and the Rubensteins liked his humble mannerisms. The gray man spoke of the past and shared with his new hosts that he served honorably in the Marine Corps, was decorated with the silver-star, bronze-star, numerous campaign ribbons and the purple-heart. He also told them that he used to be a police officer back in the late 1940s.

The couple gave their vampire guest an extended tour of their estate and showed him their personal research laboratory, which was located in a soundproof room in the rear of their house. Watkins felt safe as he was led through the mansion. Additional security cameras and a nice firearms collection were taken in confidence by the man during the trip.

Spinning the dial of the huge gun safe, the doctor turned and looked at his curious friend. "I'll show you the combination. If we ever have an emergency, you might need access to these weapons."

When he opened the fireproof box, the vampire immediately commented about the semi-automatic pistols inside. A nice assortment of long guns were neatly stacked in the racks, as well. The rifles included a nice Remington bolt-action .30-06 sporting rifle, an M1 Garand, .30 carbine, AK-47, M-14 and M-16.

"Can I borrow one of those Colt .45s?" asked the Marine. "I had one when I was alive and I wouldn't have been caught dead without one."

The doctor retrieved a matte-finished pistol from the fireproof safe and handed it to the old leatherneck. Pointing the weapon in a safe direction, Chester withdrew the magazine and pulled the slide to the rear to inspect the firearm.

Rubenstein was impressed with the safety-conscious Marine who handled the pistol with a discernable knowledge that he knew came from experience.

"Where's the ammo?"

Fabian opened a closet next to the safe and the vampire was astonished. Over a dozen ammo boxes were neatly stacked in the corner. One of the cans read .45 ACP 230-grain ball. The doctor opened the can and handed the vampire a box of ammunition for his pistol. He also handed him a cleaning kit with some patches and a bottle of oil.

"Let me show you to your sleeping quarters. My wife and I want you to feel at home during your stay, so please feel free to move about and look around any time you want."

The doctor led Chester to the center-most part of his mansion. The vampire's sleeping quarters was a house within a house. There were no windows and only one visible locking door leading in and out of the secure structure. The doctor pulled a key from his pocket and handed it to his guest and told him to open the door. Once inside, Rubenstein showed the man a secret passageway located behind the bookshelf.

"Use this in case of an emergency. It leads underground and outside to the pump house next to the swimming pool."

Watkins was extremely pleased with his new bedroom and his gummy smile was evidence of this. "This sure beats the drainage ditches."

The bookshelf contained hundreds of books ranging in many different categories. In the corner of the room was a nicely hand-carved chess table with Medieval-looking pieces. Beside it were two chairs. In the center of the room was a coffin resting on a stone pillar.

"Do you like to play chess?" Chester inquired.

"I sure do," answered Rubenstein, "but my wife and I need to retire for the evening. We have to attend a medical meeting in the morning."

"I understand."

After bidding the man good night, the doctor closed the door behind him and left the room. Within seconds, the gray vampire field-stripped his Colt .45 and inspected it thoroughly. After cleaning it Marine Corps-style, he reassembled the pistol and racked the slide a couple of times to ensure it was together properly. Satisfied that his piece was in good working order, he loaded it and set it inside his coffin.

Chester's attention was turned again to his fascinating book "*Wisdom of the Dead*." He opened the manual to the exact spot where he left off reading and resumed his studies. He continued reading for a couple of hours until a strange feeling overtook his body. When he glanced at the clock on the wall, the time read 6:05 a.m. Sluggishly, the gray vampire rose from his chair and staggered to his coffin. Once inside, he cradled his pistol in his lap, closed the lid and passed out.

CHAPTER 3, A NEW IDENTITY

Following a stressful day of work and lectures, the Rubensteins returned to their estate to find Chester standing in the living room studying the grandfather clock again. The old timepiece began to chime seven times, signaling it was 7 p.m.

"This antique is almost hypnotic," the old man stated.

"Hello Chester, how are you this evening?" queried Patricia.

The vampire turned his head, responding, "Fine, but I need something to eat."

Fabian motioned with his hand for their new guest to follow him. "Come with me to the laboratory."

The hungry old man followed the doctor straight to the back room, never uttering a word.

"I'll show you where we keep our supply of blood and how to heat it up to a comfortable temperature for consumption."

The vampire's eyes were intensely focused on the man as he gave the simple instructions. Fabian placed a medium-sized bag of blood inside the medical warmer and set the timer. The Marine remained silent as his life-sustaining meal was being prepared. His eyes shifted back and forth from the doctor and the heater as his meal approached completion.

When the timer sounded, Fabian grabbed a beautiful, gold ornate cup, emptied the contents of the bag into it and handed it to the vampire. "Let me know if it's warm enough."

Watkins quoted from his book "*Wisdom of the Dead*" as he lifted the cup to his mouth and drank, "To life."

After emptying the chalice, he handed it back to the doctor and smiled. Fabian told his new friend that he wanted to allow time for his meal to digest before taking a small tissue and blood sample. A routine physical examination followed and the statistics were entered into a secret journal that the Rubensteins kept hidden inside a small safe in the lab.

"You're completely toothless," exclaimed Fabian.

"I know, I'm a toothless vampire," replied Chester. "There's a hobo downtown with a big hickey on his neck testifying to this fact."

"Marius told me that the rogue vampire who bit you would probably be destroyed when she is found. She had no business biting an old man."

"I think she did me a favor," chuckled Chester. "All my arthritic pain is gone and I can see like a hawk."

The two men mingled around the lab for a few more minutes before returning to the living room to rejoin Patricia who was watching television. When Fabian sat down next to her, he asked if anything interesting was mentioned in the news. Only death, pestilence and destruction was her reply.

The vampire sat down in a leather chair across from them, scratched his chin and asked, "Do you have any cigars? I haven't had a smoke since I died."

Patricia rolled her eyes. "You're not going to like the taste. Your metabolism is still changing."

"I'll be the judge of that."

Fabian got up and walked over to his study, which adjoined the living room, and called for the vampire to follow him. He told Watkins that Patricia didn't like smoke, but he was also inclined to indulge in a nice cigar on special occasions.

"Please close the door behind us Chester."

Fabian opened a drawer and pulled a cedar box from his desk and offered the vampire a big, fat, Cuban cigar. The old man plucked one from the bunch and drew it to his nose to take a whiff.

The doctor handed him a lighter after applying the flame to his own cigar and said, "Light up."

Like a seasoned addict, Watkins lit the cigar, inhaled a small amount of smoke and, to his surprise, he didn't cough. The taste wasn't bad either.

"I haven't had a Cuban cigar since the Kennedy administration."

Fabian puffed his stogie and nodded as the vampire spoke. The doctor pointed to a chess set situated on the coffee table and asked, "Would you like to play a game?"

"Yes," answered the old man.

The two gentlemen sat down and engaged in a friendly game that soon became serious after the old guy checkmated the doctor.

"I didn't think you were that good," exclaimed Fabian.

"I was the Marine Corps chess champion."

The two men began another game, and the vampire beat him again. A third game, followed by a fourth, and finally the doctor conceded.

"You're a challenging opponent. Wait until you meet Vladimir."

"Who's he?"

"He's vice chancellor of the Dynasty of Immortals, the political council of ruling vampires. No one has defeated him in over two centuries."

Chester scratched his head and laughed, "I look forward to playing that guy."

The two men reset the board, placed their cigar butts in the ashtray and tidied up the study. Fabian was a compulsively neat man and the vampire picked up on this attribute almost immediately. Patricia was the sloppy one in the family according to her husband.

Both guys returned to the living room and to their surprise Count Marius was standing there talking with Patricia.

The slick-haired man waved at his new convert and said, "Watkins, I have your new driver's license and social security card. According to these documents, your new identity is Sidney Marion Kunkle, age 74."

"Why not call me Michelle?" said the disappointed man. "Do I really have to go by that ridiculous name?"

"This was the only name available. He fell overboard on a cruise ship in the Caribbean and no one noticed he was missing."

"Either that or they didn't give a damn," added Watkins.

"In the vampire's circle, you will still be known by your birth name," Marius stated. "The new identity is only for business transactions that you will be conducting in the future."

Chester took the documents from the Romanian's hand and studied them carefully. To his surprise, his picture was already on the new license. He wondered how they were able to do that, but didn't bother asking. Marius informed the Rubensteins and Watkins that the Dynasty of Immortals had organized a reconnaissance party to apprehend the rogue vampire who bit him. Once she was located, she would be liquidated for her crimes against humanity and the dynasty.

"After she's convicted, she'll watch the next sunrise," the Count said with stern authority. "She's been sighted around the Memorial City shopping mall. She won't be hard to capture."

The dignified vampire told everyone that the political party was having a meeting in northwest Arkansas and he strongly urged Watkins to attend. After the Count departed, the doctors told Chester that the Count's estate was located there and it was a beautiful place to visit.

According to the governing body, the girl's actions were jeopardizing the entire colony. Left unchecked, her carelessness risked exposing the brotherhood openly. The Count's conversation troubled Watkins. Even though this teenager murdered him, he'd forgiven her in his heart. All the pain in his body was gone and he was actually grateful.

"I hope they don't kill her," the gray vampire remorsefully said. "She couldn't help herself. She's just an irresponsible kid."

"You heard Marius," replied Fabian, "she's a nuisance."

"Maybe not. Can't you see the problem here?"

"What problem?"

Motioning for them to move to the couch, Chester pointed a

second time, saying, "I'll explain."

The three elders sat in a semi-circle as the toothless man explained his theory. He thought that the Dynasty was making a hasty decision and he wanted to find out why. Watkins reminded them of the fact that people don't become vampires all by themselves. They needed to find out who bit this young girl and the circumstances surrounding this mystery. After a lengthy conversation, Chester convinced his hosts that they needed to find the girl before anyone else did.

"If she dies, so do her secrets, including the identity of the immortal who bit her."

"We never thought of that," answered the interested physicians. "She might hold the key to something sinister."

"Exactly," replied Watkins. "Can I borrow one of your cars tomorrow night to search for her? I think I can find her first."

"Yes," replied Fabian. "I'll have Sidney Kunkle added to my automobile insurance first thing in the morning."

"I think I'm going to puke," mumbled the vampire, "but go ahead and do it."

Watkins excused himself and went back to his room to read the "*Wisdom of the Dead*." He pulled the ancient text from the bookcase and walked over to the chess table to sit down. This was the most fascinating work of literature he had ever studied. Chester reasoned within himself to commit to memory some of the parables that were written. He studied the book throughout the night and at dawn he climbed into his casket again to settle in for the day.

CHAPTER 4, REDEMPTION

Chester awoke and slapped the top of his coffin open. He sat straight up and hissed like a rattlesnake. His mouth was dry and his throat was irritated. For the first time since his transformation, he had experienced a dream. "*Impossible,*" he thought. He remembered the vivid details of his nightmare. A spiritual conflict that became physical where he confronted evil men disguised as good. He was triumphant in his encounter, but the vampires around him were burned to death in some type of ritual.

He remembered reading in Chapter 8: Darkness Keeps Us Whole. The beginning paragraph explained how a vampire's powers are greatest during peak hours of darkness when the sun is at its apex in relation to being on the opposite side of the Earth where a vampire dwells. At the end of the chapter, it detailed how immortals never remember sleeping unless their spirit departs from their body. Sucked into the conflicting darkness for a special purpose, the spirit encounters the souls of those who threaten their survival. These nightmares were spiritual truth and were an interrelated part of being immortal.

The senior citizen climbed out of his brazen coffin and walked over to the bookshelf to retrieve his vampire's manual. His hunger continued to gnaw at the pit of his stomach, but his thoughts were consumed with this strange dream. Eating would have to wait.

The vampire thumbed through the pages until he found Chapter 9: Find the Void Within Yourself. This chapter gave step-by-step instructions on how to transform into a bat or wolf. "*This might come in handy later,*" he thought. A special incantation in foreign languages was listed for the transformations. Chester was no linguist, but he recognized the words to be Latin or Spanish in regards to the wolf spell. "*El Lobo de noche translate imidiatemente.*" Translated into English, the sentence read, "*The wolf of the night translate immediately.*" The same sentence could be used to reverse the process. Any and all items a vampire had on their person, including clothes, weapons and jewelry would shrink to a proportionate size.

The vampire set the book back on the shelf and shouted the incantation in a commanding voice. Suddenly, he felt the floor vibrate and his vision seemed to be altered to a lower level. Chester shook his head and looked down at his feet and noticed two huge, silver paws. He looked behind himself and saw large, muscular hindquarters sporting silver legs. The old wolf cleared his throat with a deep growl, which sounded raspy, and he noticed something unusual. Inside of his mouth he felt sharp, canine teeth with his tongue.

"Interesting," he said. He repeated the incantation and with a whirl he felt himself elevate. Looking down at his feet, everything appeared normal again.

The gnawing sensation in his stomach was becoming uncomfortable. After a few minutes, Watkins went to the laboratory and retrieved a bag of blood from the Rubenstein's refrigerator and fed himself according to the doctor's instructions. Chester promptly returned to his private room to study his ancient manuscript again. The time was only 6:47 p.m. and the Rubensteins hadn't returned home yet.

The vampire pulled the book from the shelf and opened to the place where he left off. The words for the bat spell appeared to be written in a Germanic language and translated into English with the meaning, "*Bat of the night, take flight.*" Chester committed to memory the words of both spells and returned the book to its rightful place. This time, the old codger whispered the incantation to see what would happen. "Bat of the night, take flight."

Immediately, he felt a rush of air and a sensation of falling. He spread his arms to break his fall and flailed them to catch himself. To his amazement, he was hovering in mid-air. The vampire bat looked down at the ground and saw a tiny pair of legs dangling underneath himself. He ran his tongue through his mouth like he had done when he was transformed into a wolf and he felt a mouth full of small teeth. He took flight and flew around the room a couple of times and landed on top of his coffin.

"This is amazing."

Chester recited the incantation and to his surprise nothing happened. He was still a bat. The bat took flight again and returned to the exact spot where he was transformed and shouted, "Bat of the night, take flight!"

To his frustration, nothing happened. The bat returned to his perch on top of the coffin to reassess his situation. *"I'll try the wolf spell,"* he thought.

"El Lobo de noche translate imidiatemente."

Suddenly, the vampire bat felt a whirl and his vision was altered to a higher level. The huge, silver wolf stood perched on top of the coffin. Within seconds, his slippery paws began to give way, leaving him straddling the casket. Without thinking, he let out a blood-curdling howl as his testicles touched the icy surface.

"El Lobo de noche translate imidiatemente!" he shouted in Latin.

The old man was turned into himself as he simultaneously dismounted the brazen object.

"Enough fun and games," he thought. Chester walked into the front room just as the Rubensteins were returning home from work.

"Good evening, doctors," Watkins said.

"I'm surprised you're not standing by the grandfather clock," said Patricia.

"I've got other things on my mind. Can I borrow a vehicle tonight?"

"Yes," answered the frizzy-headed physician as he approached the gray vampire and handed him the keys to the Porsche. "I'm sorry, but I've got to do some important paperwork for the hospital. I won't be able to join you in your search for the girl tonight. I'll try to accompany you tomorrow. Good luck in finding her."

Without wasting any time, Watkins headed directly for the garage and drove the sports car to Memorial City. He knew that Marius and the others had underestimated the importance of this young girl. Whoever found her first would be privy to any special information she might have.

Chester's search continued for several months without turning up anything. Fabian accompanied him when his schedule allowed, but for the most part the old man hunted by himself. Two more weeks passed and the Dynasty of Immortals ordered the search called off until new intelligence was gathered. It was the general consensus among the ruling elders that the rogue vampire had moved out of the area entirely.

The stubborn old Marine wasn't as easily convinced. "I think she's laying low just like the Japs did in their caves."

"There's no evidence of her whereabouts," replied the doctor. "No one else has been bitten since you."

"How about other cities? Are there any new vampires turning up anywhere else?"

"Not to anyone's knowledge."

"I wonder how she is feeding?" the vampire asked, scratching his head.

"That's a good question."

Another month passed, and Chester was still continuing his quest. He extended his search to adjoining neighborhoods and still came up empty. The doctor gave the vampire a key map of the city, but late one night when Chester was studying it he began to reason within himself why they hadn't found the girl. "*We're thinking like adults and she's a teenager.*"

The calculating vampire changed his strategy and decided to include movie theaters, game rooms and hip-hop clothing stores in his new search. The Rubensteins provided Watkins with a new wardrobe and chances were the young girl wasn't wearing the same clothes either. Finding out what the teen-aged crowd was doing was essential. Every group of young people the vampire observed he scrutinized closely. Late one night, Watkins' persistency paid off. He was driving the Porsche past a movie theater and saw a bunch of juveniles standing in a circle talking. As he strained to look, he saw the young girl standing among them. His heart fluttered in his chest as he circled around the back of the cinema and parked the car in the alleyway in an inconspicuous spot.

Confident that no one had seen him, Watkins walked around the side of the dimly lit building and peered around the corner to spy. Standing next to a nice-looking young boy with spiked hair was Chester's killer. The couple was holding hands as they talked to the other youngsters in the group. Fighting his angry instincts, the toothless man emerged from the shadows and rounded the corner with such swiftness that he caught everyone completely off-guard. Both vampires' eyes were locked on one another as he shoved his way into the center of the crowd and slapped the young man's hand away from the girl. With rejuvenated strength, he took hold of her shirtsleeve in such a manner that she was unable to escape his clutches. The old Marine's face looked similar to a bulldog's as he glared at his young opponents.

With his chin sticking out he shouted, "Anyone want a piece of this?"

Like a scrapping, rutting buck, the cocky, teen-aged boy, who was holding the girl's hand, challenged the tough-looking veteran. "What the heck do you think you're doing you old geezer?"

The vampire barked as he struck the mouthy juvenile with a stiff-armed blow to the chest, knocking him to the ground. "I'm in charge around here now. Shut your face."

Looking up at his attacker, the young man responded, "That hurt. You're in for it now gramps."

"Shut up you little punk or I'll plant my foot in the middle of your ass. I'm this girl's grandfather and she's coming home."

The tough-acting gang surrounded Watkins and started taunting him. "She's not going anywhere you grumpy windbag."

The gray vampire jumped backwards, pulled his coat to the side and brandished the Colt .45 pistol that was loosely tucked in his belt. When the arrogant boys saw the business end of the barrel, they took off running in different directions.

Tears started forming in the boy's eyes who was lying on the ground and he started to plead with Chester. "Please don't shoot me, sir. I'm sorry, we were just talking trash."

"You've got three seconds to get out of here. Now, get moving."

The terrified boy jumped to his feet screaming, and bolted like a frightened animal.

The young girl was astonished and at the same time powerless against the seemingly feeble man she'd murdered. Struggling with all of her might, she was unable to break free from his powerful grip. He had twice her strength because of the steady diet of blood supplied by the doctors.

"Please don't kill me, mister. I'll do anything you want."

"I'm not going to hurt you," replied Chester. "I'm trying to save your life. Now, come with me before someone calls the police."

The gray Marine began dragging the resisting teenager by the arm as she whimpered like a helpless puppy, "Please don't hurt me."

"I promise, honey, I won't hurt you if you do exactly as I say."

Chester opened the driver's side door of the sports car and pushed the struggling vampire over into the passenger's side, never turning lose of her arm. After climbing in beside her, he fired up the Porsche and peeled out. The spinning tires and burning rubber made a screeching sound as the car yawed sideways and emerged from the alleyway and into the street.

"First thing's first, what's your name?"

Trembling, the girl answered with a cracking voice, "Marsha."

"I'm Chester," he said as he slowly released his tight grip from her purple arm. "Marius and the other vampires have been looking for you for months. If they'd gotten to you first, they would have killed you."

"Those stupid assholes. I was on to them a long time ago."

Watkins remembered reading in the "*Wisdom of the Dead*" how vampires are able to recognize one another, even in large crowds. "*The spirit of the living dead is drawn to his counterpart as a moth is drawn to a flame.*"

"So, you saw them searching?"

"Yes, and I hid from them."

Chester reached for the girl's purse and stuck his hand inside to examine the contents. While doing this, he never took his eyes off of the road.

"What are you looking for?"

"Where's your vampire's manual?"

"I threw it away after a stinky rat ate some of the pages."

"Marsha, that was foolish. Did you ever try reading it?"

"Not really."

The old man took his hand off of the girl's purse and pointed at the road. "How would you like for me to close my eyes and keep driving? What do you think would happen?"

"You'd crash. That's stupid."

"It's the same analogy. You're heading down a dark road and driving blindly. The "*Wisdom of the Dead*" is more than just a book, it's essential for our survival."

Watkins reached into the glove compartment of the Porsche and retrieved the cellular phone that Fabian loaned him. The two men devised a secret code to use if Chester was successful in finding the girl. Watkins pressed the redial button and waited for the call to go through. When the doctor answered his home phone, the message was passed, “Birds of a feather flock together.”

This was the signal for the physicians to prepare another coffin and have a warm meal waiting for their new guest. If the Rubensteins replied, “Not in this nest,” Chester would be alerted that either Marius or another vampire from the Dynasty was visiting and it wasn’t safe to return. It was essential that the girl be questioned before anyone was advised that she’d been found.

“I’m sorry I bit you. I couldn’t help myself.”

Chester started laughing as he looked at the young girl. “I’m not. My life was a living hell. If you were 80-plus years old, you’d know what I mean. Everything hurt, and what didn’t hurt didn’t work.”

“You’re not mad, really?”

“No, I forgave you the first night I woke up. No arthritis, no shortness of breath, no kidney stones.”

“You seem like a nice old man. You kind of remind me of my grandfather. He died a couple of years ago.”

“I’m sorry to hear that,” replied Chester. “Was he a military man?”

“He was in the Navy.”

“A squid and a deck ape.”

“What’s that?”

“Never mind. How long have you been a vampire?”

“Almost a year. I hate being a vampire. I had a family and friends who cared about me and then some bastard raped and killed me.”

Upon hearing this, the old man slowed the vehicle down and turned into a parking lot on their right-hand side. “Marsha, we need to talk.”

“I don’t want to talk about it. I shouldn’t have said anything.”

Chester parked the car in an empty slot next to a Dodge pickup truck and left the engine idling. “I know this is a sensitive subject, but Count Marius is blaming you for my death. You’re just a teen-aged girl. The person who bit you should be the one held responsible. Was he an older man?"

"I'm afraid. All I can remember is that this vampire was evil and he kept letting stinky farts. He was wearing an amulet around his neck and it dangled in my face while he was on top of me."

"Can you remember any symbols on this necklace?"

"Yes, it was a Pentagram with a skull in the center of it. The symbol of Satan."

Chester remembered reading in Chapter 10 of "*Wisdom of the Dead,*" titled Satanic Vampires, "*The immortal will have two choices: To serve one's self and Satan or to restrain from the lust for blood and strive to live among humans peaceably. Once the evil path is chosen, there is no redemption.*" The chapter was written to discourage vampires from choosing the practices of wickedness and it gave reference to another book that the evil converts studied, titled "*Abbadon's Priests.*" According to the ancient text, the satanic manuscript was full of evil spells and methods of practicing the dark arts. A direct link to the underworld could be accessed by black magic rituals and communication with demonic spirits.

The toothless old man wanted no part of the kingdom of darkness, and sternly questioned the young girl. "What path have you chosen? Life or death, good or evil?"

"I choose life. I choose good."

"Can you remember anything else about this vampire?"

"Not at the moment, but if I do I'll tell you. Where are we going?"

"To a safe house." Chester reversed the Porsche and drove out of the parking lot and headed towards Bear Creek. His thoughts were racing through his mind as he tried to figure out what was going on. "*Maybe there was another rogue vampire,*" he thought. He didn't want to risk exposing the young girl to the Dynasty of Immortals until he could convince Marius of her innocence, but how could he do this? He thought it would be wise to hide her out until he attended a council meeting to see if this group could be trusted.

When he approached a stoplight, he turned to look at the young girl. “Marsha, I want you to behave yourself when we get to this house. These people are risking their lives to help us. Please don’t do anything foolish like running away.”

“I promise you I won’t, but I have to ask, ‘Why are you helping me?’”

With a gummy grin, Watkins answered, “I’m helping both of us. By the way— I don’t have anything else better to do.”

Chester followed Fabian’s advice and detoured a couple of blocks out of the way, making sure he wasn’t being followed. When the vampires entered the Rubenstein’s home, Patricia greeted the young girl with a cheerful smile and tried to make her feel welcome. “I bet you’re hungry.”

The gray man gave her a nod, signaling that everything was OK.

“Yes, ma’am,” replied the teen-aged vampire. “I haven’t eaten yet.”

“Chester, why don’t you visit with Fabian while I take our new guest to the laboratory and prepare her a warm meal. After that, I’ll show her around the house so we can discuss lady stuff.”

The two men retreated to the study and closed the door. Watkins pointed to the cedar cigar box. “I need a smoke really bad.”

“Me too,” replied the doctor. “I could also use a stiff-drink.”

“I think my hunch was right. Something sinister happened to that young girl and I don’t think we should tell anyone we’ve found her.”

The doctor exhaled a thick cloud of smoke and withdrew his cigar from his mouth. “What do you think is going on?”

“I don’t know, but I do know this, we need to be very careful who we trust.”

“I’ve known Marius for 33 years. He’s a man of integrity. The Dynasty is an upstanding organization”

The vampire took a drag of his cigar and replied, "Marius is not the one I'm worried about. I think this young girl was raped by a satanic vampire and until I find out who he is I'm not taking any chances."

The men's conversation lasted late into the night. It was Friday and the doctors weren't on call that weekend. The vampire told Fabian that he wanted a copy of "*Abbadon's Priests*." Confused, Rubenstein sternly objected because he didn't know Chester's intentions. The old man reassured his friend that he only wanted to study the book for academic purposes. Reluctantly, the doctor agreed.

Chester thought to himself, *"We need to know how our enemies think and how to exploit their weaknesses."*

Fabian had no idea how to find this ancient book. It was forbidden to possess a copy according to council law. The doctor suggested that Watkins try searching in occult bookstores and if this didn't turn anything up he would contact an old college friend who was a history professor.

"My old fraternity brother has a collection of archaic manuscripts and medieval books," the doctor stated. "He probably doesn't have this book, but I'm certain he's heard of it."

Fabian and Watkins returned to the living room and saw that Patricia and the teen-aged vampire were laughing about something.

"What's so funny?" asked Fabian.

"Nothing," replied Patricia.

When Chester smiled, Marsha started giggling again. "I've got to confess, we were talking about you. I feel so guilty. Even though I was starving to death, I would have never bitten you if I would have known you were toothless."

"That brings up another question the doctor and I have," replied Watkins. "How were you feeding?"

The fair-skinned teenager readjusted her position on the couch, responding, "I broke into a couple of medical clinics and stole some blood. I stored the bags in an underground culvert and they kept fresh for several days at a time."

Both of the doctors leaned forward at the same time and Fabian spoke up. "Smart thinking."

Watkins motioned for the four of them to sit closely. "We need to talk. I don't know what we're up against, but I believe we're in a precarious situation. The demonic vampire who bit Marsha is still out there. Until we can figure out who he is, we need to be very careful. He might be part of a secret organization and if that's the case, then he's not alone."

The doctor told his wife that he was in agreement with Chester and that they were going to research a couple of things before telling the governing council of vampires about the girl.

Watkins insisted that Marsha study the "*Wisdom of the Dead*" every evening until she finished it. He also suggested that she sleep in the secret passageway. There was plenty of room for her coffin and any personal belongings she might need. The Rubensteins agreed with him and thought that was a good idea. They continued discussing their plans until the antique grandfather clock chimed six times.

The young vampire got up and kissed Chester on the forehead. "Thank you for forgiving me."

"I think we better get some sleep," replied the old man as he put his hand on the teenager's shoulder. "Everything will work out in the end, you'll see."

The Crusaders of Light assemble for another wicked ritual

CHAPTER 5, THE CRUSADERS

In a rural area near Evergreen, Texas, five musical instruments playing in disharmony signaled the beginning of the ritual. It was a full moon and the witches screamed in fits of abandon as they danced around the fire drinking booze and smoking marijuana laced with angel dust. The rhythmic beat of the drum would not cease until the meeting was adjourned. The drummer's relentless energy was induced by cheap methamphetamines, enabling him to continue pounding for hours on end. A primitive horn bellowed out of tune as the leader cast two sulfur circles in the middle of the deserted barn.

"As I will, so mote it be!" shouted the coven leader Lucious Miller. He took a drink of cheap whiskey and pointed to one of the musicians.

A gong sounded and the members took their rightful places and assembled around the circles. The musicians continued to play a horrid tune while Miller stepped inside his circle of protection and spoke his enchantment.

"Lord of the night, bringer of light, appear before us," he intoned.

With heads bowed and eyes closed, the witches anxiously awaited for their master to appear. Through a hole in the roof of the barn, the vampire bat entered the building and landed in the middle of the circle.

"Bat of the night, take flight," the vampire bat uttered quietly to himself to reverse the spell.

The members opened their eyes and standing in the other circle was a tall, handsome vampire dressed in a white tuxedo. His zipper was undone and when the cult leader made eye contact with him he quickly pointed to it in hopes that none of the other witches had noticed. The proud vampire inconspicuously glanced down and tried to pull it up, snagging the head of his penis in the process. He let out a shrieking yell as he unzipped, gritted his teeth and repositioned his privates. When he zipped it back up again, it made a distinctive sound, blending in with the wretched music.

"I'll summon the powers of the underworld," the wicked huckster said as he prepared to quote a fake incantation that he just made up.

"So mote it be!" the coven shouted in ignorant unison.

"O Lucent one, may your will be done. I give you the ancient right to speak to us tonight."

The vampire screamed as he pretended evil spirits were entering his body. He farted a couple of times during his phony act and the smell of rotten eggs filled the air. The entire group began to cough and convulse and some of the witches fell to the ground and began to slither like snakes while the others moaned and began chanting.

The vampire cleared his throat, deepened his voice and pretended that someone else was speaking through him.

"I command you, empty your pockets, wallets and purses and give tithes in the name of your god to this unholy servant. Anyone who has any money left in their pockets will be sacrificed."

A witch in the crowd began to cry as her husband emptied the contents of her purse and threw them in the circle. The sound of coins and loose change being dumped out made an unmistakable ring.

One of the warlocks slapped his wife's hand as she endorsed her welfare check in the name of the vampire.

The evil one barked, "You with the hood on, gather up the offerings and bring them to me."

"Yes, master."

He quickly counted the checks, cash and loose change, which only totaled $357.33. In a rage, he angrily hollered, "Blasphemy! Do you think this is a church social? Take off your watches and jewelry and cast them before me."

Hissing, the vampire displayed his teeth as watches and rings were thrown to the barn's dirt floor.

"You wearing the diamond-studded watch," the huckster sternly ordered, "bring it hither."

"It belonged to my dad," he cried. The pitiful man attempted to run but was knocked unconscious by the gong player who hit him in the head with his heavy stick.

"Strip him and prepare him for sacrifice. Insubordination will not be tolerated."

The man slowly regained consciousness and began weeping as he was being dragged to the wooden alter.

"Bind his hands and feet," ordered the vampire.

Lucious unsheathed a dull, rusty dagger from his belt and slit the incoherent man's wrists. A witch from the group caught the spilling blood in a sacrificial chalice as the warlock slowly bled to death. Miller, who was standing over the victim, thrust the knife into his chest to complete the sacrifice. The cult began to cheer while the hallucinating musicians played their corny-sounding instruments with maximum intensity. The noise was almost deafening. Finally, the vampire cried out, "Enough!"

All of the music stopped except for the drum, which slowed to a steady beat. The vampire stepped out of his circle and approached the altar.

"Give me the chalice," he ordered.

The woman who was holding the container handed it to the wicked guest. He lifted the cup to his mouth, spilling some of the blood on his beautiful suit. The vampire indulged himself like a glutton. When he was satisfied, he passed the cup and ordered the other coven members to partake of what remained.

Some of the witches began to disrobe, smearing blood on themselves. Suddenly, the vampire cried out, "Orgy time!"

The rustic barn became a building of debauchery as the group worked themselves into a drunken, sexual frenzy. The sacrificed body was cast into the bonfire as the party carried on into the wee hours of the morning.

The time according to the expensive watch the vampire was now wearing was 4:17 a.m. He put his blood-stained clothes back on and gathered up the rest of his jewelry and money, and stuffed all of his pockets full of loot.

The Crusaders of Light were mere shadows of their predecessors. The evil vampire knew this and capitalized on their stupidity. The cult members' ancestors had served him for generations, with each succeeding group becoming more gullible. The vampire hunters were now being seduced by a vampire who commanded them to do his bidding and kill his political rivals. With false promises of positions of power and immortality, the group followed him blindly. His ultimate quest was to become chancellor of the Dynasty of Immortals.

"Miller, here is a map of Raton Pass, New Mexico. Follow my written instructions and kill the vampires and their caretakers before the next full moon."

When he was finished giving orders, the vampire returned to his ritualistic circle. He jingled when he walked because of all the change in his pockets. After he recited the bat incantation, he could barely get off the ground because of all the weight. The vampire bat took off flying lopsided and crashed into the side of the barn wall next to a bale of hay. Hovering with all his might, he regained his momentum and exited through the same hole he had entered from earlier. When he cleared the building, the coven cheered, "Farewell, master."

Within seconds, he was far away from the hokey barn and his dim-witted servants. Feeling confident that his orders would be carried out before his next visit, he flew into the night sky, navigating home by the stars.

The following day, the Satanists attended their respective churches because it was Sunday. Most of them were never recognized for what they were because of the spiritual blindness in the denominational congregations. Infiltration of religious organizations was an important part of being a witch. The group members were constantly on the lookout for potential recruits. Apostate Christians made the best Satanists according to Miller.

The cult leader presented a heart-warming sermon to the small flock at the Baptist church where he was appointed interim pastor. His wife also taught Sunday school. She subtly taught lies to the young children and often distorted the truth. She was constantly planting seeds of doubt in their innocent little minds. The ignorant mothers in the church loved and praised her for the wonderful job she was doing. Only one family had the discernment to question her teachings. This family was strongly rebuked by the church and was soon targeted by the cult. Their names and street address were mailed to the lewd vampire's post office box so he could pay them an unsuspecting visit in the future.

A week had passed since the wild ritual had taken place and five of the cult members met with Miller at his residence to discuss vanquishing the vampires in New Mexico. Two of these men were police officers. The group agreed to take the next week off and travel in two separate vehicles. Once their mission was accomplished, they would detour through Colorado, go fishing for a couple of days and return home via Oklahoma.

"We need to strike early in the morning according to our master's instructions," Miller said. "After sunrise, we kill them"

The vampire's written directives were taken from the book "*Wisdom of the Dead*." Chapter 13: Vanquishing the Immortal. This segment of the book listed all of the implements and methods used to terminate a vampire's life. The vampire only disclosed one technique. The cult had no knowledge of the existence of this ancient manuscript. The evil master was very careful not to give them too much information. He wanted to keep his followers as uninformed as possible so he could deceive and control them. His orders were simple and basic: "Drive wooden stakes through the vampires' hearts with wooden mallets as they sleep." After that, they were to shoot the caretakers and set the buildings on fire.

The following week, the satanic leader and his cohorts were successful in accomplishing their mission. Many loyal vampires lost their lives to the hands of these murderous killers. One of the victims was a trusted council member. The caretakers were systematically tortured, raped and shot to death. The only remaining evidence of the countryside estate were the concrete foundations standing out in the smoldering ashes.

When news of the attack reached northwest Arkansas, Count Marius called for an emergency meeting of the Dynasty of Immortals. Three days later, the Rubensteins were informed of the killings.

Back in Houston, the weather was turning muggy as summer approached. It had been raining for almost two days and some of the streets in the lower parts of town were beginning to flood. When Chester and Marsha woke up, the doctors were already knocking on their door to inform them of the murders that had taken place in Raton Pass. The vampires followed the family into the front room to hear the tragic news.

"An entire estate was burned to the ground," said Fabian. "Everyone was killed, even the children."

The gray vampire's face grimaced as he recounted a similar incident that happened on an island occupied by the Japanese. The enemy soldiers were tossing babies into the air while others were trying to catch them on the ends of their bayonets. Afterwards, they torched the entire village, executing everyone.

"There's only one way to deal with people who do things like that," replied the old Marine.

"And, what would that be?" asked Patricia.

"We have to go to war, but first we need to know who we're fighting against. An invisible enemy is the most dangerous opponent of all."

Watkins was determined to find the evil vampire and his book "*Abbadon's Priests*." The doctors had been preoccupied conducting experiments on the vampire's DNA and analyzing blood samples all week. The old man didn't want to interfere with their work, so he invited Marsha to accompany him that evening and search for the satanic book. As soon as the vampires left, the research scientists returned to their laboratory to study some slide samples.

Watkins and the girl drove to the south part of Houston and took the Telephone Road exit.

"Have you got any ideas?" asked Chester.

"Everything is closed. I wish we could search during the day," she answered.

"I don't think ordinary stores are going to be carrying what we're looking for. Maybe we can find a copy in a comic book store."

The two started laughing and Marsha replied, "I really love your sense of humor."

As they traveled southward, they approached a giant neon sign with the inscription "Fortune Teller." A yellow palm was mounted above it pulsating on and off. The house behind the sign had the symbol of the all-seeing eye mounted on top of the roof and owl statues were positioned in every window.

"Slow down, Chester. Turn in there."

"What?" said the old man as he drove past the driveway.

"I think we should try that fortune-telling place."

The vampire made a quick U-turn and returned to the mystical-looking building. The two of them went to the door and, to their surprise, it was unlocked. When they entered, they could hear strange music coming from a room in the back. The two followed the sound through a hall and into another room with beads covering the entryway. Watkins parted the beads with his hands and they made a distinctive clicking, clacking sound. Sitting in a chair next to a table with a fuzzy red cloth draped over it was an old-looking gypsy woman with a thin, scraggly goatee. When the vampires entered the room, she turned her head in their general direction.

The young girl whispered to Chester, "Look, she's blind."

When the gypsy spoke, the two could hardly understand her because her voice was so hoarse. "I know what you seek, but do you understand what it is you must find."

The old vampire whispered to the teenager, "She's full of shit. Let's get out of here."

Watkins turned around to leave when the medium cried out, "What you seek entails more than just book knowledge."

Marsha clutched the gray vampire's arm and tugged on it, motioning for him to come to the gypsy's table and sit down.

"I think you're right. Let's give her a chance."

Pulling up chairs, the vampires joined the haggardly looking woman and sat patiently waiting for her to speak. Chester was gazing into the crystal ball that was in the center of the table when the silence was broken.

"Twenty dollars and I will see if the spirits are willing to speak to us tonight."

The teen-aged vampire reached into her purse and produced a crisp $1 dollar bill and placed it in the blind soothsayer's hand. She turned to Chester and winked her eye.

"Deceitfulness will only anger the spirits," the gypsy said.

Watkins reached into his back pocket to find his wallet. He placed two $10 bills on the table in front of the woman.

"You're a kind man, I can feel your warmth." The woman took the money and slid it under the crystal ball, using it as a paperweight. "I can also feel your pain."

"What can you tell us?"

"Give me your hands."

Compliantly, he placed both hands on the table in front of the old crone. She reached for them and blindly felt around until she touched something.

"Let go of my hands," ordered Marsha.

"Excuse me," replied the blind hag.

She felt around again until she found Chester's hands.

Embracing them, the woman started rocking back and forth slowly as she petitioned the spirits to speak. A couple of minutes passed and her chair started to make a squeaky sound like it was coming apart. The gypsy continued her act until one of the legs snapped off of the chair sending her crashing into the table. Trying to catch herself, she released her grip from the vampire's hands and pulled the tablecloth off as she fell to the floor. The crystal ball was launched into the air and smashed into one of the owl statues sitting on the windowsill. The impact sent glass flying in all directions.

The woman started to writhe about on the floor amidst the broken glass and the grinding, crunching sound made the vampires jump to their feet. Suddenly, the woman sat up and cried out, "The book you seek is the book of the destroyer. To live, you must destroy the evil one."

"Where can we find the manuscript?" shouted Watkins.

"The spirits need more money."

He reached for his wallet again, saying, "Here's another twenty. Where the hell can we find it?"

"There's only one occult bookstore located in The Heights. Tell them Zelda sent you."

Before the vampires left, and out of generosity, Chester handed the old lady another $20 dollar bill and told her to get her window fixed. The couple drove straight to The Heights in search of the curio shop and it took them almost an hour to find it.

The vampires parked at the side of the building and when they got out of their car Marsha spied a man who was hiding in the bushes next to the specialty store. As the two were walking toward the shop, the robber crawled out of his hiding place and sprinted into the path of the approaching vampires.

"Give me your wallet or I'll blow your head off," he demanded as he pointed a .38 revolver at Watkins' face.

As slick as an agile cat, Marsha displayed her teeth and pounced on top of the man, knocking him to the ground and pinning him. As the would-be robber lay struggling on his back, Chester reacted quickly and stomped on the man's wrist causing him to turn loose of his weapon.

Chester pulled his .45 from under his jacket and stuck it to the man's head. "How would you like it if I blew your head off instead?"

The thug stopped resisting and lay motionless in silent compliance.

"When the young lady gets off of you, I want you to roll over on your stomach and bring both of your hands behind your back. You know the procedure. I have a feeling you've been in this position before."

The old man withdrew the pistol from the assailant's head and stepped back a few feet, still keeping the .45 trained on his target. With his free hand, Chester pulled his belt from his pants and ordered Marsha to tie the man's hands. After she was finished, the stern-faced Marine pulled the man up by the belt and walked him over to the back of the Porsche. When he opened the trunk, the prisoner immediately objected, "I'm not climbing in there."

"You don't have to," Chester replied as he pulled the crowbar out of the trunk and struck the thug in the back of the head, knocking him out. With a grunt, the vampire hoisted the man up, threw him into the cramped space and slammed it shut.

"I hate it when someone wastes my time," the cagey Marine said dusting his hands off. "Let's go into the store and see what kind of stuff they've got."

Laughing, the young girl added, "I bet that chump never saw that one coming, did he?"

The two walked into the shop and woke the clerk up who was sleeping behind the counter in a reclining chair. Groggily, he wiped his eyes. "Can I help you?"

"Zelda sent us."

"Not her again."

The vampires looked at one another thinking that they had just been taken when the clerk said, "I've got an old book with a funny-looking cover you might be interested in buying."

"Can we see it?"

"Yes, we bought this old footlocker and it was full of weird junk," the shopkeeper said as he stood up. "Follow me, it's in the back."

Chester and Marsha went to the rear of the store and watched as the man opened a dingy trunk and retrieved the book from inside. He dusted the cover off and handed it to the old man. The vampire looked at the words "*Abbadon's Priests*" written on the cover.

"How much?" asked the vampire.

"Five bucks," the man said as he closed the lid. "That kind of literature isn't in demand. We only wanted the trunk and they had it stuffed full of strange things when they sold it to us."

"Can we take a look in there?" asked the toothless man as he reached for his wallet and handed the clerk $5.

"Help yourself," he answered as he was walking back to the cash register.

Marsha stooped down and opened the footlocker to examine the contents. To their surprise, there were wooden mallets, stakes, crosses and dried garlic cloves inside the old relic. The teenager hissed when she smelled the garlic and dropped the lid of the trunk.

"Let's get out of here," she said coughing.

The two vampires left the store and Chester said goodbye to the clerk as he closed the door behind them. When they approached the Porsche, they saw that it was shaking violently from side to side. They could hear muffled screams and kicking coming from inside the vehicle.

Chester pulled his keys from his pocket and quickly opened the back compartment and punched the man in the face, knocking him unconscious again. When he closed it, he told Marsha, "Let's get out of here before someone sees us."

When they drove off, she asked him what they were going to do with the would-be-robber.

"Maybe we'll ask the doctors to perform some kind of weird experiment on him. They can transplant his foreskin to his eyelids or something like that? We'll call him cockeyed Eddie."

The two laughed for almost five minutes before Chester spoke up. "I think I'll rough him up again and teach his scrounging ass a lesson. We'll dump him off at the Bear Creek golf course when we're finished."

The young vampire started giggling. "I picked his pistol up and stuck it in my purse."

"Good thinking, we might need it someday. Has anyone ever taught you how to shoot a handgun before?

"Not really, but I've watched lots of movies and television shows."

"I was afraid you'd say that."

"What?"

"Never mind, don't worry, I'll teach you the basics. Let me see it so I can unload it. We don't want anyone to get hurt."

Marsha handed the vampire her purse as he was slowing down for a stoplight. Chester reached inside to feel for the gun and when he found it, he took the weapon out of her handbag and sighed. "I don't think I'll be able to teach you how to shoot this revolver."

"Why not?" questioned the girl.

"It's a water pistol."

When the light turned green, Chester floored the gas peddle of the Porsche causing the criminal's body to make a thud inside of the tight trunk. With tires squealing, Marsha made the remark, "I don't think our prisoner made a very good career choice."

Watkins turned his head quickly and looked at the girl, "Like they say, crime never pays."

The vampires entered Bear Creek Park, turning in off of Clay Road. As they maneuvered left, they could hear the man pounding on the interior walls. Chester slowed to about 10 miles an hour and drove slowly southward toward the country club. They parked the Porsche in a dimly lit area overlooking the golf course and yanked the thug out by his legs, throwing him to the concrete driveway. Watkins pulled the man to his feet and spun him around. "Get up you son of a bitch."

Marsha flared her lips, displayed her fangs, and hissed at the frightened robber while Chester loosened his restraints. With a slapping whip, the gray vampire pulled his belt loose, freeing the man's hands.

Bewildered, the dizzy criminal's jaw dropped. "My God, look at her teeth. What kind of freaks are you?"

"Shut up you snot-nosed punk, We're going to teach you a lesson you'll never forget."

With both hands, the vampire began to rip and tear the man's clothes off of his body, throwing them in every direction. Standing naked, the shivering man looked up at Chester with terror in his eyes. With a grin, the mischievous senior punched the robber in the stomach causing him to double over. Working as a team, Marsha kicked the guy in the buttocks and Watkins barked like a Marine drill instructor, "Get out of here before I shoot your trouser-worm off."

Without hesitating, the military veteran yanked his Colt .45 pistol out of his pants and discharged a round harmlessly into the grass right between the man's legs. Frightened and disoriented, the battered crook took off screaming as he ran across the golf course and through the sprinkler systems that were just coming on. Once he was out of sight, the vampires jumped inside of the sports car and drove off traveling in the opposite direction.

"Hand me that cell phone in the glove box," the old man demanded.

The young girl did as she was ordered and gave Chester the phone. He fought back laughter as he called the Sheriff's Department and reported seeing a naked pervert running through the park. When the dispatcher asked him for his name, he replied that he was just a concerned citizen who didn't want to get involved and abruptly hung up.

The next morning when the Rubensteins were eating breakfast and watching television, a reporter came on the set and said that a streaker was arrested for indecent exposure near Eldridge Parkway. The correspondent went on to say that the man who was apprehended had a lengthy arrest record and was recently paroled from Huntsville prison. According to police records, the man only served seven years of a 20-year sentence for armed robbery and murder.

"I'm glad he's back behind bars," Patricia said as she turned the TV off.

"Me too," Fabian replied. "Let's get going or we'll be late for work."

The doctors departed not knowing that their vampire guests were the ones who were responsible for the entire incident.

Chester's pranks…El Lobo, de noche. Wolf of the night takes revenge on pesky trash eating mutts.

CHAPTER 6, CHESTER'S PRANKS

Chester and Marsha's relationship continued to flourish with the passing of each night. The gray vampire included the young girl in almost everything he did and even taught her how to play chess. Getting her to smoke cigars was a special challenge however.

Her love, respect and admiration for the old vampire grew stronger as she spent more time with him. Watkins had a way of making people feel comfortable and the young girl trusted his every word. He promised her that after he studied the satanic manuscript he would start searching for the evil vampire who murdered and raped her.

"We must find him," the old Marine repeatedly said. "I have a feeling that there's more to this situation than meets the eye."

Late one night, Chester asked Marsha's opinion about a verse he was studying in "*Abbadon's Priests*."

"You know that book scares me," she said.

"I know it does, but we have to understand how our enemies think."

Grudgingly, she agreed. "Show me the verse."

Chester opened the book to page six, verse 66.

Immediately, when Marsha saw the sequence of numbers she covered her mouth and gasped. "Six, six, six is the devil's number."

The verse read, "*Capitalize on their stupidity and they shall worship you. Kill them and they shall fear you. Rape them and they shall love you. An evil monarch must possess all of these traits.*"

The old man closed the book and turned to look at the teen-aged vampire. She shrugged her shoulders and said, "Maybe our vampire wants to be a king."

"It seems to me this verse encourages just that," replied Chester.

For months, the old man had talked about attending a council meeting in northwest Arkansas, but he kept procrastinating. His search for Marsha had interfered with him attending previous functions. With nothing else standing in his way, he felt that it was time to check this organization out. The next conference was scheduled in two weeks, one night prior to the full moon. "*Maybe this might fit into the scheme of things,*" he thought.

"We have one advantage over our enemies."

"What's that?" queried Marsha.

"The element of surprise. They don't know we're looking for them."

Chester closed the evil book and returned it to its hiding place behind another book located on the bookshelf. He hated handling it and always washed his hands afterwards. Fabian examined the book's weird leather cover and, after analyzing it in the laboratory, he determined that it was lined with human skin. The teen-aged vampire refused to touch it and she would only read from its pages looking over the old man's shoulder.

Both of the vampires left their private quarters and went into the front room for a change of scenery. The doctors were asleep and the considerate guests were being very careful to be quiet. Chester slowly opened the curtains and looked outside through one of the windows. For several weeks Fabian had been complaining about some of the neighbor's dogs running loose through the neighborhood and knocking over trashcans. The whole subdivision was in an uproar because one negligent family was responsible and they kept ignoring everyone's complaints. The old vampire looked beyond the bars of the security fence and just outside where the trashcans were stored he saw two mixed breed dogs ripping through a garbage bag. Both metal containers were knocked over and debris was strewn into the street.

The old vampire whispered to Marsha, "Watch this," as he pointed the dogs out to her.

He told the teenager to stay by the window and watch as he silently slipped through the front door and into the night. In just a few seconds, she witnessed a vampire bat flying through the yard and over the security fence in the direction of the dogs. She lost sight of the bat, but within a couple of minutes she saw a huge silver wolf approaching unseen behind the menacing mutts.

Lunging at the dogs, the wolf caught them completely by surprise. Like a tornado, he was mauling both of them so fast that they never had a chance to defend themselves. Biting off their ears and tails, the vampire canine sent both trash diggers running and yelping down the street. For the fun of it, he couldn't resist chasing them all the way home to see where they lived. After he got there, he figured he'd teach the reckless family a lesson. He knocked over their trash receptacles and had a heyday with the newspapers, shredding them in hundreds of pieces throughout the yard. The cowering dogs watched and whimpered from under the bushes as they hid from the big bad wolf.

Satisfied that revenge had been achieved, he returned to his part of the neighborhood. He transformed back into himself, picked up the Rubenstein's trash, and neatly placed the lids back on top of the cans. A few seconds after he was finished, the vampire bat flew back over the fence. Another minute passed and Chester strutted through the front door.

He approached Marsha as she was closing the curtains and she silently applauded with her hands, "I couldn't believe how fast you looked. Those stupid dogs didn't have a chance."

"I surprised myself," the old man replied. "It's exhilarating to be able to run that fast."

Marsha was so impressed with Chester's display that she asked, "What chapter is that spell in again? I need to learn that."

The gray old man smiled. "I've been telling you that for weeks. Maybe you'll listen to me now. You need to study that book."

The following morning when the Rubensteins headed out for work, they drove past the obnoxious neighbor's home and they couldn't believe the atrocious mess they saw in their front yard.

Fabian started laughing and pointed at the lawn. "Look at all the trash. Serves those stupid idiots right."

With her eyeglasses dangling off the end of her nose, Patricia responded, "My goodness, look at their dogs. They're all torn up."

"Maybe a bobcat mauled them," the lazy-eyed doctor replied as he slowly pulled away.

Later that evening when the Rubensteins returned home, Fabian told the vampires about everything he saw that morning. Patricia joined in the conversation and commented about how pitiful the mongrels looked. "It looked like a wildcat ripped them to pieces."

Both of the vampires dummied up and acted like they didn't know a thing. Marsha looked at Chester and winked her eye as the doctors continued telling their story.

Later that evening after the physicians went to bed, the vampires had an in-depth conversation about their former lives. Marsha was surprised when the old man recounted all of his previous jobs and world travels. He was a policeman, a carpenter, a vacuum cleaner salesman, a garbage collector, and he even worked for a traveling carnival.

"I wish you could have seen the snake boy," he commented. "He was a real lady's man, that silver-tongued devil."

"You've done a lot of things."

"Yes, I have."

"How long were you a police officer and where did you work?"

The former Marine scratched his big nose as he thought back in time. "About three years in a small town in East Texas. In the summer of 1949, I kicked the sergeant's ass in a donut shop and got fired for insubordination."

"Why did you do that?"

"Because he pissed me off. He was an egotistical, arrogant bully. He treated people like shit. He thought he was better than everyone else because he wore a badge. That asshole never served in the military or fought in World War II."

"So, they fired you?"

"You bet they did, and after I turned in my badge, about three weeks later, that moron shot and killed a 14-year-old boy who stole a candy bar from the general store. He accused the kid of pulling a pocketknife on him."

"Did he get away with it?" Marsha asked as she leaned toward the old man.

"Yes and no," he answered, shaking his head.

"What do you mean?"

"He planted a penknife in the boy's hand and the judge and jury bought his lie. The kid's family, who were nothing but dirt-poor farmers, sat in the courtroom during the whole trial. The atmosphere was more ridiculous than a circus act. Both attorneys were corrupt and when the case was dismissed the boy's father walked outside and waited for the officer in the parking lot."

"What happened next?" asked the inquisitive young vampire.

"His father shot him right between the eyes with a Winchester .30-30 deer rifle. It was nasty. The blast took the top of the sergeant's skull clean off. It happened so quickly that the farmer got away before anyone could arrest him."

"Really?"

The old vampire chuckled. "Maybe they didn't want to catch him."

"What do you think of today's police officers?"

"Most of them don't treat people with respect like we did in the old days," Chester responded. "I see law enforcement officers making a lot of stupid mistakes here in Texas, especially the highway patrol."

"What do you mean?"

"Tactical mistakes, like searching vehicles by themselves with three or four people standing behind them. An officer who turns his back on his suspects is inviting trouble. Some of these young studs think their cowboy hats, Sam Brown leather, shiny badges and boots make them invincible. I've got news for them, they're full of shit."

"So, these guys are taking unnecessary chances?"

"In certain situations, yes. Some of these fools display poor weapon retention skills also."

"What's that?" questioned the girl.

"Weapon retention is a state of consciousness. It's not allowing someone to snatch your pistol out of your holster unexpectedly. I see some of these patrolmen standing within arm's reach of some rough-looking dudes while writing their little tickets. All it takes is a split second to be disarmed. I always stood in a bladed stance and kept a prudent distance between myself and anyone I was dealing with, usually 10 feet or more. That way if I was charged, rushed or some ornery guy wanted to fight or stab me, I could react, draw and fire, or knock his ass out with my nightstick."

"Sounds like you really knew what you were doing."

The gray vampire smiled. "I did— that's why I got fired."

Both of them laughed for a few more minutes before retiring to their quarters. The teenager meditated on all of the things the wise man said to her that night. *"Life took on a different perspective hanging around older people,"* she thought. The Rubensteins were also a good source of information and they were very interesting to talk to. The combined influence of intellect and kindness was an overpowering factor contributing to the rehabilitation of the rogue vampire. Her rebellious attitude and nature were channeled into a positively structured environment fostering mental growth and education. In essence, Marsha knew she was being home-schooled.

Saturday evening arrived and Chester was entertaining an intriguing idea. He wanted to demonstrate to the young vampire just how sloppy the Texas highway patrol actually was. The doctors went to bed early that night, leaving the old man to freelance his dastardly prank.

"Come with me," he ordered.

"Where are we going?" she asked.

"You'll see. We're going to have a little fun."

Immediately, the young vampire became excited because she instinctively knew that Chester was up to something. The pair entered the garage and the old man grabbed a screwdriver from the doctor's toolbox and walked behind the Porsche.

"What's that for?"

"Patience, you'll see."

Watkins removed the license plates from the car and placed them on the workbench. "Get in."

Within minutes, the two were outside the gate and cruising the neighborhood. Chester drove the Porsche to the ignorant neighbor's house who owned the undisciplined dogs. He parked a couple of houses away and silently crept toward the residence. When the mutts saw him approaching, they whimpered and retreated into the bushes. The vampire took the screwdriver out of his pocket and removed one of the license plates from the car in the driveway. Marsha fought back laughter as she watched the old prankster quietly slip away and return to their car. He screwed the plate to the rear of the Porsche and unobtrusively drove away.

Heading to Interstate 10, the prankster said, "I'm going to introduce you to our state police."

When the sports car entered the onramp of the highway, the gray vampire shifted gears, pinning both vampires to the back of their seats from the inertia. Within seconds, the speedometer read 115 mph and was still climbing.

The young vampire screamed, "Go grandpa!"

Chester's speed leveled out to 135 mph after passing a few slow-moving cars. He let off the accelerator and began to slowly decelerate to the posted speed limit of 70 mph.

"Where are we headed?" asked Marsha.

"West, past Katy, Texas."

The young girl was eager to see what would transpire.

"Do you remember reading in the book "*Wisdom of the Dead*" about our immortality?"

"Yes," replied Marsha. "Chapter 13. '*Nothing can kill us except direct exposure to sunlight, fire or a wooden stake driven through our heart.*'"

"Good girl," replied Chester. "I'm going to provoke a fight with a police officer tonight to teach you a lesson in life. He probably won't have a chance to draw his weapon, but just in case he does I don't want you to be afraid."

"I wasn't afraid when that creep tried to rob us," the teenager answered back.

"You're my fearless matriarch. Hold on to your seat."

The sports car headed west past the city of Katy. The pair traveled for another 10 minutes until they finally saw a patrol car pulling over a speeding van on the opposite side of the freeway. With its wig-wag lights flashing, Chester observed a tall officer approach the suspect's vehicle.

"That looks like a black and white to me."

The two traveled to the next exit and circled back under the overpass. Chester parked on the shoulder of the feeder ramp and waited for about 10 minutes before re-entering the freeway. He wanted to see if any backup vehicles would respond to assist the officer, but he also wanted to give him ample time to write a ticket or conduct his business.

When he was satisfied that enough time had elapsed, the former Marine shifted the sports car into first gear and rapidly worked the stick shift through its gears as he drove off. He accelerated to 80 mph and headed in the direction of the action. As he approached the flashing lights of the patrol car, he could see the van slowly pulling away and merging into the light traffic. The vampire sped past the police officer who was just turning his wig-wags off. He looked into his rearview mirror and he saw the blue and white lights pop back on again.

"Now, act real polite," he said as he slowed down and pulled over to the shoulder.

The patrol car quickly pulled in behind them and the officer turned on his spotlight to illuminate the Porsche. A few minutes passed and Chester saw an approaching shadow pass through the flashing lights. He rolled the window down and looked into the blinding lights. Squinting, he made out the figure of an officer who was wearing the familiar uniform of the state police.

"I clocked you doing 80 in a 70. Can I see your driver's license?"

The old vampire feigned being weak and senile. Pretending to have a raspy voice, he replied, "I'm sorry, sonny, I was talking to my granddaughter and I wasn't paying attention."

"I'm not your son. Hurry up and let me see your driver's license," the officer said in a cocky tone.

"The senior citizen looked at Marsha and whispered to her, "See the disrespectful attitude?"

Chester purposely fumbled through his pockets and acted confused. "I'm sorry, I must have left it at home."

"Step out of your vehicle right now. Have you had anything to drink tonight?"

As the vampire opened the door, he faked intoxication and fell out of the Porsche and onto the cement. "I haven't had anything to drink in over an hour." He wallowed around on the ground for a few seconds and continued to play along.

"Get up you drunk son of a bitch and follow me to the rear of your vehicle."

Chester grabbed the side of the car door and acted like he was steadying himself as he stood back up.

"How many drinks have you had grandpa?"

"One huge Bloody Mary, but it was a double."

"Follow me," he ordered in an authoritative tone. "I'm going to conduct a sobriety test."

When the officer turned his back on the staggering vampire, the prankster quickly regained his composure and rapidly advanced, snatching the officer's pistol from his belt. With a karate kick executed with his right leg, Chester planted his foot in the center of the trooper's back and sent him somersaulting to the pavement. The officer's hat flew off while he was airborne and when he hit the pavement he landed face first, knocking his front teeth loose. Screaming, the pitiful officer attempted to crawl under his police unit to escape the enraged madman.

"You disrespectful bastard. You wouldn't make a pimple on a real cop's ass!" Chester shouted.

After placing the disarmed cop's pistol in the small of his back under his belt, the old vampire bent over and grabbed the officer by the cowboy boots and pulled him backwards. The frightened, wide-eyed man was clawing at the pavement with his hands like a scurrying rat caught by an angry tomcat.

In an attempt to call for help, the trooper attempted to pull his radio from his belt only to see it kicked into the highway by the growling vampire. Relentlessly, the old Marine taunted the inexperienced officer with insults. "Did the police academy teach you to turn your back on people?"

Chester kicked the man in the side with such force that he farted and rolled over on his back simultaneously. "Look at me when I'm talking to you!"

The struggling officer tried to negotiate. "You're committing a felony. Let me go, or you'll wind up in prison."

"You still don't get the picture!" the vampire shouted as he backhanded the man in the face. "I'm in charge now and I'm going to teach you a lesson in humble pie you insolent punk."

Chester turned the guy back over on his stomach, knelt down with both knees in the center of his back and pinned him. He pulled the handcuffs from the man's duty belt and shouted, "You know the procedure!"

He grabbed the trooper by the left wrist, bending his arm behind his back. The twisting pressure caused his right arm to instinctively retract next to the other. With a snap, the old Marine locked the cuffs, securing both hands.

"Where's your handcuff keys so I can double lock these things?"

The embarrassed trooper hesitated for a few seconds, and then replied, "In my ignition."

Chester stood up and stomped on the officer's cowboy hat, disfiguring it. He pulled the trooper up by the back of his belt and placed the funny-looking, wrinkled hat back on his head and marched him over to the side of his car. The vampire noticed that the cop was wearing an unusual ring on his left hand. At first he didn't think anything about it, but within a couple of minutes curiosity set in and he removed it from his hand to examine it.

"That's my ring, give it back."

"No shit," Chester said as he took a closer look at the strange symbols and insignias engraved on the side of it. The vampire put it in his pocket and turned the police car's ignition off so he could access the keys to double lock the officer's handcuffs.

"You better give me that ring back," he shouted, "or else!"

The vampire grabbed the complaining man by the cuffs, bending his arms upwards and causing him to arch his back from the painful maneuver.

"Ouch," he squealed. "Stop that, it hurts."

"You're not in any position to negotiate, so shut your face."

Watkins opened the back door of the trooper's car and like a rag doll he shoved the beaten man behind the metal cage that separated the front and back. Chester climbed into the front seat of the car and turned the wig-wags and headlights off. He hit the power locks to the rear compartment to ensure the officer couldn't escape.

"You're not going to get away with this."

"I thought I told you to shut up."

Being conscious of the time, the vampire knew that he only had a few more minutes left before someone would check on the trooper. He began to rummage through the console of the police cruiser until he found a can of pepper spray.

"Hey, what are you doing up there?"

"They didn't have mace when I was a cop, lets see if this stuff really works." Laughing, he stuck the nozzle through the cage and hosed the disrespectful cop down, trying his best to empty the entire can.

"Stop it, you crazy old man!" the trooper screamed as he began coughing and choking from the noxious spray. Snot, spit and tears started spewing from the man's face as he pleaded for mercy.

"Are you learning your lesson?" the vampire shouted.

"Yes. Yes!"

"Good, then I'll bid you farewell." The vampire tossed the empty canister to the floorboard of the car and he began ripping the cruiser's radio wires from underneath the dashboard. He placed the keys back into the ignition and started the patrol car up. The vampire continued to laugh as he turned the heater switch all the way up. The stagnant smell and heat, mixed with the pepper spray fumes, eventually became unbearable for the vampire. The officer started to vomit as he cried for help. Chester opened the front door and inhaled a breath of fresh air before finishing his dirty work. Holding his breath, he re-entered the cruiser and placed the idling car in neutral. He grabbed the officer's flashlight from the front seat and wedged it firmly against the gas pedal causing the engine to rev and vibrate loudly. The vampire jumped from the vehicle and turned the steering wheel towards the field that bordered the freeway.

"Have a nice ride," he said as he yanked the stick shift into drive and closed the door behind the runaway vehicle.

The squad car careened through the barbed-wire fence, knocking over a small pole and continued its journey through the hay meadow until it faded out of sight. The vampire could hear the sounds of cattle scurrying and stampeding out of the way in all directions to avoid the oncoming car. Suddenly, he heard the vehicle crash into something solid in the distance.

Chester ran back to the Porsche and found Marsha laughing uncontrollably. He jammed the sports car into gear and sped away heading back to Bear Creek.

"Did you act like that when you were younger?" the teen-aged vampire asked.

"No, I was a heck of a lot wilder back then."

The gray man figured it would be morning before anyone would find the trooper because of the obscure location of the traffic stop. The hole in the fence was so small that it was barely noticeable.

"Tonight's lesson is titled pride," stated the toothless vampire.

"What do you mean by that?" the teen-aged girl inquired.

"Pride is the downfall and weakness of fools. The trooper was your first example. He thought he was invincible, so he turned his back on me. Never underestimate anyone and never let your guard down. Invincibility is an illusion."

The girl looked at the old man and said, " I remember that night I bit you. You shocked me when you hit me in the stomach with your cane. You knocked the daylights out of me."

"If I was ten years younger, I believe I could have gotten away from you."

"You're probably right," she admitted. "I'm kind of glad you didn't though."

"Me too, Marsha."

The Porsche exited Highway 6 and shortly thereafter the vampires returned to their neighborhood. Chester parked in the same spot beside the obnoxious neighbor's house and removed the license plate from the back of their car. He returned it to its rightful place, screwing it tightly to the license plate holder on the same car from which it was stolen. The dogs hid in the bushes and cowered as the vampire growled at them.

When he got back in, Marsha asked, "Do you think they'll trace that plate?"

"You bet they will, but they won't be able to tie it to us. Next time when we go out, we'll play it safe and borrow the Town Car."

The pair returned home and Chester immediately placed the original plate back on the Porsche. Both vampires retreated to their private bedrooms and settled in for the remainder of the night.

The next day when the doctors returned home from work, the entire neighborhood was saturated with law enforcement officers. A SWAT entry team with a battering ram crashed into the front door of the unsuspecting neighbor's home while tear gas grenades were being fired through the front room windows. Snipers took aim from behind squad cars to maintain tactical advantage and cover the charging, black-uniformed team. The trashy family quickly surrendered and vehemently protested as they were being led away in handcuffs wearing only their underwear. The other neighbors watched in disbelief as they saw the debacle unfold. When the officers began placing the angry man in the paddy wagon, his loose boxer shorts fell down to his ankles causing him to stumble.

"Pull 'em up!" an officer shouted.

"I can't, I'm handcuffed, someone help me."

The neighborhood erupted in applause and laughter as the door was being closed.

"I bet they were dealing drugs," Fabian said. "I knew they were up to no good."

"Probably cocaine," replied Patricia. "That man sure had a little penis."

That evening when Chester revived, he punched the lid of his coffin open with both hands and bailed out, pulling his Colt .45 from his belt. With a sweeping motion, he scanned his surroundings, pointing his weapon in every direction he looked. As his vision and thoughts cleared, he realized that he had experienced another nightmare. This dream was different from his first one. The vampires in this setting were pitted against him in a violent altercation. His handgun was useless against these immortal creatures and because of his age he was physically weaker than they were. Parts of the vision were fuzzy, but the spiritual revelation ended with him standing over their vanquished ashes.

Marsha entered the room through the secret passageway. "What's all the noise out here?"

"Nothing," replied Chester as he placed the pistol back into his belt.

"Why did you have your gun out?"

"I had a bad nightmare."

"That's strange. I had a dream also, but it was a good one. You were presented a golden crown with diamonds, rubies and all sorts of sparkling jewels embedded in it. When it was placed on top of your head, all of the vampires knelt before you in reverence.

"Who placed it on top of my head?"

"I did."

The old man took the weird ring out of his pocket and handed it to the young girl. "I want you to look at this thing."

Marsha hissed as she examined it. "Where did you find that? I saw a picture of something like that in "*Abbadon's Priests*."

"I thought that you didn't want to read that book, let alone touch it."

"I don't. I was looking over your shoulder when you were reading it."

"Oh."

"I took it off of that trooper's hand last night. I forgot to show it to you." The old vampire went to the bookshelf and retrieved the wicked manuscript from its hiding place. He turned to the folded page where he stopped reading and to his surprise he saw the same satanic symbols that were etched on the ring.

The wicked book read, "*Behold, this ring is bestowed upon*

all of Lucifer's children who abide by secret right and partake of human sacrifice at night. The blood of the living shall be drink for the dead. So mote it be."

"I'm frightened," said Marsha. "It's getting hard to tell the good guys from the bad."

"That cop was an asshole. I'm glad he's not on our side."

"Do you think all of the troopers are crooked?"

"Certainly not, but I believe there are more satanic sympathizers than we're aware of. I'm certain that they've wormed their way into other organizations, too." Watkins returned the book back to its special hiding place and set the ring beside it before covering them up.

"You mean you're not going to wear it," Marsha jested.

The former Marine grinned as he walked over to his casket, reached inside and pulled out the trooper's Glock .40-caliber pistol. "I think it's time I teach you how to use a real handgun."

Eagerly, the teen-aged vampire agreed, nodding her head.

The gray instructor led the young girl by the hand to the chess table and gently pushed the pieces aside to make room for both of the pistols. In seconds, he unloaded the weapons and then proceeded to field strip them so he could teach his student the names of all the basic subcomponents. That evening, he taught Marsha all of the fundamentals of firearms safety. He showed her how to field strip and reassemble both sidearms, and how to properly hold and aim each pistol. Loading the magazines presented a challenge for the girl because of the spring pressure, but with practice she eventually got the hang of it.

"In my Marine Corps company, we had a saying, 'It's not the rounds you fire or the noise you make. It's the hits that count.' Tomorrow night, we'll find a place to go target shooting."

"I'm excited," exclaimed Marsha.

Chester quizzed the girl to make sure she remembered the most important thing. "What the first rule?"

"Treat every firearm as if it's loaded and never point the muzzle at anyone unless you're going to shoot them."

"You're the smartest student I've ever had. You're a genius."

"What did you expect? I have the best teacher in the whole world."

The old man reloaded both pistols and placed the extra one in his coffin. He promised Marsha that he would give it to her the following evening after her shooting lesson was over. "We need a few boxes of .40-caliber ammunition. I'll ask Fabian if he has any in stock."

Both vampires headed to the laboratory to quench their hunger and shortly thereafter returned to their room.

"Are you still going to attend the council meeting?" Marsha asked.

"You bet I am."

Chester told the young girl that he was pleased with the organization's logistics. His fake social security number and bank account were bringing in a steady flow of income. His desire was to take a good look at things in Arkansas and approach the Dynasty of Immortals with an open mind. Even though they had enemies, the old vampire also knew that they had friends in high positions of authority. He hoped that the counterbalance would offset the evil organizations that he was learning about.

Count Marius proved to be a man of his word and someone to be trusted, but Watkins still wasn't ready to reveal to anyone that he had located the teen-aged vampire.

The next couple of days passed quickly and were uneventful. Marsha's pistol lesson went smoothly and Chester gave her the trooper's weapon as he had promised. The trip to northwest Arkansas was at hand and the toothless man eagerly packed his bags in anticipation of his flight.

CHAPTER 7, DYNASTY OF IMMORTALS

Fabian drove the gray vampire to the southwest side of Houston to catch a private jet that was scheduled to depart Hobby Airport at 10:15 p.m. This was the first time Chester and Marsha would be separated.

"Take good care of my little girl," Watkins said as they drove into the airport's parking garage.

"We'll make sure she keeps sleeping in the secret passageway," replied the doctor. "Patricia is going to home school her in algebra because she's weak in that subject."

"I told her to stay inside," the old man said as he tugged at his seatbelt. "She's got plenty of reading materials and she's expressed an interest in studying martial arts also."

"Patricia really loves that young lady. She's so polite and she just adores you Chester."

"I love her too. I'm glad we found her, it nice having a young person around."

After finding a parking place, the pair entered the building and quickly passed through the airport's security checkpoints. They briskly walked to the designated terminal to catch the private jet that was taxiing toward the pickup zone.

"Looks like the plane just landed," the gray vampire said. "It'll be nice to get out of town for a few nights."

"The Dynasty's timing is impeccable," the doctor added.

Chester boarded the shiny blue plane and Fabian waved as the aircraft re-entered the runway and flew off into the smoggy night sky.

Two hours later, the jet landed at a private airstrip located just outside the city limits of Bentonville, Arkansas. After disembarking, the old man was greeted by a gorgeous blond vampire with a shapely figure and stunning blue eyes. She smiled as their eyes met.

"Like a moth drawn to a flame, they were of a kindred spirit," Watkins thought.

"Welcome to Bentonville," the beautiful woman said. "My name is Destiny.

The former Marine extended his hand in a respectful manner, gently taking hers. "I'm Chester Watkins, alias Sidney Kunkle."

Smiling, the pretty woman asked, "Did you have a nice flight?"

"Yes, I did, but the restroom accommodations are more user-friendly when you're a soaring bat."

The woman grinned. "Now I know who's responsible for all the acid rain. Marius told me you had a tremendous sense of humor. I think we're going to get along really well."

Watkins grabbed his small suitcase and followed the foxy vampire away from the runway and toward a flashy, white limousine that was waiting in the distance.

The chauffer stood poised next to the rear door and opened it, helping the pretty, blue-eyed lady inside.

"May I take your bag, sir?" the friendly driver asked as he reached for Chester's suitcase and, opening the trunk, tossed it inside.

The dignified vehicle drove slowly away as the vampires exchanged in sociable conversation. The old man's eyes were fixed on the women's cleavage when he thought to himself, *"If I were younger, I'd make a pass at this blue-eyed beauty."* When she finally disclosed her age, the frisky guy didn't feel so guilty. She was over 200 years old and worked in a uniform factory during the Civil War.

"You sure look happy," the woman said. "Are you having a good time?"

"You bet I am. It's nice to have a change of scenery. I'm looking forward to meeting some more of our kind."

"You don't have long to wait, we're only 15 minutes away."

The limo traveled westerly and passed an Arkansas state trooper who was writing a ticket on Highway 71. The gray vampire commented, "Now that guy looks professional."

"He is," replied the beautiful vampire as she brushed her golden hair away from her ears. "He's one of our informants and sometimes works security detail for our dignitaries."

The automobile proceeded through the intersection, crossing the thoroughfare and turned left onto a winding county road leading into the heavily wooded foothills.

After climbing several small mountains and traveling approximately seven miles, the chauffer turned left and passed through a huge metal gate mounted in stone pillars. Each supporting structure was decorated with concrete lions in the center. Wrought iron fences spanned in both directions. An armed security officer stepped from his guard shack and motioned with his hand for the stretch limo to stop. The driver rolled his window down so the man could see his familiar face and immediately he was waved through.

"That's a sharp-looking guard," Chester commented.

"He's another state policeman who works security for our estate when he's not on patrol duty," answered Destiny. "At one time, he was stationed at the governor's mansion in Little Rock."

Chester turned his head in both directions and admired the lavishly landscaped estate. The car drove up a gentle slope and when they reached the top of the hill the headlight beams shined on a bus parked in the driveway bearing a huge banner that read "Blood Drive."

"I see that they've catered in dinner," the old man joking said.

The pretty vampire responding in a humorous tone, commented, "It sure beats eating out."

Behind the Winnebago stood a handsome building with a stone foyer jetting over the driveway. Four butlers standing at attention were waiting by the front doors and when the limo approached two of the men broke ranks and ran to the vehicle.

Both rear doors of the luxury car were opened by the servants and the vampires climbed out together, thanking the men.

"May I take your luggage, sir?"

"Sure, it's in the trunk," replied Chester.

Like royalty, the vampires were treated with the utmost respect. From the looks of the stately building and the hired staff, it was obvious to the gray senior citizen that the Dynasty was throwing around a lot of money and paying these employees substantial salaries.

When the two vampires entered the mansion, Chester was impressed with all the artwork that he saw hanging on the walls. "*From the appearance of these masterpieces, they were originals and were worth millions of dollars,*" he thought.

"Early Renaissance," the blue-eyed beauty said as if she were reading his mind.

"Do you like artwork?" the old man asked.

"I do, and if you'd like I'll introduce you to one of the vampires who personally knew Leonardo Da Vinci, Rembrandt and many other famous painters. He's an artist, architect and interior decorator. He's responsible directly, or indirectly, for many of the things you see in here. He's also gay and very sensitive about his sexual orientation, so please try not to offend him."

Chester wiggled his eyebrows at the girl. "Do you think he'll try to pick me up and seduce me?"

"Trust me, you're not his type."

"Darn- always a bride's maid, and never a bride."

Amused at the old man's humor, the pretty girl led him through the front rooms of the building and to a set of elevators located around the corner of the hallway.

"Where do these go?" he asked.

"You'll see," she said as she punched the button.

With a dinging sound from the elevator bell, the doors opened to reveal a menacing-looking black vampire with matted dreadlocks and piercing, bloodshot eyes. With a Jamaican accent he spoke, "How are you doing Destiny? Who's with you, mon?"

"This is Chester."

Watkins noticed that the black vampire was wearing excessively baggy trousers and dusty leather sandals. His long, yellow toenails immediately caught Chester's attention as he stepped out of the elevator. He approached the couple and extended his hand. "Nice to meet you."

After a short introduction, the gray vampire followed the pretty blond lady inside. The small compartment reeked from the smell of perspiration and ripe underarms. Chester turned his head around to get a second look at the strange creature as he lumbered down the hall and away from them. Watkins laughed to himself when he saw that his pants were hanging down so low that they revealed the crack of his buttocks.

"Is it a full moon tonight or tomorrow?" he queried in a whispered tone.

"That guy is disgusting. Most of the black vampires I know won't even associate with him." answered Destiny. "I wish he'd quit creeping around here and buy some clothes that fit."

"Is he a council member?"

"Certainly not, but he attends every meeting."

Both doors began to automatically close and with her index finger the female vampire pushed the button labeled B for basement. Suddenly, the two vampires felt their stomachs go into their throats as the trolley jolted downwards and began to quickly descend. When they reached the bottom and stepped out, Chester was amazed to see a small city completely underground.

"I'll show you to your room," the pretty girl said.

The old man followed her through a beautiful corridor decorated with stained glass flowers. Each pane was illuminated from behind with florescent lights. Colors of red, yellow, green and violet reflected off of their faces as they passed through. When they exited the other side, Chester saw a martial arts room to his left with mats on the floor. Eight vampires wearing white karate gis and black belts were standing in a semi-circle sparring with each other. One of the men turned to look at the passing vampires and when Chester saw his face he recognized that he was Japanese. It was also obvious that he was the instructor. When their eyes met, both men nodded their heads in friendly respect signaling hello.

Screaming violently in a foreign language, two men charged the Oriental vampire and attempted to throw him to the ground. Taking a defensive posture, the little man blocked their punches and ducked their roundhouse kicks. Switching to the offensive and changing his style, the little warrior used a sweeping slide kick and floored one of the attackers with a single move. Without hesitation, he aggressively leaped in the direction of the other opponent and applied a scissor hold with his legs, snaring his body and tumbling him to the floor. The wise martial arts practitioner jumped to his feet and with a bladed karate stance stood over his defeated students. The men picked themselves up from the mats and bowed their heads in the customary fashion, waiting for their comrade to acknowledge them. The Japanese man turned, faced the pair and with a smile he rendered a quick, snapping response.

Chester turned to the female vampire and said, "I'd like to study with him sometime."

She smiled and then said, "He's a fantastic teacher. He has a black belt in kung fu, karate, judo and just about every martial art form known to exist. He's also a skilled Samurai.

Destiny and the gray vampire walked side by side as she escorted him through the underground maze of elaborately furnished rooms and chambers. As they passed the council hall, Chester paused to take a look at the political podium that was located in the back of the auditorium. The solid oak platform looked like a stage surrounded by plush theater chairs. Two desks flanked each side of the room and there were six chairs positioned neatly next to them. Political slogans and paintings decorated the walls. Some of them didn't make any sense to the old Marine. A picture of Hitler with his face painted like a clown and wearing nothing but a diaper hung prominently on the left winged wall. Naked pictures of Joseph Stalin and Napoleon wearing jackboots and standing in pigpens full of manure were among the oddities that caught the old man's attention.

"What's with all the kinky pictures?" he asked.

"The paintings are an example of the foolishness of mankind. They hang as a reminder to our species to avoid the temptations of power and lust."

The pretty vampire advised Chester that there were seven governing vampires who were elected by a complicated voting process. It was almost impossible for tyrants and dictators to seize power in their governing body.

"Almost impossible?" the old Marine questioned.

"Possibilities do exist, but through education and constant vigilance we've maintained a stable form of government for nearly 500 years."

Watkins chuckled as they resumed their journey down the hall and toward his temporary sleeping accommodations. "*Everything inside the entire complex is pleasing to the eye except for some of the political works of art,*" he thought. Wisdom was a complicated learning process according to the vampire's manual and the display of fallen, failed rulers in stupid, compromising poses was appropriate the more Chester reasoned in his mind.

"The thousand-year Reich was the joke of the millennium according to Count Marius and the other vampires," Destiny stated. "The world is too big for any single person to rule by himself. History has proven this time and time again."

Shaking his head in agreement, the old vampire asked, "What did the Dynasty of Immortals think of the Emperor of Japan?"

"You need to ask Katsumi that question."

"Was that the man who just whipped the other vampires' asses down the hall?"

"Yes," answered Destiny with a smile as she pointed to Chester's room, which was at the end of the hall.

Watkins couldn't believe what he was seeing—a gold-plated sarcophagus with intricately inlaid artwork bearing symbols and writings that were only found in the ancient vampire manuscripts. The coffin sat prominently on a solid granite pillar and each one was uniquely different. There were five of these coffins in this particular room evenly spaced with beautiful inscriptions written in gothic-style penmanship displaying the vampires' names to whom they were presented. Next to each slab of stone was an antique brass footlocker with a personal lock and key where the visiting vampire could store his personal belongings.

"No one is allowed to sleep in your private coffin except for you," stated the woman. "This is our eternal gift to all of the living dead."

"Thank you. I'm honored to receive such a gift."

Chester took the key and opened the big storage box, placing his belongings inside. He secured the padlock and slipped the key into his front pocket. The curious man began to look around and admire all of the decorations. The tapestry in his room was remarkably tasteful. Scenes of eagles and birds of prey were woven into each rug mounted on the main wall. There were two walnut tables with matching chairs and a couch big enough to seat six people on the opposite wall. Two crystal chandeliers with adjustable wall outlet settings provided adequate lighting for the spacious quarters.

"Do you like your room?"

"This beats the Scottish Inn any day."

"The door in the rear of the room leads to the lavatory if you need to freshen up before tomorrow evening's council meeting." The foxy vampire turned around and looked down the hallway. "May I show you around some more?"

"Yes." The Marine closed his eyes as he ran his hand down the side of his expensive, golden coffin, feeling every contour of the detailed workmanship. He looked at the woman and smiled, affirming his satisfaction.

"Come with me to the game room, you'll really enjoy it." The blond girl started walking down the hall and turned her head to make sure Watkins was following her. "Do you like to play cards, backgammon, shoot pool, watch the Sports Channel?"

The old man caught up to the friendly woman and, walking next to her, he said, "I hear there's a vampire around here who's a really good chess player.''

"Vladimir," she answered. "I've never seen him lose a match."

When the vampires were passing the Dynasty hall, they could see down the passageway as the martial art students began filing out of the dojo single file. Chester wanted to talk to the instructor and asked Destiny if they could spare a few minutes before going to the recreation room.

"Sure, I'll introduce you."

The Oriental man bowed to the spirits of the temple as he exited the sacred room. Closing the door behind him, he turned to face the approaching vampires. Having an understanding of Eastern culture, the old Marine stopped a few feet in front of the humble-looking man and, looking him squarely in the eyes, he said hello in Japanese. Both men bowed together.

"Nice to meet you. My name is Katsumi Nakata."

"I'm Chester Watkins."

The two men shook hands in the customary Western fashion and through the act of physical transference a spiritual awakening took place. The wise man immediately recognized that he was speaking with another warrior. His psychic awareness alerted him to Chester's internal mental anguish he experienced from the war. At that moment, both men looked deeply into one another's souls and a mystical bond was formed

"I can feel your Zen. Our ancestors would have embraced

you as a brother 400 years ago. Instead, our children fought you and brought disgrace to our land."

The soldier fought back tears as he remembered his fellow Marines being machine-gunned in their amphibious landing crafts and dying on the beaches of Tarawa and Guadalcanal. Chester knew that in the heart of every good soldier was the desire for peace and not war. Killing was easy, but the pursuit of brotherhood and neighborly love was what living on this Earth was really about. He could see this wisdom in his Oriental brother's facial expressions and he instinctively knew that the other vampire could see the same love radiating in his own face.

"Forgiveness is divine," the gray man said. "We must always press forward."

The Oriental man made a head gesture signaling he agreed. "Human stagnation is the path of fools."

"May I train with you some time?" Watkins asked.

"Yes. If you are available tomorrow evening, I can give you a private lesson. Fate has caused our paths to cross and I believe that you were brought here for a reason. It's nice to meet you, brother." The black-haired Oriental turned and slowly walked down another corridor and away from the other vampires.

"Katsumi is very spiritual," stated the blue-eyed lady. "He is also one of the ruling council members."

"He has my respect," added Chester.

Walking next to one another, both individuals strolled through the elaborate network of underground hallways. The toothless man marveled at all of the beautifully furnished rooms full of golden caskets. Each sarcophagus was similar to his own, but no two were exactly alike.

"How many vampire's can this facility hold?"

"Over 500."

Destiny told Watkins that she had never seen the facility filled to capacity since living there. Every meeting was always coordinated. "We are highly organized and I can tell you exactly how many vampires will be sleeping here tonight and how many will be attending tomorrow night's council meeting."

"How many vampire are there in the world?"

"Europe has the largest underground population, but our exact numbers are still unknown. There are innumerable rogues who wander aimlessly throughout Eastern countries and they risk exposing all of us."

"How did Katsumi arrive in America?"

The beautiful girl explained to Chester that the Japanese vampire was a stowaway on an enemy World War II transport vessel disguised as a Merchant Marine ship. Five caretakers posing as deck hands, smuggled him onboard inside of a crate. Every night, they would release him so he could feed on the unsuspecting Imperial sailors. When he finished someone off, he would toss the drained body overboard into the perilous waters. The captain couldn't figure out why hundreds of sharks kept following the ship. This continued until there was nothing left but a skeleton crew. With rumors of phantoms and ghosts roaming onboard at night and murdering people, the five men easily incited a mutiny and seized control. Once in charge, they piloted the ship to Brazil seeking political asylum. When they arrived, only six of them remained.

Katsumi and his loyal friends lived in South America and patiently awaited for their country to lose the war. They planned to return to their homeland, but the Merchant ship was detained by international authorities when Japan surrendered. The men settled in Rio de Janeiro and slowly grew old until they eventually died. The vampire offered them a life of immortality, but each man refused to be bitten, desiring to cross over into the spiritual realm and join their deceased ancestors.

Marius found out about Nakata's plight and made arrangements for him to travel to the United States. After he arrived, he proved himself an honorable man. With growing popularity and support, he was soon elected as a board member to the governing body of vampires.

"That's some story," Chester said. "I could feel his pain also, but I didn't want to offend him by saying something."

"Intelligent people are hard to offend," Destiny remarked. "It's the stupid ones who get mad because they usually have issues with vanity."

"I can agree with that."

When the vampires entered the game room, it exceeded Watkins' expectations. He couldn't believe his eyes. The plush setting was fancier than any tavern he'd ever seen. Dart boards, backgammon games, poker tables, pool tables and a big-screen-set televising a heavyweight boxing match via-satellite were the first things he observed. The man turned his head back and forth, quickly scanning the entire room, until he saw what he was looking for. Sitting prominently in one of the decorated corners of the bar were three chess tables. Familiar liquor and beer signs were displayed on the walls, but when the vampire took a second look he noticed the advertisements were slightly different. The Bloodweiser sign brought a smile to his face. "*I think I'll have a glass of that stuff,*" he thought.

Two younger vampires were engaging in a Ping-Pong match and the sounds of them smacking the little plastic ball back and forth with their paddles added to the excitement of the game room atmosphere. The upbeat tempo of jazz music playing from a jukebox located in the corner of the room and sounds of a pool table being racked filled the air. The commentary provided by the TV sportscaster giving a blow-by-blow report of the ringside action blended in perfectly.

The vampires approached the stately oak bar and Destiny ordered them a shot of life-sustaining fluids. When the bartender set their glasses in front of them, the two lifted their drinks and toasted.

Quoting from the ancient book "*Wisdom of the Dead*," they said, "To life," as they drank.

"Boy, I needed that," said the old Marine as a feeling of exhilaration swept through his body.

With his mind and soul feeling sharper, the gray vampire asked Destiny if she could point out the champion chess player to him. She looked around, but didn't see him.

"I don't think he's here. I'll ask around."

The pretty woman left Chester sitting at the bar and walked over to one of the pool tables to speak with a husky-looking vampire who was engaged in a friendly game with a similarly dressed individual. The impressive-looking man was wearing a leather biker's jacket and black boots with shiny, metal buckles. The pair started laughing when she motioned for the old man to come over.

Leaving his comfortable stool, the gray Marine headed in their direction. When he reached them, the leather-clad man took aim at the eight ball and called a bank shot. With a smack, the cue ball struck the black ball and bounced off the other end of the table and neatly rolled into the corner pocket.

The losing vampire discouragingly said, "You're hot tonight. That makes five games." He shrugged his shoulders and walked over to the rack of pool sticks and placed his back into the empty slot hanging on the wall.

Destiny asked the two guys if they had seen the vice chancellor. She spoke up, trying to keep her voice slightly louder than the TV commentators. "Our new guest wants to challenge Vladimir in a game of chess."

Upon hearing this, the bartender grabbed the remote control and turned the volume completely down on the big screen. The entire pub seemed to come to a standstill and when Chester began looking around he saw that everyone was staring at him. Suddenly, the whole room came to life, roaring with laughter.

"Let's find Vladimir!" shouted one of the vampires.

The gray vampire walked over to one of the chess tables to examine the fancy pieces and when he turned around to see what all of the commotion was behind him he realized he was being followed by 20 or more vampires.

"I can't wait to see this," came a voice from among the crowd.

Pulling up chairs next to the tables, the entire group encircled Watkins and one of them challenged him to a game.

"I bet I can beat you," the opponent said.

"Choose your color," was the old man's response.

Picking white, the smart-looking challenger sat down and adjusted his chair. Chester took his place across from the man and waited for him to open the game.

Recognizing his strategy, the sly, gray vampire piped up, "Queen's Gambit."

"You seem to know the terminology, but let's see if can you play."

The group's attention was focused on the unfolding game, but when the audience spoke they were very careful to keep their voices audible only above a whisper. The bartender, who was interested in the outcome of the heavyweight fight, turned the TV's volume back on, but kept it at a lower level in an effort not to disturb the game. A few minutes elapsed and the old Marine Corps chess champion began capturing his adversary's pieces. Chester watched as the vampire exposed his queen and made a serious blunder.

The old man quickly advanced his knight, forking the king and queen and called, "Check."

In three more moves, Watkins declared, "Checkmate!"

Smiling at the cagey senior, the other vampire graciously accepted his defeat and stood up. "You're a really good player."

"Thank you."

Speaking softly among themselves, the crowd grew silent when Vladimir entered the room. The vampire behind the bar muted the sound on the television in anticipation of the Russian saying something entertaining because he knew that this was his style.

Loud, boisterous and flamboyantly, he proclaimed, "Who is ready to lose tonight?"

"We've found you another victim!" a short, skinny vampire from the congregation blurted out. Word spread fast throughout the multi-million dollar complex and the bar began to fill to capacity as more of the living dead came to watch in expectation of a good chess match. Soon, it was standing room only as the opposing vampires faced off.

"I'll let you have the first move," the flashy vice chancellor said as he took his place across from Chester.

Knowing that he would be opening with the white pieces, the gray vampire began to set his men back up in their proper positions. Vladimir did the same and collected the black pieces and reset his side of the board.

Both vampires' faces seemed to turn to stone as the intensity of their countenances made them look animated. Their eyes looked like fiery coals burning in their sockets as they engaged in the most prolific game the underground castle had ever witnessed. Not a single vampire had beaten this man in over 200 years and everyone knew it. He was the undisputed champion and openly bragged about it.

The first two games ended in stalemates and the onlookers couldn't believe that the toothless man was still holding his own against the infamous Russian. Some of the vampires started placing bets, while others began to root for the old underdog.

Arrogantly, the cocky vampire reset the board as the men alternated colors again. He detested the fact that this gray codger was still sitting across from him and refusing to lose. In an attempt to distract Chester during the first two games, he used his left hand to move his pieces while he flashed his fancy, diamond-studded watch across the board.

Playing with white again, Watkins opened with his knight. Suddenly, he smelled something similar to putrid sulfur. Some of the vampires in the audience began coughing, while others covered their noses to filter the nasty smell. Seven vampires walked out of the pub, while the others who remained looked directly at him like he was the one who was responsible. Chester gummed down, shook his head no, and tried to breathe. As the funk dissipated, he intuitively knew that the Russian had farted. "*What a nasty trick,*" he thought. "*Silent but deadly.*"

Pretending like nothing happened, Vladimir responded with his opening move, advancing a pawn two spaces in front of his king. The final game was on and unbeknown to the Russian the old man had figured out his strategy. Five minutes into the match, someone in the audience sneezed and when Chester turned to see who it was, the immoral opponent flicked his wrist, knocking Watkins' rook to the floor. The old man had a mental picture of the board ingrained into his mind and when he looked back at his pieces he quickly recognized one was missing. He glanced around and then turned his attention to the floor where he saw his castle laying. He returned it to its rightful place and looked the cheating vampire squarely in the eyes and smiled.

"Nice try," he mumbled.

As the final game drew to a close, the old Marine could see deeply into his opponent's psyche, and he didn't like what he saw. There was something about this boastful vampire that didn't set right with him. The gray man glanced down at his modest watch and the time read 3:45 a.m. He thought about placing a bet against the other vampire and swindling him out of the fancy watch he was wearing, but he didn't want to press his luck.

"The end game strategy is what sets matches like this apart," affirmed the old man as he prepared to sacrifice his queen to clinch the game.

Chester held his breath as he patiently waited for the handsome vampire to take the bait. Within seconds, the huckster captured the forsaken piece and grinned, showing his fangs as he placed it among Chester's other fallen men.

Noticing that Vladimir's king was now exposed, the old gamester quickly advanced his castle and called, "Check." A look of hopelessness swept over the defender's face when he realized what Chester had planned. In three moves, he saw that checkmate was inevitable. His mind raced as he scanned the board trying to calculate another way out, or a counter move. Seeing the gravity of the situation, he stood up hollering obscenities in the Russian language. In a sightless rage, he flexed his arm and smashed his fist into the expensive table, breaking it in two and sending it crumbling to the floor. The fierce blow sent chessmen hurling through the room and some of the vampires in the audience had to duck to avoid the soaring, fragments.

The enraged creature tried to regain his composure, but to no avail. The cheers and laughter from the crowd only rekindled his wrath. He turned around and stormed out of the recreation room like a castrated-bull. Anyone, or anything, standing in his way was pushed or knocked to the floor.

"Get out of my way!" he screamed. "This was a set-up."

The atmosphere in the pub turned jubilant as the crowd of vampires surrounded Chester, while others shook his hand and congratulated him.

"That was the best match I've seen in 200 years," one of the men cried out. "I can't believe you beat him."

The humble man enjoyed all of the attention he was receiving. When he stood up in the center of the splintered mess, he turned around and noticed that his chair was the only piece of furniture within arm's reach that wasn't destroyed. With a sexy grin, Destiny ran up to the gray-haired senior, threw her arms around him, and kissed him on the cheek.

"You're funny, smart, and you've got nerves of steel."

Modestly, he made his way through the crowd of vampires toward the doors leaving the pub. Destiny was close in tow as she followed him out of the chaotic room.

"Thanks for watching the game, and rooting for me."

"Believe me, it was well worth it," she replied, brushing her hair from her ear.

"By the way— that wasn't me who farted."

"I know it wasn't. I saw Vladimir squinting his eyes right before everyone started coughing."

"Boy, am I glad to get that off of my chest. I didn't want you to think I was uncouth or something."

"Don't worry. I recognize a gentleman when I see one."

The couple walked down the corridor and away from all the ranting and raving commotion. When their footsteps became audible again, the Marine paused momentarily to speak with the blue-eyed girl.

"What did you think of Vladimir's display back there?"

"I'm not very fond of him, but keep that to yourself. Be it known that no one speaks out openly against Count Marius' anointed ones."

By the outrageous display of anger exhibited by the Russian, Chester feared that he had made an immortal enemy. From the reaction of the other vampires, he also knew that he'd gained some respect and made a few allies. "*Hopefully, this will benefit me,*" he thought.

When the pair reached a stairwell leading down to another level, Destiny turned to Chester and said, "It was nice meeting you. Can you find your way back to your room?"

"Yes, no problem."

"Good, I'll meet you tomorrow night at Nakata's dojo."

The polite man gently reached for the girl's hand and brought it to his lips to kiss it. "Thanks for the nice evening. You're a wonderful hostess and a gracious lady."

When he released her hand, she slowly turned and walked away. Watkins watched the woman traverse the stairs like he was in a trance. Admiring the charming elegance of her hips as they swayed like clockwork from side to side, he wished to himself that he looked younger.

The myths that vampires cast no shadows or were unable to see their reflections in mirrors was strictly a fable. Every time the gray man looked at himself, he was constantly reminded of what Marius told him. His age regression would take decades before it was accomplished.

Being in the company of the sexy vampire that evening rekindled feelings and emotions Chester hadn't experienced in years. He felt alive and vibrant when he was with this woman. Realizing the foolishness of all this, the old man was torn from his whimsical thoughts and snapped back into reality when he remembered something crucial that Marsha told him. The teenager recounted that her killer kept releasing terrible-smelling farts when he was raping her. *"Could the flamboyant Russian be the satanic vampire?"* he speculated.

When Chester returned to his room, to his surprise he was greeted by the Jamaican vampire who was bunking next to him. When the strange creature opened the lid of his sarcophagus, an aroma similar to rancid vinegar filled the air. The smell reminded him of the sewer system back in downtown Houston. He watched as the mop-headed man climbed into his casket and closed the lid. Feeling sleepy himself, the old vampire followed suit and slipped into his fancy box to retire. When he closed his eyes, visions of the beautiful vampire's facial features and her slinky, cat-like stride paraded through his mind until he drifted into unconsciousness.

Shortly after sunrise, the caretakers and security personnel were relieved of duty by the dayshift employees who faithfully assumed control of the mansion. A swing shift routine was implemented and every six months the graveyard workers would alternate back to dayshift and vice-versa. This ensured peace of mind to the vulnerable vampires who were sleeping underground and who were powerless during the day. Every mortal person working at the estate was personally known and trusted by the living dead and the council of vampires.

While the immortals slept in confidence, acting on their infallible advice, the stockbrokers followed their instructions precisely, buying, selling and trading with pre-selected companies. The vampires' financial holdings grew daily and were worth trillions of dollars. The accounts were subdivided into fictitious names and foreign currencies to avoid detection and rouse suspicion among non-believers and enemies of the Brotherhood. Large accumulations of fiat money were exchanged for hard assets such as real estate, gold and silver bullion, precious gems, artwork and antiques. Being present throughout history taught the vampires the invaluable lesson. When governments failed, so did their paper money.

Vampire safe houses were being established throughout Third World countries and trusted human beings were constantly being recruited in these regions to solidify the security of this growing sect. According to the wisest members of the living dead, political division and global disharmony was a direct result of ignorance and self-glorification. According to Marius, evil men wanted to be gods.

Chester opened his eyes and, shoving with a gut-felt grunt, he opened the heavy golden lid of his decorated coffin. When the top flung open, he could smell his stinky roommate. The sour stench of underarms, stinky feet and dirty, nasty, vinegar-smelling laundry was almost overpowering.

The old man remembered his days in Marine Corps boot-camp where they taught a filthy recruit a lesson he would never forget. They had a blanket party, throwing a cover over his head rendering him immobile and then beating him unconscious with their fists. They tossed him into the shower and scrubbed his body with shampoo, toilet brushes and steel wool pads until he woke up screaming. Chester thought about doing the same to this crumb.

After climbing out of his sarcophagus, the old veteran

addressed his fellow vampire. "Did you want to take your shower first or did you want to wait for me?"

Ignorantly, the man replied, "You can go first. I don't want to wash my natural oils off. I believe it defiles and weakens the body."

Watkins stared in disbelief at the man as he bent over in his underwear and pulled a dirty, wrinkled suit out of his footlocker. The hash marks and fecal streaks in the back of his drawers looked repulsive. He continued to watch in amazement as the Jamaican walked over to one of the chairs to get dressed. When he sat down, he threw his leg over the other one and attempted to put his socks on. His long, yellow toenails punched through the material and made a tearing sound as he pulled them up.

Restraining himself from saying anything, Watkins shook his head as he pretended not to notice the fiasco. Holding his breath, he grabbed his travel bag and sprinted to the bathroom, closing the door behind him and locking it. Chester removed his clothes and stepped into the spacious, walk-in shower. He admired the tile work as he turned the water on and adjusted the settings to a comfortable temperature. In a few minutes, the room began to fill with steam as he soaped up, washing the proverbial jet lag from his body.

After 10 minutes of pampering himself and feeling refreshed, he turned the water off and walked over to the sink to shave. Looking at his reflection, he noticed a couple of small black hairs growing in his stubbly beard, but nothing significant to make him look any younger. The lavatory smelled nice and he dreaded opening the door and breathing the rotten air.

Out of nowhere, a thought came to mind, so the old vampire doused himself with aftershave and applied an extra spray of underarm deodorant. Feeling confident and clean, he turned the exhaust fan on in the bathroom and reversed the settings, adjusting it to blow outward instead of venting inward. He pointed his scented can of aerosol spray at the slotted opening and emptied the contents until the can made a sputtering sound. Next, he turned the overhead heating lamp to a setting of approximately five minutes and waited until the temperature reached a sweltering level that was almost unbearable. In an attempt to conquer the repulsive odors in the outside room, the clean vampire burst through the door wearing nothing but a towel soaked with men's perfume. Like a victorious king, he proudly marched in the direction of his grubby roommate.

The black vampire snapped his head to the right when he heard the door swing open and squinted to see through the prevailing steam. All of a sudden, he began to cough as the clean old man strutted past him followed by a cloud of fresh air. The warmer air from the bathroom pushed the colder air into the hallway and was predominantly stronger. The clean Marine opened his footlocker as he watched the Jamaican quickly collect his things and vacate the room.

Calling out, Chester shouted, "Please close the door behind you."

After hearing the slam, the cagey vampire ran over to the man's filthy coffin and lifted the lid. He uncapped his bottle of aftershave and sprinkled a few drops inside in an attempt to extinguish the repulsive smell. When he looked at the interior, it reminded him of a rat's nest littered with filthy underwear, socks and sweat-soaked towels.

"How could someone sleep in such deplorable conditions?" he wondered.

When he returned to his footlocker, he quickly put his clothes on and walked over to one of the fancy tables. Still holding the bottle of aftershave in his hand, he unscrewed the lid again and bent down, strategically hiding the open bottle behind one of the legs of the table.

"Next time, I think I'll buy scented candles," he mumbled to himself.

After completing his mission of purging the room of foul odors, Chester stepped into the hall and in the distance he could see Katsumi opening the door to the dojo. The gray vampire looked forward to speaking with the wise councilman in private. He was sincerely troubled by the Russian's display of anger and he wanted to talk to him about the game-room incident.

The old vampire entered the sacred martial arts room and saw a few things that he hadn't noticed the night before—speed bags, heavy punching bags, chin-up bars and a complete set of universal weight training equipment. All of these items were neatly positioned against the far wall. There were also mirrors where a weightlifter, or martial arts practitioner, could observe his form while he trained. According to the Japanese vampire, these items were available to anyone visiting or residing at the complex. The only rules he enforced was proper treatment of the gear, and cleaning up after yourself before leaving the gym.

"Good evening, Katsumi," Watkins said as he reverently bowed, giving honor to the instructor and the mystical forces in the dojo.

With a warm smile, the master quietly replied, "Please lock the door behind you and place the 'Do Not Disturb' sign on the doorknob. I would like both of us to use this time to briefly meditate."

The two men stood in the center of the room and, with eyes closed, they lowered their heads. Several minutes elapsed while visions of peace, harmony and serenity engulfed their minds.

The silence was broken when the Oriental vampire asked, "I sense something is troubling you. May I ask what it is?"

"Did you hear about the chess match last night?"

"Yes, I did."

"What do you think?" whispered Watkins.

"Sometimes, winning has its disadvantages," the wise man replied. "Have you ever considered that a well-calculated loss can also be a victory in due time?"

"Yes sir."

Chester had many questions he posed to Nakata during their

private karate session. Out of respect, he was cautious not to divulge exactly how he felt or his suspicions regarding Vladimir being a satanic vampire. Somehow, he knew that trying to conceal his emotions was foolish in the presence of such a great man who could see deeply into the soul with transparency. Even though they were born in different cultures and thousands of miles apart, he knew that they were somehow spiritually linked.

The Oriental spoke in parables to his new friend. "Humans and vampires are similar to fruit-yielding trees. We must watch them grow over the course of time before we can see if they will produce fruit that is pleasingly edible. All evil trees must be uprooted."

After they finished discussing philosophy, their attention was turned to martial arts training. Watkins told Nakata that he earned a green belt in karate back in the 1950s, but he had to quit because of his job. Being a person who always liked to finish what he started, he resumed classes in the '60s, but the week before he tested for his brown belt, his wife was in a serious car wreck and almost died.

"Would you like to test for your belt now?" asked the Sensei.

"I don't know if I can remember the katas."

"You can and will," replied the wise master with an air of confidence. "Everything we see, hear and learn is retained in the deepest recesses of our minds. All we have to do is harness that perfection and strive to function on a spiritual plane. Karate and all of the martial arts teach us to tap into these powers on a higher level of consciousness. To perfect your art, you must envision an action before performing it."

The talented instructor ordered the old vampire to close his eyes and with all of his power seize control over his mind and inner being.

"Now, recount your last lesson and re-enact it through visualization," he ordered. "Karate is mental, not physical."

With all of his mental concentration channeled, the gray Marine began to remember things that he thought he'd forgotten.

Within minutes, he was performing a flawless martial arts rendition of punches, blocks, flips and kicks.

"Like a river, let it flow. It's all in your mind!" the Japanese man yelled. "Continue to focus!"

Watkins had barely broken a sweat when he finished his series of simulated fights. "I never realized this was so mental."

"Last night, when you were watching me spar with my students, what did you think?" the Sensei asked. "Do you believe that I am physically stronger than my opponents?"

"They were much larger and muscular than you are," the old Marine answered. "You looked so fast, I didn't give it much thought."

The wise martial arts expert spoke in confidence to Chester and explained to him that both of the vampires he defeated the night before were as strong as 10 men combined. In spite of their tremendous power, he was able to subdue them at the same time. He said that his strength was limited to the physical capacity of three men because of his small stature, but his mind had no restrictive bounds. This made him faster and far more powerful.

"If you're not physically stronger than your opponent, you must be mentally superior. This is your first lesson. All good students must learn this discipline."

The instructor expounded on the subject, explaining that there were documented cases of mortal human beings performing great feats of strength during emotional times of duress. "Have you ever heard of the case where a woman lifted a vehicle weighing several thousand pounds because her child was pinned underneath?"

"Yes, I have."

"As immortals, our minds are capable of functioning at higher levels than those of ordinary humans. On rare occasions, and always by accident, mortals tap into these hidden powers and you see them performing feats of supernatural ability. When asked how they did what they did, they always reply, "I don't know."

Katsumi asked the old man another question. "Have you perfected the art of transforming into a bat or a wolf?"

"Yes," he answered. "Except I got hung up the first time I tried the spell."

"It's the same concept," he explained. "You did it because you believed you could do it. I have one more lesson to teach you tonight," the Japanese man said as he assumed a martial arts stance.

Chester drew a deep breath and assumed a bladed position facing his teacher. The 400-year-old vampire told him he would receive his brown belt if he could successfully deliver one blow to his midsection. He ordered the Marine to focus all of his attention on his torso and not to be distracted by head fakes, arm or leg movements, or anything else. His emphasis was the center of mass.

"Wherever the center of the body goes, the rest of the body must follow," he explained. "Now, strike me!"

Watkins' first attempts of engagement were fruitless until he realized that he was fighting in a physical mode. His flurry of punches and kicks were thrown aimlessly into the air. He redirected his energy and efforts to a mental plane, keeping his attention on his smaller, swifter opponent's stomach. Time seemed to slow down as his thoughts intensified. When he finally saw an opening, he seized the opportunity and in a millisecond he planted the palm of his hand directly into the teacher's midsection, sending him sideways to the mat.

With a smile of satisfaction, the black-haired vampire regained his composure and stood up. "I've been trying to teach my other students this lesson for months and they still can't fathom the basics of self-control. Most of them still can't hit me."

The smaller vampire commanded Chester's respect because he realized that his opponent wasn't punching back, only blocking and dodging his aggressive moves.

Both men smiled as they faced one another and when their eyes met, they bowed, ending the productive lesson that evening.

Before Watkins left the dojo, the instructor presented him with a brown belt and a very old martial arts book. Looking through the pages, he saw that all of the words were written in Japanese. Next to the illustrations, Nakata penciled in the translations in English.

"Study this book and bring it back when you are finished. When you return, we will see what you have learned."

"Thank you," Chester said as he was unlocking the door.

Standing outside in the hallway was Destiny. The old vampire asked her how long she had been waiting and she told him only a few minutes. The council meeting was scheduled for midnight and they still had over two hours to spare.

"Can I show you around some more?"

"Yes. It's kind of stuffy down here, can we go upstairs?"

Tucking in his shirt, the old man asked the pretty vampire why she didn't tell him beforehand that the Jamaican would be sharing the same room with him. With a mischievous grin, she lightheartedly told him that she didn't want to spoil the great surprise.

"You sure smell nice tonight," Destiny added. She moved closer and sniffed the man's collar. "What kind of aftershave are you wearing?"

"Some out-dated stuff. They call it High-Karate."

Chester's guide steered him to a fire escape stairwell that led upstairs into a secret room in the back of the mansion. She warned him that in the event of an emergency to always take the stairs and to avoid the elevators.

"How many exits are down here?" he asked.

"Five."

The vampires stepped outside of the secluded room and into the hallway. When Watkins regained his bearings, he recognized the hallway that led to the elevators. The time was approximately 9:50 p.m. according to his watch. The muffled sounds of people talking were filtering down the hallway as they approached the front rooms of the mansion. From all of the commotion, it sounded like a party.

Destiny placed her hand on Chester's shoulder. "Some of our last-minute guests are starting to arrive."

Aromas of eucalyptus filled the air as the two vampires entered the main lobby where the growing group of immortals was congregating. The old man started looking around to see if he recognized anyone from the previous night's rendezvous in the game room and to his satisfaction he didn't. There were so many folks talking that it was hard to distinguish any specific conversation unless you were standing right next to the ones who were talking.

Chester's escort remained close by his side. When a sissified-looking vampire wearing a white snakeskin cowboy hat, silk shirt, pink-skintight pants, and Italian leather boots entered the room, she tugged on the senior's sleeve and urged him to follow her.

As they approached the wimpy-looking man, Chester realized that this was the gay vampire Destiny warned him about.

"Is that guy wearing lipstick?" Watkins whispered into the girl's ear.

"No," she replied. "I think he just had something to drink."

When the pretty girl introduced the two men, the homosexual vampire shook the old man's hand with a firm grip.

"Hello, I'm Leslie."

"Chester Watkins. Nice to meet you."

The Marine's attention was immediately drawn to the man's eyelashes, which were twice as long as Destiny's. The thick mascara he was wearing made him look like a raccoon, and his glitzy, exaggerated movements reminded him of a pantomime. When the strange fellow spoke, he kept batting his eyelids. The gray vampire became so distracted by this facial-tic that he couldn't grasp what the man was saying.

Avoiding eye contact and looking away, Watkins refocused his attention. "Can you repeat yourself, please?"

"I said, is this your first time visiting the estate?"

"Yes, it is."

Being open-minded, the senior citizen regained his composure and asked the stylish man another question. "So, I hear you like fine-art?"

"Yes, I do. Exquisite would be a better choice of words. See the picture above the fireplace mantle?"

Chester turned around to see what the man was pointing at, and to his amazement he saw an oil painting of a beautiful, naked woman sitting in a chair. He thought to himself, *"I bet she didn't feel threatened when she took off her clothes and posed for this fruitcake."*

Smiling, he commented, "That's very nice. What year did you paint that?"

In a feminine voice he replied, "Sixteen fifty-nine, the year Rembrandt died."

The gay artist explained to Chester that he was inspired by the Dutch painter's portrait of Bathsheba at her bath. Emulating his style, it took him months to complete the masterpiece. Finding a harlot to pose for him who didn't have venereal diseases was the hardest part because most of them were covered with sores from the syphilis epidemics that were spreading throughout Europe.

"Although I was fond of Rembrandt, Leonardo De Vinci was my favorite because we had the most in common. We studied architecture together and drew up designs for helicopters."

"How many artists did you know?"

Rolling his eyes while fluttering his eyelids he replied, "How many stars are there in the sky? I knew Michelangelo, Buonarroti, Bellini, Tintoretto, shall I continue?"

"No," replied Chester, "I think that's amazing."

"I knew all of their quirks. They were all eccentric and highly overrated."

The old man was admiring all of the artwork hanging in the luxurious room until something bizarre caught his eye. Standing in a corner by itself was a wicked-looking marble sculpture of a muscular centaur with horns, huge biceps, hairy, goat-like legs and clothespins attached to his nipples.

"What the hell do you call that thing?" the Marine blurted.

"I didn't sculpt it, one of my students did," the queer answered. "He calls it Pan's Patience."

"I call it pain," the gray vampire said as he cringed at the thought of the excruciating objects. "Look at his face. He looks like he wants to kill someone."

Destiny started to smile as she tapped on the old man's foot with hers, signaling for him to be quiet. Watkins' comments ceased and he changed the subject to architecture. Out of respect for the gay vampire's gifted abilities and diligent work, Chester complemented him. He voiced his approval of all the security precautions, damage control equipment, fire sprinkler systems and escape routes.

"You've done an excellent job around here Leslie."

"Thank you sir, I'm glad someone appreciates my efforts."

Watkins looked around the room as it began filling to capacity with newly arriving vampires. All of the strangely dressed creatures representing different cultures and ethnic backgrounds reminded him of a United Nations convention. He pulled up his sleeve again, and looked at the time on his watch, which read 10:35 p.m. As the noise level intensified, he strained to hear Destiny and Leslie while they conversed. When the beautiful girl finished talking with the motley-dressed man, she led Chester into the hallway again where they could hear one another a little better.

"Let's go back downstairs. I want to show you something."

"What did you have in mind?"

"Have you ever heard of Chupacabras?"

The old man piped up, "I thought they were mythological creatures."

"They are, and so are vampires, werewolves, ghosts and the Loc Ness monster," the foxy girl jokingly replied. " Did you know El Chupacabra means 'the goatsucker' in Spanish?"

"Yes, I did. I read a magazine article about them a long time ago."

Chester followed the blue-eyed woman and she led him back down the same stairwell they used earlier. When they passed the dojo, she guided the old man to another secret passageway with a thick, steel door. When Watkins saw the entryway, he marveled at the heavy-duty rivets and thought to himself, *"This door must weigh over 1,000 pounds."*

The female vampire unbolted the heavy object and the noise of the steel lock-work retracting sounded like hammerheads slamming against one another. Behind the door was a winding staircase leading down to a deeper sublevel. The old man knew that whatever lived down there, the council didn't want it to escape. As they descended, Chester could see a dimly lit tunnel with red lights. The setting reminded him of the nocturnal bat houses found in public zoos. The smell of animal feces, urine and mildew filled the air. Echoes, howls and shrieks reverberated throughout the concrete tunnel.

"I sure hope our centaur friend with the funky tits doesn't live down here," the old Marine said.

Destiny giggled. "I detest that marble statue."

The deeper they traveled underground, the more powerful Chester began to feel. He remembered reading in the "*Wisdom of the Dead*," "*Inside the Earth, there is power.*"

"How many creatures live down here?"

"Two Chupacabras. A male and a female, and some young goats."

When they reached the bottom of the spiral staircase, the man's night vision had already adjusted to the environment and he could see steel bars set into concrete walls. It looked like an underground dungeon.

"Come with me," Destiny said. "I love Chupacabras because, like us, they're susceptible to light and they drink blood to survive."

The pair walked up to the first cage and hiding in the shadows was an indistinguishable black figure. Chester saw the carcass of a dead goat lying at the bottom of the cold, cement deck. Its lifeless eyes were glazed over and the animal's neck had two prominent puncture wounds in the side of it. Dried blood mixed with saliva caused the bristled, coarse hair to stand up where the Chupacabra sucked its meal.

"I see our friend has eaten," Chester said.

"Quiet," whispered Destiny. "He's never seen you before and he's curious."

Without warning, the creature emerged from the deepest recesses of his cell and slowly crept in the direction of the vampires walking upright. The strange beast stepped over the slain goat as it progressed forward. The hairy creature stopped a few feet short of the metal bars and cocked his head sideways as he studied Watkins' face. His cat-like pupils contracted to narrow, vertical slits as a reaction from the ambient red lighting. With nostrils flaring, his long gangly arms, baring sharp claws, pulsated by his side like they were ready to slash.

Destiny smiled at the old man and said, "Isn't he cute?"

"He's adorable," the gray vampire uttered rolling his eyes. "Where's his mate?"

"She's in the next cell. They bred last month and we wanted to give the female some extra space during her pregnancy. I'm so excited. This will be the first Chupacabra born in captivity."

"Wow," whispered Watkins. "Why don't we have a baby shower?"

"Stop being silly," the pretty girl ordered. "I thought you would appreciate seeing this."

"I do, I do," replied the old vampire. "I just had a brain-storm. Why don't we lock the Jamaican up down here and let the Chupacabra trade places with him. Do you think anyone will notice the difference?"

"You're too much," the pretty girl chuckled. "That's not a bad idea."

Watkins changed his demeanor and began to seriously examine the peculiar animal. Conflicting thoughts entered his mind and he wondered if the intelligent-looking beast had the ability to reason and make calculated decisions, or if it just survived and acted by instinct. While he was contemplating these things, Destiny did something that enabled him to draw a conclusion.

"Watch this," she said as she extended her arm and reached inside of the bars with her left hand signaling for the creature to come closer.

Without hesitation, the Chupacabra approached and, in a submissive posture, he lowered his head. The beautiful girl began to scratch the back of his neck as he grumbled in a low, rumbling tone. Suddenly, the creature did something that shocked both Destiny and Chester. He withdrew himself to the center of the cell and began to levitate. The creature hovered for several minutes and when he returned to the floor, he opened his mouth and let loose with a nasty-sounding belch. The vampires looked at one another and started laughing until the nauseating smell drifted toward them.

"One thing's for sure. He's definitely not housebroken."

Coughing from the smelly gas, the blue-eyed vampire covered her nose and walked over to the next cage to check on the female. Sitting on the floor next to the bars, the other animal glanced up at the approaching vampires. Cradled in her lap was a young billy goat with fresh bite marks in his neck. Acting hypnotized, the animal's eyes were transfixed as he bleated and lay immobile. Like a feeding parasite, she resumed her meal and locked her fangs to the throat of the helpless mammal. When the billy stopped breathing, the dainty bloodsucker stood up and tossed his limp body aside.

"What's the purpose of keeping these animals down here?"

"Marius keeps them as pets."

"Can you tell me more about them?"

"They thrive in darkness and actually like it down here. Occasionally, we release them, but only during special times of the year, or if we deem it necessary for them to serve our purposes."

"Purposes, what purposes?"

Destiny went on to explain that two of the estate employees had a land dispute with a rival cattle rancher who was trying to swindle them out of some property. Marius heard about it and was infuriated. Unbeknownst to the faithful servants, the king of vampires released both creatures every night until the cattleman's herd was completely eradicated.

"What happened to the rancher?"

Smiling, the pretty girl replied, "He eventually filed bankruptcy and left the area. The Chupacabras were another story. The male gained 40 pounds and the female put on about 30. It took them months to lose all of that weight."

While the two vampires carried on with their conversation in the dungeon below, the other vampires began assembling in the auditorium with expectations of an enlightening, profitable meeting. The halls in the underground chambers were beginning to get crowded as folks filtered in. Inside the political room, the governing body took their rightful places and waited patiently for the appointed time to commence business.

"Chester, we better go back upstairs."

"Yes, we don't want to be late."

Vladimir was always the last governing member to arrive and this agitated Katsumi because he knew that it was Count Marius who should be the last one to enter the room. The wise Oriental knew that Vladimir's tardiness was a subtle ploy to usurp authority, but the ruling prince of vampires continually ignored the obvious, as did the other council members. "*Maybe they just couldn't see,*" Nakata thought.

Suddenly, a man's fuzzy voice came over the intercom and said, "Fifteen minutes and the meeting will be called to order."

Many of the vampires hissed as the feedback from the microphone let out a deafening ring. A few more minutes passed and the living dead began to find their way to their assigned seats. Chester and Destiny pushed their way through the crowd and found their places toward the back of the council hall.

Chester told Destiny that he always liked sitting in the back of a room during meetings so he could observe everyone. Sometimes, the people sitting in the audience were funnier than the ones onstage.

He whispered to the pretty escort, "I like watching to see who picks their nose, scratches their balls and stuff like that."

Grinning, the pretty girl replied, "You're silly."

The old vampire looked at the clock on the wall, which was hanging next to Hitler's picture, and the time read 11:59 p.m. He turned around and looked back at the chamber doors and saw two armed guards toting submachine guns with extra magazines in their belts. As he continued staring, he saw the flamboyant Russian pass through the doors and strut like a rooster between both sentries. He was dressed in a pinstripe suit and wearing shiny alligator shoes.

Watkins entertained the thought, *"He looks like a mafia kingpin."*

The security personnel nodded their heads and snapped to attention. Vladimir nodded, "Carry on."

Both guards turned and simultaneously bolted the doors shut.

"The meeting will be called to order!" shouted one of the council men. "Quiet everyone."

Marius walked up the stairs and approached the podium as the crowd grew silent. The dark-haired Count was dressed in an expensively tailored blue suit, with matching shoes. He had a serious look on his face. Watkins saw two vampires rise from their seats in the front of the room and making their way toward a huge chest situated on wheels next to the stage. The decorated box was exactly 12 feet in length and four feet in height. Stooping over, the taller man struggled to open the heavy lid and when he lost his footing it slammed shut on his fingers.

Snapping his head back like an agitated coyote, he let out a yodel, "Yow, Son of a bitch!" He kicked the side of the chest as he pulled his hands free.

All of the vampires sitting in the front row winced as they saw the expression on the man's face.

Chester nudged the pretty blond and spoke softly in her ear. "Clumsy fool. I bet he won't pull that stunt again."

The assisting vampire rushed to his friend's side and together they opened the cumbersome lid. Inside of the container were chalices of fresh blood. Acting like church deacons, the two men began walking down the center aisles passing out glasses to everyone seated. When they were finished, they walked to the front of the stage and waited for the Count's signal.

The prince of vampires lifted his chalice into the air and proposed a toast. "Tonight is a special night. We drink- in memory of our brethren who were slain in New Mexico."

Harmoniously, all of the living dead shouted, "To life!" as they partook.

When they were finished toasting, they placed their cups into the holders that were situated on the backs of the seats in front of them. Chester was looking around and when he saw the Jamaican vampire he noticed that he was scratching his armpits and sniffing his fingers. Watkins quietly nudged Destiny so that she could witness the comical stunt, but she didn't respond in time to catch him in the act. "*What a nasty habit,*" the old man thought.

Marius began lecturing the group about finances and investing their personal funds to acquire wealth. Annuities, government bonds and long-term investments were the wisest choices according to all of the experts. Once a substantial profit was made, he advised the group to immediately turn paper assets into tangible holdings such as real estate, silver and gold.

The chancellor said, "Because we are afforded the privilege

of time, we can invest for longer durations. Always reinvest the principal into another long-term, interest-bearing product. Manage your excess profits accordingly."

Watkins remembered when he rolled his IRA into an annuity how it supplemented his income throughout his retirement. It was a sound investment and he always had a steady flow of income. He knew the death benefit would be passed on to his heirs without the delays of probate or public exposure. He liked the advice Marius was offering and considered investing his new social security checks into another insurance product. His current bank account was more than $12,300, but his money was earning less than one percent interest.

When he was alive, the gray old man saw many of his elderly neighbors who were too stubborn to invest their hard-earned money into anything except for certificates of deposits. They believed FDIC was the government. Several died broke and impoverished because they lost their entire estates to nursing homes and medical bills. Watkins knew that failure to plan was to ignore the inevitable.

Count Marius changed the topic and began warning the group to employ extra security precautions because of the recent attacks in New Mexico. While the leader was speaking, Chester began looking around again. He noticed how Vladimir had a strange look on his face.

"We will find those who are responsible for their deaths," Marius said as he pounded his fist on the podium.

Watkins took another look at the Russian and an interesting thought came to mind: *"This guy is a bald-face liar. He's probably the one responsible for all of this mayhem."*

When the Romanian finished speaking, everyone stood up and gave him a round of applause for his wonderful words of wisdom. As he walked off stage, another councilman, dressed in a red suit, got up and made his way toward the stand. Just before reaching it, he skidded on a couple of pencils that were onstage. Resembling a man on roller skates, he slid hands-first into the pulpit, sending it flying into the audience. One of the ladies in the front row ducked as the wooden missile sailed past her face and crashed into an unfortunate guest sitting behind her.

The enraged vampire stood up with his bleeding head sticking out of the side of the splintered podium and hollered, "Why the hell isn't that thing bolted to the floor!"

The entire room erupted with laughter and mixed rebuke from some of the visitors. In the midst of all the confusion, Vladimir leaped on top of the stage like a springy high jumper and screamed at the top of his lungs, "Silence! This meeting will not be made into a sideshow mockery!"

The serious-looking vampire began pointing at people in the crowd and ordering them to remove the pulpit from the man's head and return it to its rightful place onstage.

Watkins didn't like the way the Russian was barking orders at everyone, but refrained from saying anything. He thought the accident was funny and he knew that the councilman who was responsible was probably embarrassed by the incident.

As things began to return to normal and the broken podium was replaced onstage, the humiliated council member began to speak about etiquette and treating one's caretakers with dignity. Vladimir sat back down and started glaring at certain people in the audience who were laughing under their breath at the clumsy councilman.

Destiny whispered to Watkins, "Etiquette? That blundering idiot is constantly tripping over himself."

"Quiet, he's preaching to the choir."

Chester looked at the Jamaican again and saw that he was taking notes. When things began to settle down, surprisingly, the council member started talking about some interesting topics. He spoke of medical research that was taking place in New York State by sympathetic scientists, and the possibility of a serum that might permit vampires to experience brief exposure to sunlight.

One of the vampires sitting in the seat directly in front of

Watkins and Destiny turned around and looked at them, saying, "I haven't seen a sunrise in over 300 years. With my luck, the day I take the vaccination it'll be cloudy outside."

The pretty vampire looked at Watkins. "I've heard this talk before. Don't be too optimistic."

"I'm not, but it sure sounds nice."

The councilman changed the subject and warned the immortals to always use discretion while in public. Except for the chosen few, the entire world was oblivious to the fact that vampires existed. Most of those who did believe were either discredited or living in mental institutions. Watkins' thoughts began to wander again as the lecture continued. He kept noticing how evil Vladimir looked and he knew in his heart that this man couldn't be trusted. He wondered why Marius and some of the other council members couldn't see this.

When the red-suited vampire finished speaking, he quietly returned to his seat. The only one clapping his hands was the Jamaican vampire. He quickly looked around the room and realized that he was the only one standing and promptly sat back down. A few seconds passed and then Vladimir got up and walked onstage. Suddenly, everyone in the auditorium began to whistle, cheer and applaud, except for Chester, Destiny and the dreadlocked vampire.

When the Russian reached center-stage, Chester could see from his vantage point that the man's zipper was undone. The old man turned his head just in time to see Count Marius discreetly signal the oversight. Vladimir glanced down, stepped behind the oak stand and pulled it back up virtually unnoticed.

The flashy vampire proclaimed, "In order to be successful, you must surround yourself with successful people."

Immediately, the large group of vampires applauded. Every eye was riveted on the vice chancellor, except for Watkins, who was fashioning spitballs out of notebook paper and flicking them at the Jamaican and some of the other goofy-looking vampires.

With a serious look on his face, the Russian continued. "Failure is a direct result of negativity. We must always press forward, attaining wealth, knowledge and securing influential friends in high places."

Again, the group began to clap while the flamboyant vampire looked on like he was the president of a global community. Chester started to laugh under his breath as he saw spitballs clinging to the vampire's dreadlocks. Destiny lightly kicked his leg when she realized what he was doing and quietly said, "Be careful. You're going to get caught."

The gray joker whispered back, "OK, I just wanted to see how many wads I could land in his hair."

Vladimir began to talk about history and the dilemmas vampires faced from past generations. He arrogantly implied that vampires were superior to mortal human beings. "We must always be conscious of who the masters are, and who's subservient."

Chester knew that if the Rubensteins and other caretakers were not sympathetic to their cause, most of them would still be sleeping in sewers, caves, or graveyards. He took a second look around the room, and saw the starry-eyed vampires falling for the oldest trick in the world— sedition.

An unusual-looking female vampire with her hair pinned back in a bun, sporting disproportionate ears, snaggleteeth and dingy, green incisors stood up in the third row and shouted, "Hail Vladimir!"

The creepy-looking woman reminded Watkins of a wicked-looking, carnivorous Easter bunny. Chester made a mental note of all the living dead who openly supported the Russian. He decided to make it a point to be careful of what he said or did around these folks because he knew they probably couldn't be trusted.

The supercilious egomaniac finished his speech by emphasizing the probability of financial world domination by vampires within the next 25 years.

"We shall achieve our political and economic purposes through peaceful measures."

The old veteran knew that Vladimir was alluding to a form of global government. The only obstacle standing in his way was the powerful rays of the sun. Taking things into consideration, Watkins was thankful for their physical weakness. *"Maybe it was nature's way of balancing things out,"* he thought.

Bowing for a standing ovation, the Russian walked offstage and returned to his desk as if he'd already conquered the world. The cheering crowd rose to their feet. Acting inconspicuous, Chester and Destiny stood, but neither one of them clapped. The commotion carried on for about five minutes until the final speaker got up and strolled to the podium.

The stout vampire was a humble-looking man who appeared to be of Spanish descent. His dark, curly hair and black mustache made him look dignified, and his snug-fitting suit complemented his muscular physique.

"Welcome, friends and visitors, my name is Julio Vasquez. Even though you might live in another province, you are still an intricate part of this fraternity. All members of the living dead are one in spirit."

A projector screen slowly descended from the top of the auditorium ceiling as the lights dimmed to a mere flicker. The Hispanic man stepped aside as the voice of a narrator came across the speakers and echoed through the council hall. The video footage was shot in the jungle and numerous artifacts and primitive architectural pictures flashed across the monitor.

The commentator began going into more detail as the footage continued and he said, "In Mexico, the ancient ruins of a lost civilization are being unearthed by archeologists and strange hieroglyphics are currently being studied and deciphered in Mexico City. Anthropologists are puzzled by the carbon testing results performed on skeletal remains, which indicated some of the inhabitants of this village lived to be approximately 500 years old. A strange temple depicting the sun and moon is being excavated and the statue of a Caucasian man wearing a cape was found in the sacrificial chambers."

The reporter also mentioned that these strange findings baffled all of the scientists who were taking part in the exploration of this unusual site.

Using a remote control, Vasquez paused the tape and muted the sound. Slowly, the lights returned to normal, and the man spoke. "These tribal people revered this man as a god. Of course, we all know that this person was a vampire."

The Spaniard shared his theory with the audience and said that he believed this individual was hibernating in some underground temple in the jungle. It was essential he be located by his own kind before any archeologists found him. He asked for volunteers to assist him in his quest to find this historical link to their past.

A couple of men raised their hands and the Hispanic vampire pointed to them, saying, "After the meeting is concluded, please meet me behind stage concerning the specific details, and we'll make arrangements for you to travel to the jungles of Mexico."

Another vampire sitting in front of Chester and Destiny stood to his feet and blurted out the question, "Do wc have any idea who this man is you're searching for?"

Vasquez answered his question with a question. "No, but do you think we should take the risk of letting the mortals find him first?"

"Certainly not," replied the inquisitive vampire. "That's why I want to volunteer also."

The Spanish man finished his presentation and Marius signaled Katsumi to adjourn the meeting. The instructor quickly stood up and, using both hands, motioned for the entire group to rise.

Quoting a popular verse in Chapter 19 from the ancient manuscript "*Wisdom of the Dead*," he said, "Unification is the end result of separate individuals striving to accomplish a common objective. We are many, but we are one."

"We are one!" the group shouted collectively, ending the meeting.

Chester observed which vampires talked to Vladimir after the session was over and also noted the ones who avoided him. The big room slowly emptied and within 10 minutes everyone was gone except for the volunteers who were gathering details from Julio concerning the expedition.

Destiny and Chester were standing outside the council hall doors when she asked him, "What are your plans when you return to Houston?"

"I don't know. I think I'll purchase an equity-indexed annuity with some of the money in my savings account and probably buy a few gold coins with what's left."

"So, I take it you liked the advice that was offered."

"Yes, I did, and I plan to come back."

The blue-eyed woman asked the charming man to accompany her upstairs once more so they could take a walk outside and get a breath of fresh air. Chester thought that this was a good idea and followed her.

When they walked outside, the night air smelled refreshing and the beautiful moon looked like a gigantic blue lamp floating in the sky.

Watkins asked, "Is tomorrow night the calendar full moon?"

Scratching her chin, she looked at him and shrugged her shoulders. " I guess so."

Both vampires strolled a short distance away from the mansion where they could converse privately. They found a small picnic bench beside a little pond and sat down together to collect their thoughts. After a few minutes of silence, they spent the remaining hours of the evening chatting about hopes, dreams and aspirations. Destiny shared her interest of becoming the first female council member ever elected, but she knew that this would never transpire as long as Vladimir was vice chancellor. Feeling confident that Chester could be trusted, she disclosed her innermost feelings. She told Watkins that she hated the Russian vampire with a passion. In her next breath, she said that she also feared for her life if anyone ever found out.

"Don't worry, I won't tell."

"I don't know why I'm sharing this with you. I've held these feelings in for so long, I needed to get them off my chest."

"What are friends for?" replied Watkins. "I take it that you don't trust very many people around here."

"Not really, and I'm worried that if anything ever happened to Marius, this place would become a living hell.

"Do you trust Katsumi?"

"Yes, but Vladimir is waging a false campaign of prejudice against him. Some of the vampires are under the impression that he can't be trusted because of his Eastern heritage."

The more intimately they shared, the more Watkins was tempted to confide in her about Marsha, but his instincts guided him to refrain. He remembered how some of his Marine buddies were tortured into submission and they divulged anything the enemy asked.

As he looked into this beautiful woman's eyes, he thought to himself, *"If anyone ever hurts her, they'll taste my revenge."*

When the couple finished sharing secrets, they returned to the mansion and noticed that the parking lot was almost empty. The morning sky was beginning to turn a dull orange, and they instinctively knew that it was time for them to return underground. Most of the visiting cadre had departed and the other vampires were already settling in for the day. Standing outside next to the front doors was Vladimir and another sinister-looking vampire, named Lloyd Buckles. The two hateful creatures glared at Chester and Destiny as they approached the entryway.

"Where have you two been?" quizzed the sarcastic Russian.

"Did your toothless friend take you out on a date?"

With a sneer, Buckles piped up. "We have a wheelchair in the lobby just incase gramps can't make it back downstairs."

Pretending to be cheerful as they passed, the old leather-neck winked at them and pointed at the woman's shapely rear-end. "Sometimes being old and worldly has its advantages."

Destiny forced a smile from the side of her face. "Good night Lloyd, see yah later Vladimir."

CHAPTER 8, FLYING FIRST CLASS

The same limo driver who picked Chester up at the airport returned to the mansion and shuttled him back to the runway. Unfortunately, the same jet that brought him to Arkansas was no longer available. Acting on the vice chancellor's orders, the plane was diverted to the East Coast on urgent vampire business. Vladimir allegedly made last-minute arrangements for a substitute pilot to fly the old man back to Texas.

Fulfilling her escort duties, Destiny accompanied her new friend back to the airstrip. Acting on her instincts, she gave him her private cellular phone number and asked him to stay in-touch. Although they'd just met, she was confident that Chester was an honorable man, and someone she could trust.

When they pulled into the parking lot, they were both startled when they saw the pitiful-looking heap of aeronautic junk sitting on the runway. The old, yellow Piper Cub appeared to be listing to one side and the crooked tail looked as if it had been struck by lightning.

Astonished, the pretty girl whispered into the old man's ear so the chauffer couldn't hear her. "That Russian bastard. I'm telling Count Marius what he did."

"Everything will be alright. Don't make any trouble for yourself."

"I don't feel good about this Chester. We better go back."

"It's too late for that now. We don't want to make any waves. Trust me."

"OK, but please call me as soon as you get back to Houston."

"I will, I promise." Watkins reassured the pretty woman by telling her a small white-lie. "I've flown in uglier-looking planes than this one, and nothing ever happened."

Standing beside the unstable-looking craft was a slipshod-looking man with a beer gut, baggy coveralls, and a dirty ball cap. Acting like a drunken Arkansas moonshiner, he waved at the approaching limousine.

The driver started chuckling when he saw the decrepit plane and its goofy-looking pilot. When he glanced into the rearview mirror and looked at the vampires, Destiny hissed showing her sharp fangs. Immediately, the mortal looked forward, and tried to suppress his laughter.

When the shiny limo pulled beside the dingy plane, Chester noticed the dry-rotted rubber tires. He wondered if the aircraft was capable of taxiing down the runway. The air pressure looked unbalanced, with the left tire appearing to be over-inflated, and the right side almost flat.

Retrieving the luggage from the trunk, the chauffer was conscientious about his facial expressions. Blank-faced, he handed the old vampire his bag and said, “Have a nice flight, sir.”

“I’ll take that,” said the wire-eyed pilot as he stepped between the two men and grabbed the suitcase. “There’s a storm brewing around Texarkana and I want to make sure this luggage is securely lashed down. We don’t want it sailing around the cockpit if we hit some turbulence. ”

Interrupting, Destiny exclaimed, “You’re not flying into a storm are you?”

“Nah,” the crusty man replied, “we’ll go over it if we have to.”

Introducing himself as Captain Randy, the pilot opened the passenger door of the two-seat plane and asked the senior to climb inside. *This thing looks like a flying coffin,* Chester thought.

Once inside, the vampire buckled his seat belt and waited for the captain to join him. When he peeked out of the window at the pretty girl, he could see the look of concern on her face. Pretending to blow a kiss, Watkins silently mouthed the words “thank you.”

Taking off wasn’t as easy as the pilot promised. A strong gust of wind practically blew the little plane into the barbed-wire fence at the end of the runway. Once they were airborne, the old

Marine released his death grip from the dashboard and settled in as they ascended into the sky. With the full moon illuminating everything below, the trees looked like they were a strange shade of blue, as did some of the houses.

The pilot's bad breath filled the cramped cabin, prompting Chester's creative imagination to figure out a way to combat the irritating smell. The old man took a cigar out of his pocket and without asking permission, he quickly lit it up.

"Have you got an extra one of those?" the captain inquired.

"Sure do," replied the vampire. "These are the best, they're Cuban."

After lighting up the second cigar, the bitter aroma subdued all of the other smells inside the aircraft. A few minutes passed and the entire compartment filled with a thick cloud of smoke, making it hard to see through the windows. Chester looked over at the wild-eyed pilot and smiled when he saw a glowing red ember hanging off the end of his cigar. A sudden jolt of turbulence sent the hot cherry right between the man's legs, and with a scream he began fanning his smoldering pants in an attempt to extinguish it.

"Yikes," he bellowed.

"Are you all right?" Watkins asked.

"Yeah, but my family jewels aren't," answered the red-faced man.

The plane began to sway and dip as the struggling pilot fought to put out the fire in his crotch. A few seconds passed before the man regained his composure and resumed monitoring the controls. Chester looked over at the instrument panel and questioned the man about all of the flickering lights blinking on and off. The silly captain told him that an electrical short was the problem and not to worry. Everything was functioning normally.

Traveling southbound, the pilot received a radio transmission warning him of severe weather over East Texas. As the tiny plane approached the Red River border, Chester saw a solid wall of clouds with bolts of lightning surging through them.

"Hang on," Randy said as he adjusted the throttle and attempted to climb above the ensuing storm.

"You're not going to fly us through that shit are you?"

"No, we're going over it."

As the plane's altitude leveled out, the old vampire posed another question, "How long have you had your pilot's license?"

With a ridiculous grin, the stupid-looking man told Watkins that he never received his pilot's license because he had dyslexia and couldn't pass the written exam.

"Why the hell didn't you tell me that before we took off?"

"You never asked."

"What's with all this captain stuff?"

"That's just my nickname. Everyone in Bentonville calls me that because I'm the captain of my softball team. We were undefeated last season."

"Who gives a damn," mumbled Watkins. "You better turn this thing around."

"Got-cha covered boss. If things get too hairy I will."

Bright flashes of light and thundering booms enveloped the sky, as they continued their journey. The gray vampire increasingly protested as the wannabe pilot maneuvered the Piper directly into the danger zone. The ignorant man tried to reassure his passenger that everything would be OK, because he worked at the airport as a custodian and knew a lot about aeronautics.

"You mean you're just a stupid janitor! Who does this plane belong to?"

"I don't know. Someone made arrangements for us to borrow it and they paid me $5,000 to fly you to Hobby Airport."

Suddenly, a loud clap of thunder shook the delicate craft and shockwaves reverberated throughout the fuselage. Memories of the Pacific campaign flashed through the old Marine's mind as he closed his eyes and cringed. The loud noise and bright flashes of light reminded him of a nighttime artillery barrage that wiped out an entire platoon of Americans.

Looking through the cloudy haze, the pair found themselves directly on top of the vicious storm. Rising in front of them at an altitude higher than the single-engine plane could safely climb was the eye of the storm. The thunderous tempest was more than the inexperienced pilot had bargained for.

Seeing no way out of the perilous situation, the wise vampire tried to figure out an escape scenario just in case the plane went down. Looking around for a parachute and seeing none, he knew that his options were practically nonexistent. Within minutes, they were surrounded by thick clouds, and the unstable turbulence began shaking the rickety craft like a matchbox. The brutal beating was beginning to take its toll on the antiquated engine. A series of mechanical vibrations shook the plane, and the motor started bellowing white smoke. With a sputtering sound, oil began spewing all over the windshield.

"We're losing altitude!" screamed the pilot. "I can't control her."

In an attempt to clear his field of view, he turned the half broken wiper on, only to see it jerk in slow motion and spread oil across the glass. Acting like a panicking maniac, he fumbled around trying to turn the switch off. When his hand found it, he flicked it so hard that it snapped loose, falling to the floor. The sluggish wiper kept traveling from side to side smearing its mess like peanut butter. Eventually it was ripped free from the window by the torrential winds. Chester looked as the thing whizzed by the passenger's side, and out of sight.

Rain mixed with pea-sized hail began pelting the helpless J-3 as it slowly descended through the wicked maze of Mother Nature's wrath. Inside of the cockpit, it sounded like a cheap popcorn machine. The pitiful engine started whining like an out-of-tune siren as the propeller's speed varied from fast to slow, and then repeated its weird cycle of peculiar repetitions again. The stalling craft's altimeter began spinning like a slot machine and both men's ears popped from the sudden drop in altitude.

Like a vacuum, the fierce winds began sucking the plane deeper into their destructive paths. Horrified, the softball captain fought in vain to regain control of the aircraft. Passing through the pulsating electrical fields and watching the bolts of lightning narrowly missing the J-3 caused the pilot to lose his ability to reason.

"We're going to die," the man screamed. With his next breath he started repenting of his sins. "Lord forgive me for visiting message parlors, siphoning gas from my neighbor's cars, and cheating on my taxes."

Plummeting like a rock, the Piper broke free of the clouds and was now underneath the storm. Feeling the full brunt of its ravaging force, the terrified pilot started ripping and clawing at the plane's instruments like a raving lunatic. Watkins looked out of his foggy window and through the torrential downpour, he saw the lights of a small town growing closer. Knowing that impact was inevitable, the vampire closed his eyes and focused all of his strength to perform the impossible feat he quickly thought up. With a martial arts yell, he smashed out the passenger side window with his elbow, and unbuckled his seat belt. A loud whooshing sound filled the cabin, as rain, wind, and broken glass blew back inside.

Randy turned his head in the direction of the enraged warrior and looked on in disbelief as he saw him preparing to fight for his own life.

Screaming like the Marine he was, he recited the powerful spell, "*Bat of the night, take flight!*" Chester was transformed into a vampire bat and launched himself out of the doomed Piper. The horrific force of the 120 mph winds caused the diminutive creature to hit the side of the faltering plane as he bailed-out. Flapping his wings with all of his strength, the disoriented creature fought to stabilize himself. He quickly recovered his faculties and watched from high above the ground as the plane spiraled out of control like a smoking boomerang.

The forsaken J-3 crashed into a hardware store, exploding upon impact. The collision sent fragments of metal and glass soaring into the rainy mist. Within seconds, the entire building was engulfed in flames as secondary explosions rocked the small town.

Hovering in midair, the vampire bat spotted a gas station on the other side of town approximately a mile away. It didn't take him long to make up his mind to get out of the rain. Watkins flew as fast as he could in the direction of the 24-hour store, and landed behind it undetected. When he reversed the spell, he noticed that his pants were ripped and his underwear was showing. Dripping wet, the man ran around to the front of the store and went inside. As soon as he entered, he came face-to-face, with a deputy sheriff standing by the cash register.

Politely, the law officer pointed. "Sir, your trousers are torn, and your skivvies are showing?"

"Sorry, they got ripped on something while I was trying to get out of the rain."

Before the law officer could ask anymore questions, his police-radio squelched. The dispatcher made an urgent plea for everyone on call to respond to the fire at Finn's hardware store.

"Sorry, I've got to go," he said. "Have a nice evening Nancy."

The deputy ran to his patrol car, and with blue lights flashing and sirens blaring, sped off. Another minute passed and a fire department truck drove past the little store heading in the same direction.

Chester turned around and looked at the lady who was standing behind the counter. Her attention was diverted to the police scanner sitting on the windowsill. Unfamiliar with how the device worked, she tried to locate the frequency that the Sheriff's Department was using. When she finally located their radio transmissions, she turned around and saw the drenched man who was standing by the doorway.

"Let me get you a towel from the back. You're soaked to the bone, you might catch pneumonia."

"Thank you. I appreciate your kindness."

"Follow me sir."

The friendly lady told Watkins that there was a pair of blue overalls and matching T-shirt in the storage room next to the walk-in cooler. The outfit belonged to an employee who resigned and he never returned to collect it. She said he was welcome to dry off and change clothes if he wanted to. Without thinking twice, Watkins took her up on the offer and stepped inside the room.

After putting the loose-fitting clothes on, he returned to the front of the store and found the clerk behind the counter listening to the police radio again.

Pretending like he didn't know anything, the vampire asked, "Did they say what caused the fire?"

"They think it was a plane crash, but they're still not certain."

Chester looked outside and saw that the rainstorm was beginning to break. The light drizzle slowly trickled down to a fuzzy mist. A few more minutes passed, and all of the precipitation stopped. Not wanting to stick around any longer than he had to, Watkins thanked the nice woman, and said goodbye.

When he left the store, he could see the glowing lights from the fire on the other side of town. Looking down the street, he noticed a news van heading in the direction of the action. Chester walked behind the building again and recited the bat incantation. He flew off into the muggy sky and headed to Highway 59. He knew that following the southerly route would make navigating easier.

After reaching a comfortable altitude, the gray bat began thinking about everything that just happened. It was obvious that the Russian plotted his murder. The more he thought about it, the angrier he got. An evil contingency of immortals was jockeying for power within the Dynasty, and they would kill anyone who got in their way. Chester was perceived as a threat and dealt with accordingly. The old Marine decided to lay low and let his enemies believe that he was killed in the crash. By doing this, he could pick and choose his day of revenge. There was one thing the Marine Corps taught him to do well, and that was fight. His adversaries made the first move and failed. If possible, he would never give them this opportunity again.

As the bat continued flying, he thought to himself about the luggage that he lost onboard the plane. *"Nakata's martial arts book was among the items destroyed."*

Off in the distance, Watkins could see some approaching headlights as he angled towards the highway. Traveling 2,000 feet below him was an 18-wheeler heading south. Watkins' wings were beginning to tire, so he decided to land on top of the trailer and ride for awhile. Because the vehicle was traveling faster than he could fly, he knew that he had to time his landing perfectly. Right before he touched down, a thick cloud of diesel smoke spurted from the exhaust pipes and shot right into his face. The truck began jake breaking as its pipes roared and belched more nasty smoke into the air.

Coughing and cursing, the angry bat spread his wings and flattened himself out as low as he could to avoid the fumes.

A half-hour later, the vehicle turned into a truck-stop to refuel. Chester flew off into the piney woods behind the store and reversed his spell again. He headed for the restroom to freshen up, and when he walked inside of the café, he noticed that everyone was staring at him and laughing. When he saw his reflection in the mirror, he realized why. His face was completely black from all of the soot. Feeling embarrassed, he splashed some water on his head, rinsed his hands off, and started looking for another way out. His attention was drawn to the small window located above the toilet. Standing on his tiptoes, he pushed it open, and transformed into a bat again so he could fly away.

Once outside, he circled around to the front of the store

looking for another truck. Traveling for long distances was too strenuous for his tiring arms and he knew that he could make better time hitching a ride. The vampire saw a flatbed trailer with some heavy equipment chained on top of it. He flew overhead and landed right next to a bulldozer that had an enclosed cabin. The wise bat saw a small opening in the window that was just big enough for him to crawl through. Once inside, he fluttered under the seat and was met by a stray cat that wanted to make a meal out of him.

Springing on top of the tiny bat, the hissing feline caught Chester by the wings and opened his mouth to eat him.

Thinking quickly, the old Marine shouted, "El Lobo de noche translate imidiatemente!"

The terrified tomcat didn't know what to think as he balled up on top of the wolf's head yowling, clawing, and fighting like a small tiger. Watkins shook his head to dislodge the hissing cat. When the animal lost his balance and fell off, he leaped out of the cab through the partially open window. Jumping up on the seat, the silver canine saw the scared cat streaking through the parking-lot with his hair standing on end. Chester decided to hide on the floorboard and remain a wolf until a change of situation warranted another transformation. Hopefully, the truck driver wouldn't look into the cab until he reached his final destination. If he was lucky, it would be Houston.

Back in Evergreen, Texas, Vladimir was just arriving for the scheduled full moon ritual. Cloaked in secrecy, the witches always tried to cover their tracks and they seldom met in the same place twice. This time they chose a Presbyterian church to practice their abominable black magic and to offer a special sacrifice to the immortal vampire. An unsuspecting hitchhiker was picked up by one of the seductive coven members and offered a spiked beer laced with sleeping pills. After being drugged and hogtied, the group held the man prisoner in a rural root-cellar to await execution.

Pertaining to human offerings, the high priest ordered his

cronies to always pick someone who would never be missed by society. Hookers, homeless people and young babies who were specifically bred within the coven were perfect examples of the unknown victims tortured and killed by these demented souls.

The Russian bat landed in front of the country church and peered through the stained glass window to look at his faithful followers who had congregated to worship the forces of darkness.

Working his drums over like a madman, the intoxicated warlock kept a steady beat going as some of the female witches were lighting candles and placing them in their holders. Dancing barefoot in front of the stone altar, some of the other Satanists spit at the tied up man who was bound and gagged. One of the devil worshippers noticed him struggling in a feeble attempt to loosen his restraints and, in a fit of drug-induced anger, belted him in the face, knocking out his front teeth. Moaning, the hitchhiker spit them out into the filthy rag wrapped around his mouth.

Knowing that everything was in order, the flamboyant vampire stepped through the front doors of the church like he was royalty. The musky smell of marijuana and smoldering candles filled the air as he drew in a breath and looked around. Dressed in a brilliant white suit with gold-trimmed pockets, the satanic creature strolled down the center of the pews and nodded his head from side to side as a gesture of approval to his unholy brethren.

With raptured ecstasy, the coven shouted, "Welcome master!"

Miller approached the Russian and whispered into his ear, "Did you have a chance to visit the troublemakers yet?"

"Are you referring to the address you mailed to my post office box?" questioned Vladimir.

"Yes."

"I'll pay them a visit next week," the vampire stated with a sinister smile. "You know I hate troublemakers."

The brown-robed witches assembled in an orderly fashion as

their wicked master took his place behind the pulpit to address the coven. He looked down at the primitive alter and began to salivate when he saw his meal struggling to break his bonds. One of the witches blew on a croaky-sounding horn and it made a deafening noise. This was the signal to commence torturing the hitchhiker.

"Remove his gag!" shouted the blond-haired huckster. "I want to hear him shout praises to Lucifer. I want to see him beg for clemency."

One of the witches sprinted to the altar and ripped the cloth from the man's face, scratching his cheeks in the process. His loose teeth fell to the floor. With a scream, the homeless man pleaded for his life. "Please let me go. I promise I won't tell anyone about you."

"I command you to tell everyone in hell about us," roared the evil vampire, "because that's where we're sending you tonight."

"So mote it be," chanted the Satanists.

"Prepare to purify our sacrifice!" shouted Miller.

The gong player struck his instrument and one of the warlocks took a leather whip out of his robe and started flogging the helpless man. The cat-o'-nine-tails ripped flesh, clothing and hair from the screaming man's arms, neck and back. With each cracking lash, the sounds of laughter from the crowd began drowning out the pleas for mercy. Working themselves into a satanic stupor, the members waited for their devilish visitor to complete the sacrifice.

When he approached the altar, the handsome vampire was drooling from the mouth as he prepared to feast on his bleeding victim.

"If you shout, 'Hail Vladimir, Satan's servant,' I might let you live. Now, give praises and no faking it."

The hell-bound hobo began telling everyone in the desecrated church that he loved Vladimir and the devil more than anything else in the world. He looked around at all of the hooded witches and said that he forgave all of them for what they did to him and that he deserved to be beaten.

"I really mean it!" he yelled. "You can beat me again if you want to."

"You don't sound very convincing!" shouted the slanderous creature as he bit into his neck.

Kicking and gargling, the condemned vagrant began to convulse as the vampire sucked all of the life from his body. Amidst cheers of blasphemy, cursing and rebellious laughter, the poor man quickly lost consciousness and succumbed.

"We don't want him to regenerate," ordered the Russian. "When we're finished celebrating, set the church and his body on fire. Make sure this rat hole burns to the ground."

"Yes, master!"

"Also, if there's anything worth stealing, don't forget to snatch it before torching the joint."

One of the hallucinating witches started jumping up and down on the pews, shaking her tambourine shouting praises to Vladimir while she puffed her marijuana cigarette. "Hail to the king of the vampires."

Lucious told the evil master that the stoned lady was a science teacher at one of the local schools and she was doing a wonderful job with all of her students. Next, he pointed to onc of the drunken men who was vandalizing some of the church equipment and said, "Look at him, he's the principal."

The warlock began pounding on the church piano with his fists until he smashed all of the keys, rendering it inoperable. He guzzled a bottle of beer and threw the empty longneck at a sacred statue, narrowly missing it, and striking one of the women in the head who was standing beside it. Laughing, she threw it back and hit him in the groin, making him double over.

The isolated country church looked like a sacrilegious party from hell with all the coven members desecrating every religious symbol inside the building.

Vladimir pulled Miller aside and the two began plotting and

conspiring with their demented criminal minds how they were going to capture Count Marius and wrest power from his loyal subjects. The strategy was fairly simple and entailed luring the prince of vampires to one of the safe houses in Tennessee and subduing him after sunrise. All the concierges would be murdered and the chancellor would be transported in a Moving-van to Cold Springs, Texas. His casket would be secured with chains and padlocks, and packed with garlic cloves to prevent him from escaping. After the Satanists extorted all his financial holdings, they'd torture and vanquish the Count in a satanic fire ritual preformed around Christmas.

"When I seize control of the Dynasty of Immortals, you and this coven will be rewarded financially."

Back at the truck stop, the flatbed was just pulling out of the store and onto the highway. The silver wolf began to get carsick from all the rocking back and forth going on inside the cab. Feeling like he was on a Navy troop transport carrier, he held his breath until they gained some speed and things smoothed out. Once he was comfortable, he settled down and enjoyed the ride. According to the clock Chester saw inside the café, he estimated they would arrive in Houston around 3:30 a.m. if the trucker didn't take any detours or stop at a rest area.

By now, Watkins figured that Fabian and his friends had probably heard about the plane crash and assumed he was dead. He planned on sneaking back to Bear Creek and laying low until he figured out how to get even with his adversaries. As long as everyone thought he was dead, he didn't have to worry about someone trying to kill him again.

When the 18-wheeler passed through Cleveland, Texas, Watkins conjured up the idea that he would transform into a bat again around the Beltway 8 area and navigate home from there. To his surprise, when they got to the expressway the driver took the exact route Chester needed. Heading for the west side of the city, all he had to do now was watch for the Clay Road exit. From there, he could fly home in approximately 15 minutes.

Things were going good until the driver had a blowout on top of the 290 overpass. Sounding like a shotgun blast, rubber tire fragments smacked into the flatbed and littered the highway. After pulling his rig over to the side of the bridge, the small bat flew out of the cab, never looking back. Watkins headed directly for Clay Road and within 20 minutes he was back in his familiar subdivision.

Being cautious, the smart vampire flew around the block a couple of times making sure someone wasn't spying on the Rubenstein's home. Confident the coast was clear, he landed undetected in the back yard behind the swimming pool and next to the outbuilding. He reversed the bat incantation and entered through the secret passageway that led to his private quarters. It only took a couple of seconds to disarm the security system, because he'd memorized the code. As his eyes adjusted, he saw that the teenager's belongings were still hidden inside the tunnel. He politely stepped around them before entering the room through the hidden door behind the bookcase.

Without making a sound, Chester quickly checked his room out. When he was satisfied that everything was undisturbed and where it belonged, he retrieved his .45 pistol from inside his coffin and stuck it in the small of his back under his shirt. He opened the door leading into the hallway and went directly to the front room. Before stepping inside, he paused for a few seconds to eavesdrop. He heard the doctors trying to comfort the hysterically sobbing teen-aged girl.

"Just when I was starting to believe things were turning around, something like this had to happen. Chester was like a father to me. I hate this stinking world."

Sporting a smile from ear to ear, Watkins walked into the living room. "It's nice to know when you're appreciated. That was one heck of a eulogy you delivered Marsha. Keep up the good work."

The trio looked as if they'd seen a ghost as they gazed in disbelief. Marsha leaped to her feet and ran into the old man's arms, embracing him tightly.

"We thought you were dead," she cried. "Thank God, you're alive."

"I've been dead for months," the cagey senior answered. "So, what's new?"

Both doctors told Chester that they were going to contact Count Marius immediately and let him know that everything was all right.

"Don't call anyone," he ordered. "The vice chancellor conspired to have me murdered."

"He did what?" asked Patricia. "You've got to be kidding."

"Vladimir arranged for my flight back with an uncertified pilot who was paid $5,000 to commandeer a cracker-box Piper Cub from hell."

"Are you certain about this?" Fabian asked with a puzzled look.

Watkins related the entire story, starting with the chess match. He told his friends that he believed the Russian was planning a coup d'état. "He's got a lot of blind followers who are just as wicked as he is, and it's obvious they want more power."

"The council won't allow this to happen," Fabian stated. "There are too many devoted vampires who would resist such a thing."

"They won't see it coming. Vladimir is a cunning individual. I promise you, he won't stop until he seizes control of the Dynasty of Immortals."

The gray Marine told the doctors the only two vampires he trusted on the governing board were Nakata and Marius. If a power ploy was executed, he was certain that the Japanese man would be overlooked because of his cautiousness. The karate instructor wasn't the type of person to divulge his thoughts or convictions to just anyone, and he had the fortitude of a survivor.

Most of the other vampires were followers and would go along with whatever form of government was at hand. The only thing they cared about was hanging out in the game room, drinking blood, and indulging themselves. Chester worried about Destiny because he knew her motives were pure and her friendship was genuine. As much as he wanted to let her in on what was going on, his intuition told him that he would be jeopardizing her life if he did so.

Playing opossum was the wisest thing to do until their enemies made the next move. The only question that came to mind was, *"How long could they hold out?"*

CHAPTER 9, MEXICAN JUNGLE

Deep in the recesses of the sweltering jungle, an expedition of six volunteer vampire archeologists began their quest to find the hibernating vampire and repatriate him to their fold. Little did the explorers know, that Vladimir planted a mole among them, to spy out their activities and have them murdered if they were successful in locating the legend. The jealous Russian was concerned that this man might be a strong leader because the ancient villagers had constructed a temple in his honor and placed his idol inside. The insidious creature wasn't going to allow any competition or diversions to interfere with his plot to seize control. His demonic tentacles of influence were far stronger than anyone realized, and he would stop at nothing until he accomplished his goal.

Vasquez made arrangements with a high-ranking staff member at the local hospital to supply the group with blood and supplies in exchange for some silver and gold bullion. The greedy doctor was well aware of the existence of vampires and he'd always cooperated with them in the past. Experience had taught him that the financial rewards were substantial. Unbeknownst to Julio, the physician had been recruited as one of Vladimir's pawns, and he began reporting all intelligence gatherings to him immediately. The Russian promised the crooked man that he would double his pay if he cooperated. The deceived doctor was unaware that he'd just made a pact with the devil's emissary.

From the onset of their quest, the exploration team was plagued with mosquitoes, biting flies and no-see-ums. As they made their trek through the jungle, hacking away with machetes in hand, their patience was wearing thin as the bugs nibbled away. The tiny pests drank as much blood as the vampires did and they resented it. The worthless insect repellant they applied to their exposed skin seemed to be attracting more critters than it did to ward them off.

Leeches, snakes, scorpions and feral dogs were also giving

the team problems. Two of the vampires in the search party decided to transform into wolves and fight off a pack of wild canines that were following the team. The pair was successful, killing three of them and wounding two more.

The Yucatan Peninsula was home to several ancient cities from centuries past. The vampires were only 50 miles from the Chichen-Itza ruins and they marveled at all the stone architecture they were encountering. Temples, sacrificial chambers, courtyards and pyramids were among the interesting things the explorers found hidden in the jungle.

Three days and four nights elapsed and the volunteers were growing impatient having to sleep underground in rat-infested burial chambers. One of the vampires who had fair skin looked like he had chickenpox from all the insect bites on his face and arms. Another man with the nickname "Hacker" awoke to find that vermin had gnawed off part of his ear and nose while he slept. Even though he was aware that he would regenerate the missing body parts in a couple of months, the thought of what happened to him was humiliating. There was only one lady in the expedition team and she kept teasing her friend, telling him that he looked like a hog-nosed snake.

Every night the expedition team would start out from the same excavation site, which was their base of operation, and navigate using a map and compass. The handheld global positioning system, GPS, enabled them to mark waypoints and stay on course with extreme accuracy. This particular evening they set out with a heading of 192 degrees heading southward. The explorers fanned out in pairs and began their search. The same two vampires who transformed into wolves did so again and used their keen sense of smell to sniff their way through the jungle. The roving group passed through a small village causing the town dogs to bark, but when they saw the wolves they quickly retreated, hiding under vehicles, bushes and farming equipment.

Julio was an expert with the GPS. He only turned it on to check his bearings and maintain a heading. By doing this, he was able to conserve his battery power for days on end. He'd power the system up quickly to get a satellite acquisition, and once he adjusted the course reading with his compass, he'd turn it off.

"I can't wait until we find our immortal," Vasquez said. "From the looks of his statue, I'm certain he's an astute leader. His ancient wisdom will be an attribute to our society."

"He does look pretty smart," one of the men added. "I remember reading an article in a health magazine and it stated that a large forehead indicates intelligence."

The vampires' superior nocturnal eyesight enabled them to see with clarity in the dense foliage as they continued to chop through the underbrush. Continuing south on their present heading brought them to another primitive site approximately 10 kilometers from the closest village. These ruins weren't marked on their map or any of the other topographical maps they were using to study the area.

"Look at this," Vasquez said as he pointed to a small temple. "Let's go inside and explore. Maybe our friend lives here."

Tasha, the female vampire, was the first one to enter the small opening located in front of the stone building. The two wolves reversed their spells and were transformed back into themselves so they could aid the others in their search. The girl turned on her flashlight to illuminate the way because the inside was pitch black. With no ambient light available, the vampire's night vision was ineffective.

As he was walking around inside probing the wall for a secret chamber for some clue, Hack mentioned the fact that he noticed a strange odor. "It stinks in here like dirty socks."

"It does," replied Julio as he flipped on his pocket Mag Lite. "That smell indicates someone, or something, is living here. I think we're on to something."

The group walked down a narrow corridor that was so shallow everyone had to stoop down as they pressed forward. When they reached the end, it opened back up where everyone could stand erect. Once they were comfortable, the group saw another hallway leading to a set of stone stairs. When they descended, they entered a sublevel and found an old, dusty carcass with a stake driven through its chest. Everyone in the group hissed as they beheld the body of a would-be mummy vampire.

"Subterfuge," whispered Vasquez. "This is a diversion. Our friend is far wiser than the average vampire."

The Spaniard kicked the body and it broke apart spilling candy, gum and chocolate bars all over the floor. "It's a piñata."

"Someone must have stolen it and placed it here to scare off intruders," said Tasha. "It sure looked real."

After regaining their composure, the group turned around to leave and were caught completely off-guard by the impressive-looking creature who had snuck up behind them. The tall, light-skinned, Caucasian man was wearing a golden cape and his features looked identical to the statue they saw inside the first excavation site. When Vasquez shined his flashlight into the man's eyes, they took on a wild look as he screeched and hissed, bearing his fangs.

"Do you speak English?" one of the vampires questioned.

The creature shook his head up and down, motioning "yes," and then he shook his head from side to side motioning "no."

"I think he's confused," said Tasha.

"What's your name?" Julio asked in a calm tone as he raised his arms and showed the creature the palms of his hands.

"Ra!" the creature screamed. "Ra, Ra, Ra. I am Ra."

"Isn't Ra the name of the Egyptian sun god?" queried one of the men.

As the group looked into the madman's eyes, they realized that he was mentally impaired. Slobber was dribbling out of his mouth and dripping down his chin as he growled at all the vampires who he perceived as threatening intruders.

"Calm down. We're not going to harm you."

The disturbed man began to cry as he pointed to the busted piñata. "You hurt my buddy. Me no like you."

While the distracted group was trying to converse with the retarded vampire, Vladimir's mole turned his flashlight off and quietly slipped out of the chamber unnoticed. He made his way to the upper level towards the exit, but as he distanced himself from the group he could hear their echoes from below. The deranged lunatic began screaming in a shrilling voice. "Get out! This my cave!"

Once outside, he reached into his backpack and withdrew five sticks of dynamite that were duct-taped together. The evil pawn was careful to conceal them from his peers, who might have grown suspicious as to why he was carrying them. The sinister traitor wedged them into the rocks above the exit and, taking out his lighter, lit the fuse. With a gut-wrenching laugh, he transformed into a bat and flew high into the sky to watch the explosion. The blast rocked the jungle, shaking trees and spewing rocks into the air. After the shockwaves ceased, thousands of pieces of gravel pelted the forest, sounding like a rainstorm. Inside the temple, the doomed vampires and their mentally deficient host were forever entombed.

Confident that his mission was almost accomplished, the wicked little bat flew back to town to meet with the doctor—and seal his fate. *"I'll tell him to meet me at the excavation site so I can pay him his reward for faithful service. Two fangs in his neck and a nice bonfire cremation will be his compensation,"* the vampire thought to himself.

After receiving his instructions from the traitor, the greedy physician drove his beat up, oil burning station wagon to the secluded ruins. Thoughts of lavish vacations, new cars, a mansion in Cancun, a bank full of money and lots of naughty women to fulfill his fleshly desires flashed through his reprobate mind.

An hour later, the doctor arrived at the dark, abandoned ruins to meet with Vladimir's cunning emissary. Holding a gunnysack, the vampire said, "Look what I've got for you, doctor."

"Do you have the silver and gold, Señor Marcus?"

With a stone cold look on his face, he deceptively answered, "Yes, it's inside this big, heavy bag. It weighs so much I can barely lift it."

When the Mexican physician was within arms reach of the murderous creature, the vampire lunged at him, throwing the burlap sack over his head and kicking his legs out from underneath him. The man balled up inside the empty bag in a fetal position on the ground while the torturous vampire began kicking him like a soccer ball.

Pleading in Spanish, the betrayed man cried, "Alto, alto. No mas."

"So, you want me to stop?" shouted the tormentor. "OK, I think I'll have a bite to eat now."

The heinous imp yanked the sack off the beaten man and jerked him to his feet by the scruff of his shirt. The trembling doctor's face grimaced as the powerful creature bit into his carotid artery. Savagely, the blood-lusting devil finished off his victim and stuffed his unresponsive body back into the burlap sack. With one arm, he dragged the bag over to a scrap pile of discarded lumber and plywood that was used to construct scaffolds next to the pagan temple. A can of kerosene used for torches and lanterns was close at hand, so the vampire took the liberty of dousing the entire trash pile and setting it ablaze.

The vampire meditated for a few seconds on the verse in *"Abbadon's Priests,"* Chapter 13:13. *"Kill everyone you owe a debt to and spare not thy wrath. By doing so, you shall gain double. Greed is an unquenchable fire in the belly of the dominant. Burn your enemies before they burn you."*

As he stood next to the fanning flames, the creature reached into his pocket and retrieved his cellular phone. When his party answered, Marcus said, "Mission accomplished, my lord."

"Did you derive pleasure in deceiving everyone, including that money hungry doctor?" Vladimir asked.

"Yes, I did master and you should have seen the surprised look he had on his face when he saw the empty sack I was holding for him. His facial expression was priceless."

"Good, keep 10 percent of the silver and gold for yourself and give me back the rest. Also, if there are any valuable artifacts, steal them and we'll make arrangements to smuggle them out of the country."

"Yes, my lord."

"Do me a favor," Vladimir asked. "Take a sledgehammer and smash the head off of that damned statue in the temple before you leave."

"Yes, sir."

The Russian congratulated his wicked servant and told him to hide on the island of Cozumel until the revolt was finished. Before hanging up, he added, "Well done, my wicked servant. I'm promoting you to ambassador. Picture this, you can travel the world and make hundreds of fake deals and renege on all of them."

Vladimir's plans were taking root. The expedition group contained five loyalists who would have fought to the death supporting Count Marius. With each staged murder, the vice chancellor's dominance was growing stronger. His coup d'état was almost within his grasp. His next step was to ensure that the prince of vampires would take a permanent vacation. The Romanian would just disappear one night, with everyone believing he went to Europe on extended business. The Russian would pretend to be carrying out strict orders by proxy, and in the process he would change their democratic form of government into a fascist dictatorship. All of the false directives would be carried out, the blame shifted to Marius, and no one would be the wiser.

The subjugated mob would soon grow to hate their former leader. The Russian would continue his farce until everyone was sick and tired of all the restrictions. Once his political façade was accomplished, he would announce to everyone that Marius was accidentally vanquished during his trip, and pronounce himself chancellor. Restrictions would be relaxed and he would feign kindness to the gratefully seduced hoards.

CHAPTER 10, MEMORY LANE

Even though the vampire's manual discouraged it, Chester wanted to take a drive through his old neighborhood and see what had become of his former home and personal property. He'd been dead for over six months and it was his desire that his estate be divided equally between his two adopted children, Peggy and Reggie.

Driving the Lincoln Town Car that night was a big change from cruising around in the doctor's sporty Porsche. Chester turned off of Long Point onto his familiar street and when he drove by his house, to his surprise, he saw a big pile of trash in the front yard and a "For Sale" sign planted right next to it. His beloved home was dark and all the curtains were gone from the windows. The grass needed to be mowed, the sidewalk edged and the hedges trimmed. The place was a mess.

"Is that where you lived?" asked Marsha.

"Yes."

The old man put the Lincoln in reverse and pulled alongside the curb, parking next to the mailbox. When he got out, a strong feeling of emotional sentiment swept through his mind. Ruby, their children, Thanksgiving, birthday parties and all the good ol' days were gone forever. Time and the existence of mankind was no more than a vacuum, sucking everything that ever existed into its relentless black hole of death.

Watkins went over to one of the trash-pails and removed the lid. When he looked inside, he saw the oak shadow box containing his World War II medals and Marine Corps emblems lying on the top of the stack. He rummaged through all of the discarded items and was deeply grieved at what he found. Photo albums, pictures of Ruby and himself, precious keepsakes and everything pertaining to their life were tossed into the garbage.

"Those wicked children. We gave them everything—college educations, their first cars and even helped them with the down

payments on their houses," he grievously remembered. *"They didn't even have the gratitude to take our pictures into their possession and cherish our memories."*

The old man never liked his children's spouses. They were cold and cynical. Maybe they didn't like him either and were probably the ones who were responsible for trashing everything.

Chester quickly collected some of his mementos and placed them in the back seat of the Town Car. "Give me a few more minutes," he said as he grabbed the family photo album.

"Sure, Chester, take your time," answered the sympathetic teenager.

After collecting a few more items, the duo left the neighborhood and drove to his daughter's house in North Houston. He wanted to pass by, look from the street and see if they benefited from their inheritance. The old man's mind was concocting thoughts of how he could regain the money he entrusted to his adopted children. His annuities, CDs, money market accounts and oil stocks totaled $512,500. *He would have been better off donating it to the Salvation Army or a homeless shelter,* He pondered.

Immortality afforded him the advantage of seeing things as they were. Another thought entered his mind: *"Sometimes the truth hurts, but it's better than believing a bunch of lies."*

When they reached his daughter's home, he saw a large speedboat sitting in the garage and a bright, shiny sport utility vehicle parked next to it. He rounded the block, leaving the neighborhood and drove straight to his son's place, which was located in Baytown, east of Houston.

"Are you all right?" Marsha asked. "You're awfully quiet."

"Just upset. Ruby and I did everything for those kids, but when their real parents were released from Huntsville prison Peggy blamed us for them being locked up."

During the drive, Chester explained to Marsha how the children's mother and father were arrested for money laundering, racketeering and swindling their church congregation out of thousands of dollars. The couple was also practicing veterinarian medicine without a license. The preacher put his customer's sick and dying animals to sleep with a 12-gauge shotgun and charged his clientele full price for euthanasia.

"Their father was known as the Reverend Deep Pockets," Chester said.

Bewildered, the girl blurted out, "They were ministers?"

"Crooked as a snake and evil to the bone."

Watkins took the Main Street exit when he got to Baytown and within a few minutes he found Reggie's home. Just like his daughter's place, there was a fancy truck parked next to an expensive bass boat. The house had a fresh paint job, a new roof and a newly constructed deck.

"I've seen enough," groaned the gray vampire. "I don't mind them prospering, but it's obvious that they didn't appreciate what Ruby and I did for them."

"I've got an idea how to get even with them and I think you're going to like it."

"I just want to forget it and let it go."

"Please hear me out," the girl demanded. "Let's pull an identity theft scam on them. They deserve it."

The gray vampire's eyes perked up as he looked over at his mischievous convert. "What did you have in mind?"

"We establish a line of credit in their names and ruin their reputations. After I'm finished with them, they won't be able to charge a nickel's worth of merchandise."

"Who taught you how to do this?"

"My Uncle Ed lived like the sultan of Arabia. He was a counterfeiter, credit card king and a big time gambler. When the law tried to catch up with him, he split for Canada. My parents didn't approve of his cons, but he was family. He always stayed one step ahead of the cops and the IRS."

"I like this guy already," Chester said, "and I don't even know him."

Marsha confided in Watkins about the fun weekend she spent with her shiftless uncle in Las Vegas. She was 15 when he came for a quick visit and offered to fly her to Nevada, all expenses paid.

"What girl would pass that offer up?"

He taught her how to play blackjack, count cards and watch the slot machines for big spenders who dumped a lot of change in the one-armed bandits and lost. Ed's advice was to grab that machine as soon as the person left and continue playing. A jackpot large or small was inevitable because of the odds. By following his simple advice, she made around $7,500 in two days. Her lazy uncle had about 30 credit cards, three different forms of identification, passports, social security numbers and driver's licenses.

"When Uncle Ed got drunk, he told me how to establish credit in someone else's name and leave them with all the bills."

The old vampire balked at the idea at first, but as he continued to think about it, he realized that it might just teach his kids a lesson that he had neglected to show them.

Deciding to go with her plan, Chester said, "Identity theft it is."

"Good, when we get back home I'll need you to give me their full names, dates of birth and any other information you have. The more the better," the girl said as she rubbed her hands together. "Boy, are they going to be in for the ride of their lives."

Watkins made it clear that he only wanted to charge the amount they inherited and no more. Marsha agreed, promising to quit when they were indebted $250,000 each.

"I still can't believe that they threw all of your pictures in the trash," the teenager said shaking her head.

"Me either," Watkins replied as they drove past downtown Houston.

When the vampires returned to the mansion, the first thing

Marsha did was to write down all the information that Chester could recall concerning his adopted children. She was pleased that he remembered both of their social security numbers. This would make things a lot easier.

"We want to establish a new line of credit for each person and pay off the balances on time so the credit card companies will increase our spending limit. In the beginning, we want Peggy and Reggie to be very responsible, having the highest credit score possible. After we've built an excellent reputation, we go on a spending spree and wipe them out."

"You naughty little girl," the old Marine laughed. "I hate to admit it, but they deserve this."

"They sure do." The teenager thought back, remembering when her grandfather died. All she wanted from his estate was a picture to remember him by. He left her $5,000 in a college fund.

Three weeks passed and Marsha was successful in acquiring six new credit cards, two in Reggie's name and four in Peggy's. Chester drove the teenager to the mall a couple of times so she could make several small purchases. He gave her some money from his checking account to pay off the incoming balances and by August she had 11 more cards and a substantial credit line. Marsha's plan was to max out all the cards during the Christmas holidays, make some cash withdrawals and open a Swiss savings account.

The old vampire told Marsha that he would much rather see her benefit from his money than his unappreciative family.

Jokingly, she stated, "It's OK to kill you, just don't trash the family photos."

"You've got that right girl."

CHAPTER 11, TRAGEDY STRIKES

Late one evening when the Rubensteins returned home from work, Chester and Marsha immediately noticed that Fabian had a solemn look on his face. The old vampire was so preoccupied with all of the recent turmoil in his life that he failed to notice most of the warning signs concerning his friends. Over the course of two months, Patricia began losing weight and kept complaining of constant fatigue. The doctors had such a grueling work schedule that everyone assumed she was just putting in too many hours at the hospital. When she left the room to change out of her work clothes, the old vampire approached his friend to see what the problem was.

"What's going on Fabian?"

Discreetly, the doctor responded, "My wife has cancer and she's dying. The test results are conclusive and there's little anyone can do."

The gray vampire shook his head in disbelief. "Surely, with all your connections in the medical community there's got to be someone who can treat her."

"Radiation, chemotherapy and all conventional methods known to medicine can't prevent the disease from spreading. The mortality rate for this type of cancer is 100 percent per person. Our friend and colleague Doctor Watongazine, who's the foremost cancer specialist in the state, recommends that we try alternative treatments."

"What did he have in mind?"

"He gave me the address to an African witchdoctor who lives in Bellaire. He suggested that we pay him $200 to do a ritualistic dance to appease the cancer gods."

"You've got to be kidding."

Fabian sat down on the sofa and placed his hands over his face. Fighting back tears and with a cracking voice he said, "Damn it, I've studied medicine all of my life and there's nothing anyone can do to save her. We're powerless."

Chester stood over the sobbing doctor and gently placed his hand on his shoulder in an attempt to comfort him.

"All of our research, our dreams, our ambitions, all of it is in vain. We've devoted all of our spare time studying vampires in the hopes of conquering death and for what?"

Looking at the old Marine, Marsha spoke up. "I hate to interrupt, but do you remember the psychic who told us how to find the satanic book?"

"Yes," replied Watkins.

"You thought she was full of crap, but she pointed us in the right direction."

The old man turned his attention to the doctor and insisted, "I think we should give this medicine man a whirl."

Trying to reason in his educated mind, the doctor's logical thoughts fought against his compelling emotions of desperation to try anything. "Bullshit and horse-hockey. I'm not going to watch a voodoo dancer try to heal my wife."

Challenging his disbelief, the teenager said, "If you love her, you will."

"She's right," added Chester. "I would have done anything to save Ruby, even something as ridiculous sounding as this."

The disheartened doctor took the crumpled piece of paper out of his shirt pocket and handed it to the gray vampire. He smoothed it out on the end table and lifted it up to his face to read the address and phone number. Handing it to Marsha, he asked her, "Can you read this doctor's handwriting? I sure as hell can't."

The young girl took the note and went over to the phone and called the number listed. When someone answered, she said, "Yes, I'd like to book an appointment."

When she was finished talking, she hung up the phone and asked Fabian to go get his wife. "We're going to Bellaire. The priest said he can fit us into his schedule, but we have to hurry."

Chester and Marsha took the Town Car and drove the doctors to the intersection of Beechnut and Bissonnet to look for the witchdoctor's church. The old vampire looked out the window as he was driving and saw a gang of interracially mixed hoodlums rapping to some funky music.

"Look, we're in Africa. We must be getting close."

"That's not funny," replied Patricia. "Those underprivileged children need education and guidance."

"From the looks of them," added Watkins, "the only guidance they need is how to find the nearest pawn shop to fence their stolen goods."

The vampire turned into a shopping strip where he saw the words "Pan African Church of the Serpent Healers" painted on a sign. "There it is."

Chester parked the vehicle in front of the shabby-looking building right next to an old Ford pickup truck with Illinois license plates. The bed of the truck was filled to the top with empty beer cans, scrap aluminum and old copper pipes. Painted on the window of the church was a black Madonna holding an African baby sporting an Afro. A caption located next to her mouth read, "Did you know some of God's children are black?"

The four made their way to the entrance and were taken by surprise by a homeless man who was sprawled out beside the front door. "Alms for the poor," he said in a drunken stupor as he tried to sit up.

Watkins reached into his front pocket and handed the man a five-dollar bill, which he gladly accepted. The bum pointed to a liquor store across the street and told the gray vampire that he was going to purchase a bottle of discount wine in the name of the lord. "I'm drinking for Jesus." Acting disgusted, Marsha showed her fangs and hissed at the wino as he jumped up and ran towards the package store.

When the patrons entered the colorful church, they saw that it was decorated with an amalgamation of Christian, Jewish, Muslim and New Age symbols. Dressed in ceremonial garb, three African men motioned for the group to come to the back of the building.

"I am Lahoonta," one of the men said, "spiritual advisor and high priest of our humble congregation."

The embarrassed Dr. Rubenstein tried to conceal his identity, but the men already knew who he was because Mr. Watongazine had already informed his friends about Patricia's situation. One of the assistants extended his hand and said, "Hello, I'm Jim, nice to meet you. I've been a Christian for over 10 years and was recently enlightened that Jesus was black."

"I thought he was a Jew," replied the gray vampire.

"Yes," added Fabian. "In the synagogue, they taught us that he was Jewish."

"He was Jewish, but those people had darker skin back then," replied the black man. "The ancient paintings of the Madonna are proof that he was black. The white man has distorted the truth to keep all of us under his bondage."

"Are you referring to that painting on the window?" questioned the old Marine. "Heck, give me some red paint and I'll make her an Indian."

Lahoonta interrupted the men as they were speaking and said, "Jim, let's not get into a theological discussion. These people are here for our help."

"Sorry, your Excellency."

"Thank you," replied the doctor as he removed his glasses to dust them off.

"Can you present us with an offering so we can get started?" questioned the priest. "It is better to give than to receive. We call it planting a seed of faith. The bigger the seed, the greater the harvest."

"Yes," answered the Doctor. "Hand me your checkbook Patricia."

Fabian endorsed a check for $500 and handed it to the

witchdoctor who placed it in the offering box.

Waving his hands, the priest cleared his throat and said, "Bow your heads and pray silently to the supreme deity as I prepare to bind the devils of affliction."

Both of the religious assistants assembled next to their instruments and began softly playing them while the priest took a scary-looking African mask off the wall and placed it on his face. He ordered everyone to form a loose circle and for Patricia to stand in the middle. The dirty organ began spewing smoke from its pipes as Jim pushed the keys. The witchdoctor started dancing around the cancer-stricken woman and he pulled two shakers from his robe and began flinging them into the air.

The musical rhythms grew louder as the peculiar ceremony intensified. After 10 minutes of dancing around in circles, the dizzy, out of breath priest placed both his hands on Patricia's face and shouted, "I command this illness to leave and be gone!"

He ripped the ugly mask off his face and threw it to the floor. After stomping on it and breaking it into tiny pieces, he advised the woman that the evil spirits were crushed. In his next breath, he proclaimed, "You're healed!"

His assistants shouted, "Hallelujah!" and began clapping their hands.

The teen-aged vampire looked over at the organ player and noticed that he was making eyes at her legs. She gave a crooked smile, showing one of her fangs, and the shocked man quickly looked away.

When the group left the church it was almost midnight. As Watkins was driving out of the shopping strip, he saw the black priest in his rearview mirror sprinting over to the liquor store in an attempt to beat the 12 o'clock lockdown.

The drive back to Bear Creek was a quiet one. Fabian knew in his heart that the healing ceremony was probably a sham, but he also knew that the power of suggestion could be an influential factor in his wife's recovery. It was a medical fact, and there were documented cases where terminally ill patients were completely cured from diseases by the power of prayers. These anomalies often baffled doctors who believed entirely in technology and logic as a means of treating illnesses. Only time would tell if Patricia's mind was powerful enough to channel her cancer into remission.

As the weeks slowly passed, it became obvious to both of the vampires that the frail woman was losing her battle. Fabian refused to admit it and placed his wife on a strict vegetarian diet. He instructed her to purify her immune system by eating healthy foods and drinking plenty of green tea. In her struggle against death, her bodily functions began slowly shutting down and she began turning away meals and eventually refused to eat altogether. In a few more days she was completely bedridden. Too feeble to get up and use the bathroom by herself, she began crying out for help.

On a Thursday night, Chester found the doctor sitting in his study alone trying to read another alternative treatment book. "I can't concentrate," the doctor said as Chester entered the room. "She's not going to make it."

Watkins sat down across from the doctor and looked him squarely in the eye. "There's a way we can save her."

"No," replied Rubenstein, "she's too weak to travel to Bombay, India. The flight would kill her."

"That's not what I had in mind. Why not let Marsha bite her. That's our only hope of saving her."

"Brilliant," stated the doctor in a sarcastic tone of voice. "And, why not let her bite me also and we'll all live happily ever after."

Watkins tried reasoning with his friend when the doctor offered another rebuttal. "She's got enough garlic in her system to repel 10 vampires."

Wisely, Chester replied, "Yes, but she hasn't eaten in almost two weeks. Her system is probably purged by now."

"Even if you're correct, she'll probably refuse to be bitten."

In Chapter 17, *"Wisdom of the Dead,"* detailed instructions were given on how to administer the *"Kiss of Life."* The process was occasionally used by hopelessly romantic vampires who fell in love with mortals and wanted to spend the rest of eternity with their soul mates. As with all things pertaining to life, there were certain variables and risks that factored in with the transformation process. On rare occasions, the bitten person's personality would change, while others would go totally insane, becoming menaces to society. A select few would be compelled to seek the darkened paths of *"Abbadon's Priests,"* becoming unredeemable and eternally damned.

The old vampire laid out all the facts to his trusted friend because he didn't want to be held responsible if things turned sour. "For the most part," he said, "my personality is entirely intact. The only marked change is when I first became hungry. The thirst turned into a consuming rage."

"I understand," replied the doctor. "The choice will be left up to Patricia."

Chester and Fabian walked into the bedroom and stood next to the dying woman who was sleeping. The pain medication she was taking was the strongest dosage the hospital allowed. The doctor gently nudged his wife with the palm of his hand and whispered, "Honey, wake up. Chester and I have something we want to ask you."

The emaciated woman turned her head and strained to speak. "I was dreaming that I went to purgatory and I saw your mother sitting down there eating non-kosher foods like pork chops, fried catfish and frog legs. I asked one of the devils, who was dressed in a fiery red suit, if I was in the right place and he said no. He was holding a giant pitchfork with barbecued spareribs skewered on the points. He said that because I was related to this woman, I was obligated to see her before going to heaven. She was being punished for telling everyone that Santa Clause and the Easter bunny were dead."

"Interesting," answered Fabian. "She never allowed us to color eggs, celebrate Christmas or have a tree either. My brothers hated her for that."

"I saw the Easter bunny in northwest Arkansas," Chester jested as he joined in the conversation. "She was real ugly, too. Maybe your mother-in-law will earn sainthood when the real buck-toothed bunny dies and goes to hell."

Patricia tried to smile as she nodded her head. The men pulled up chairs and sat down beside the bed in anticipation of helping the dying woman make her final decisions. Fabian explained the situation to his wife and pleaded with her to allow Marsha to bite her.

"I don't want to lose you," Fabian said, struggling to conceal the sadness in his face. "We can continue our research together and you can conduct experiments on yourself. You'll have firsthand knowledge by being a vampire yourself. Who knows, this might just be the medical breakthrough we've been looking for."

To everyone's surprise, Patricia immediately agreed and whispered, "I feel like death warmed over and it would be a relief to get this agony over and done with."

"I'll talk to Marsha," said Chester. "I'll be right back."

The old vampire got up and left the room to consult with the young, dark-haired vampire and fill her in on their lifesaving plans. When he finally found her, she was in the laboratory preparing her evening meal. She was just placing a refrigerated bag into the warmer when Chester entered the room.

"You might want to hold off," Watkins stated. "I've got something I need to talk to you about."

When he explained what was going on, the teenager expressed her willingness to help. She told him that she had been entertaining the thought of biting Patricia for weeks, but she was too afraid to tell anyone.

"I don't want to be held responsible if anything goes wrong," the girl added. "Does Fabian know all of the risks?"

"He probably knows more about vampirism than we do," answered Chester. "He's willing to do whatever it takes to save Patricia's life."

Marsha placed the bag of blood back into the icebox and followed Watkins into the Rubenstein's bedroom. Even though she knew everyone was in agreement regarding this decision, she was still reluctant to bite Patricia. The hunger pains in her stomach subsided because of the anxiety surrounding the situation. "*Maybe it was stage fright,*" she thought.

"Can you leave Patricia and I alone for a few minutes?" she asked.

"Come on Fabian, let's go into the front room and let them talk."

When the two men left the room, Marsha and the dying woman shared their thoughts. "The pain is almost unbearable," the feeble woman mumbled. "Even though I'm miserable, I'm still afraid of dying. What was it like when you passed away Marsha?"

The teenager paused for a moment before answering. She knew that the doctor didn't know all the specific details surrounding her death. The memory of her sexual assault, the evil creature who murdered her and the panic she felt was something she didn't want to convey to her beloved friend. She blocked out the ghastly memories and searched her heart for the right words to say.

"It was kind of like going to sleep. When I woke up, all of my physical pain was gone."

"Good," replied Patricia. "I want to tell you something before we proceed. When you first entered our home, I was glad you came into our lives. I want you to know that I love you like the daughter Fabian and I were never able to have."

The doctor shared a very private matter with the teenager concerning her intimate relationship with her husband. She confided that they were unable to conceive and have children because her husband was attacked by a vicious Pit-Bull and the dog mangled his testicles, rendering him sterile. Reconstructive surgery was cosmetically successful, but the physical damage was permanent. Fortunately for both of them and their marriage, their sexual lives were minimally affected and he could still perform.

"In fact," Patricia said, "things got very interesting after that. Fabian became more attentive of my needs and always satisfied my desires."

Marsha faked a smile as she envisioned in her mind the ferocious dog clamping down on the doctor's balls.

The dying woman looked up at the young girl and said, "Let's get this over with."

Fortunately for both of them, Marsha's hunger pains were starting to return as the two of them relaxed.

"Close your eyes," the teenager kindly whispered as she brushed Patricia's hair away, exposing her neck. "Think happy thoughts because you're going to live forever."

The vampire licked her fangs before biting into her friend's neck. A final thought came to mind before proceeding with the terminal act. Patricia had become a mother figure to the girl and she loved her very much. Because of this, she had to focus entirely on the words of wisdom written in the book *"Wisdom of the Dead." "The kiss of life will conquer death. Your passing sustains my life. Together we die, together we shall live."*

When the vampire's fangs penetrated the woman's neck muscles, she began quivering as her body fought with every ounce of strength to stave off death. All of the medication in her system was emitting repulsive odors through her breath and perspiration. Marsha also noted that a strange ammonia smell was emanating through her urine as it streamed down the side of the bed. Just moments before her passing, Patricia let out a shrilling scream as her soul departed her body. At that second, Fabian burst into the room as his wife was sighing her last breath.

"Oh my god, she's gone."

Marsha withdrew her face from the woman's throat and wiped the blood off her lips with the back of her left hand. Meals that were taken directly from a living human being always tasted better than blood that was stored for consumption. This scenario was different, however, because of the woman's illness. Her blood had a weird, medicine taste.

"Calm down," Watkins said, assuring his dear friend that everything would be fine. "Her incubation period is starting right now. Let's go back into the front room."

The humble old vampire pulled the sheet over Patricia's face and told the distraught doctor that it was time for nature to take its course. Following Chester's advice, the three of them left the bedroom to let the dead woman rest in peace.

"Now I understand your plight," Fabian said. "I'm sorry for being sarcastic earlier. Maybe I'll join the ranks of the living dead when the time is right."

"It would be an honor to share eternity with you doctor. When Patricia wakes up tomorrow evening, we'll all be laughing about this, you'll see."

The doctor walked directly into his study and told both of the vampires in the front room that he'd be right back. A few minutes passed before he returned with an expensive bottle of Scotch whiskey in his hand.

"I think I need a few belts," Rubenstein said as he uncapped the bottle and took a sip. His face winced as he swallowed a second shot. "Boy, did I need that."

Marsha looked up and politcly asked, "Doctor, can I get you a glass with some ice?"

"Yes, that sounds like a good idea. I think I need to finish this bottle off tonight."

The gray vampire agreed with his friend and added, "I think I'll keep you company. Let's have a cigar."

Both of the men returned to the study out of respect for the dead woman who didn't like them smoking in the front room. Only time would tell if her incubation period would be successful. A calculated risk was better than having no options available to them at all. Both men were well aware of the facts, knowing that approximately one in a thousand people who were killed by vampires were incapable of resuscitating.

A couple of hours passed and the effects of the 100-proof Scotch were beginning to take hold of the doctor's emotions. When he attempted to stand up from his chair, he lost his balance and crashed into the end table, knocking the lamp over and falling to the floor. As he wallowed around on the carpet, he began rebuking the hospital and the staff members with slurred words. "If she doesn't regenerate, I'm going to slap the piss right out of that physician who referred us to the witchdoctor. Then, I'm going to work my way down the totem-pole one doctor at a time."

The gray vampire blew a huge puff of cigar smoke in the air as he looked down at his animated friend. "Come on, Fabian. It's not their fault. You know as well as I do that everyone did their best trying to save her."

"Bullshit! If they did, then she'd still be alive." The intoxicated doctor started getting teary-eyed as he tried standing back up. "When I sober up, someone's got to pay."

"Who did you have in mind?" Watkins asked, trying to humor his friend.

"I haven't figured that one out yet, but when I do you'll be the first one to know." The drunken man lost his grip on the end table in the middle of his sentence and fell backwards onto the carpet. Suddenly, his mood shifted and he started laughing. "Piss on the whole world, piss on you, piss on me, piss ants. I think I just pissed my pants."

"You did what?" the gray vampire replied. "Give me your arm and I'll help you up."

When Chester reached down to take hold of the doctor's hand, Fabian tricked the vampire and pulled him to the floor. Immediately, both men started laughing because they saw the humor of the situation.

"I'll be OK, Chester. Thanks for being here for me. I'm just a little drunk."

"I know," Watkins, said as he smiled back at the doctor and helped him to his feet. After regaining their footing, Watkins put his arm around his friend's shoulder and assisted him to the living room couch. "Sleep it off and we'll regroup tomorrow evening."

Within minutes, Fabian was fast asleep and snoring like a buzz saw. Chester went to the hallway closet and got a pillow and blanket for his snoozing friend and tucked him in for the night.

CHAPTER 12, A PASSIONATE REUNITING

As soon as Watkins and Marsha revived the following evening, they went directly into the doctor's bedroom to check on Patricia. When they entered the room, they saw Fabian sitting by her bedside crying.

"She's dead!" he hollered. "What went wrong?"

Chester walked over to check things out and when he pried the woman's mouth open, he observed that the roof of her pallet was a bright, golden-black color. "She's going to make it. She's still incubating. Let's leave her alone."

"Are you sure?"

"I'm certain. Take a look for yourself."

When the doctor put his glasses back on, he could see that Chester was correct. "Why didn't I think to look into her mouth?"

"Don't feel stupid. Even though you're a doctor, this situation is far too personal and it's affecting your reasoning. I've been there and experienced this before."

The old Marine thought back, remembering how some of the medics on the island of Tarawa lost their cool when they saw some of their close friends wounded or killed by enemy fire.

"Whatever you do, please don't open another bottle tonight," Marsha begged. "It took me over an hour to clean up after you guys."

"I don't think I'll be reliving that memory. My pounding head can't take it. I've got a hangover from hell," Rubenstein said as he removed his glasses and rubbed his eyes.

The three of them went into the front room and as they were about to sit down they heard a thrashing sound coming from the bedroom. They turned and bolted back into the bedchambers to find Patricia yanking the covers off of the bed and throwing them to the floor.

"Damn it!" she angrily screeched. "These covers are soaked with urine and this place smells like a stinky ass nursing home!"

The woman turned around and hissed at the two vampires and her husband. A few more seconds passed and then she came to her senses, realizing that she had overcome the greatest enemy humanity has ever faced, which was death. When the magnitude of everything began to sink in, a warm feeling of joy swept through her inner being. She smiled at them, showing her yellow fangs and then blushed, feeling embarrassed for her inappropriate behavior.

Fabian ran to embrace his skinny wife who flung her arms wide open to receive him. "My god, I thought I'd lost you forever."

"You're not that lucky," she replied with a dry voice. "My throat is parched. Get me a glass of water."

Chester began remembering back at his first attempt of ingesting a meal and shook his head no as he tried to gain the woman's attention. "You won't like the taste. Have you ever drank salty mud?"

"I'll be the judge of that. Please get me a cold glass of water from the refrigerator Fabian."

"Yes, dear," the humble doctor answered as he was leaving the room. "I'll be right back."

Both of the vampires tried reasoning with their new convert, but to no avail. She refused to listen to them. Chester told Marsha to retrieve the *Vampire's Bible* from their room because Patricia was going learn the hard way. "*Some people are just stubborn,*" he thought.

When Fabian returned, he handed his wife the sparkling clear glass and without thinking she snatched it from his hand and brought it to her lips to drink. In a split second, she spewed a mouth full into the air and both of the vampires started laughing at her.

"We told you so," Chester said. "Follow me to the laboratory. You need to drink something to give you a kick start."

The woman nodded her head and apologized to the old man. "I should have listened to you."

Watkins knew from experience that the first drink of blood

was always the best. The euphoria a vampire would feel was unparalleled. After heating the blood to a comfortable temperature in the medical warmer, the gray vampire poured the contents into the beautiful chalice and handed it to the woman. She closed her eyes, refusing to look into the golden goblet and the old Marine recognized that she was repulsed by the thought of taking a drink. In an attempt to ease her apprehensiveness, he assured her that the taste would be more gratifying than anything she had ever eaten.

"This stuff beats the socks off of the best sirloin you've ever sank your teeth into. Trust me."

With eyes shut, the woman took a small sip to sample the contents of the cup. To her surprise, the old vampire was correct. After doing this, she quickly tipped the large cup into the air and drank it like an alcoholic guzzling an expensive bottle of champagne.

"Another glass," she demanded. "I need more."

Chester couldn't heat the blood up fast enough to satisfy the starving woman. Everyone knew that because of her illness she was physically incapable of eating for almost 13 days. Her weakened system was craving sustenance and the life-giving fluids were her redemption.

After finishing her second glass, she thanked everyone for being so patient with her demands. "I felt like I was loosing my mind."

"The hunger takes on a negative effect like nothing you've every experienced. It can dominate your personality. You have to learn to control it or it will control you. Give it a few minutes," the experienced old vampire said. "You're going to feel better than you've felt in years."

"I already do," Patricia replied. "I felt a surge of energy pass directly through my body when I drank the first cup. My mind is clearing and I just remembered something. Fabian, did you pay our satellite TV bill?"

"I knew that I had forgotten to do something," the absentminded physician answered. "I'll send the check off in the morning."

"Don't worry," Marsha piped up. "You're too late. They shut it off last night."

After finishing their meals in the lab, the group of vampires returned to the living room to discuss some personal business. Fabian had to come up with an intelligent excuse for his wife's disappearance to satisfy her extended family members, friends and all of the other people who knew her at the medical center. Another concern was their blood supply. Because of his wife's absence, the staff might become suspicious regarding Fabian's alleged phantom research, which was now going to require additional volumes.

Logistics were becoming very complicated and the small group had to devise a feasible plan. Another worry to contend with was the Dynasty of Immortals. The Rubenstein estate was a certified safe house and was receiving special funding from the organization. If some of the governing vampires showed up unannounced for a surprise inspection, their secret would be exposed. The rogue vampire was now responsible for two deaths, so if anyone discovered that she was still alive, her fate would be certain.

"We might have to find another place to live if things continue to snowball," Watkins said. "Maybe we should pull up roots and move to a small town in East Texas."

"I like the Piney woods," replied Fabian, "My wife and I have a little cabin around Cold Springs, Texas, and it's very secluded."

While the group was discussing business, Patricia let out a quiet hiccup, causing everyone to pause and look directly at her. "Excuse me," she said. "I have no idea where that came from."

"I do," said Marsha. "You're stomach has been empty for almost two weeks and now it's full."

Everyone smiled and resumed their conversation. After another hour of planning, the small party decided to wait things out for as long as possible to see what would transpire within the political organization of vampires. They figured that if Vladimir assumed power, their nights would be numbered and they'd be forced to make some sort of hasty decision.

"Does anyone have any short-term ideas?" the sophisticated woman asked.

"I've got a couple of things I'm kicking around," her husband answered.

Chester's intuition was telling him they were safe for the time being, but for how long was uncertain. His combat experiences in the Marine Corps taught him an important lesson in life: Always be prepared and try to think one step ahead of your enemies.

The gray vampire inquired, "What's on your mind, Doc?"

Fabian told everyone he was entertaining the idea of contacting a real estate agent and trying to acquire some property west of Alamosa, Colorado. He was very familiar with the Rio Grande National Forest because he had hunted there consecutively for 10 seasons. The trophy hunter pointed to the fireplace and reminded everyone that he killed the majestic 4x4 bull-elk hanging above the mantel with his .30-06 rifle. He remembered there were lots of properties for sale back then and the prices were reasonable, but 1986 was a long time ago.

When Marsha asked him if they were financially able to do this, the white-haired scientist grinned and said that he might file for his retirement at the hospital, liquidate his 401 (k) account and invest part of his earnings in some more land. Rubenstein's net worth was well over five million dollars he told the curious vampire.

"We'll buy our own mountain and become survivalists," the doctor lightheartedly said. "We'll horde food, guns, gold and lots of blood."

"It would be nice to get out of this stinking city," Chester added with a serious-looking expression. "The fresh air would do us some good."

The doctor advised everyone that he was going to switch his

schedule to second shift when he returned to the hospital in January. With the exception of a couple of administrative meetings, he was free until then. Spending more time with everyone, was now a priority. While he was thinking of more ideas, he coined a special name for their newly formed group, which he called "The Eternal Family."

"It's important that we try to stay on the same schedule," he concluded. "The only way we're going to survive this mess, is by working together."

When they finished their short-term planning, Fabian excused himself and said that he had something to do outside before the sun came up. It was kind of a surprise for his wife.

The doctor ran to the garage and started cutting up some cheap plywood with an electric handheld ripsaw. When he finished his sloppy, jagged cuts, he hurriedly nailed together a makeshift coffin to secure his wife's body. When Chester went outside to see what all the commotion and hammering was, he couldn't believe what he was seeing. Bent nails, a crooked, splintered box and rusty Chinese hinges were being duct-taped to the sides of the ugly object.

Ringing wet with perspiration, the physician asked, "Hand me that knife on the workbench so I can cut this thick tape. This hatchet is too dull to slice it."

The old vampire was taken by surprise because he'd never seen anyone using a roofing hatchet to frame something before.

"What are you making, Doc, a doghouse?"

Feeling embarrassed, the man answered, "Stop making fun of me. She's got to sleep somewhere and it's almost daylight I'll purchase a real casket in a couple of days.

"I know you will," replied the gray vampire, "but you should have asked me for some help. I'm a pretty good carpenter."

"I didn't want to trouble you. I just wanted to surprise her, that's all. It doesn't look that bad, does it?"

"Trust me," the vampire said with a gummy smile, "she's

going to be very surprised."

When the two men carried the pitiful-looking box into Fabian's bedroom, Patricia and Marsha had no idea what the ugly thing was going to be used for. At daybreak, when the doctor's wife got sleepy, she cringed when she suddenly realized what the unsightly thing's purpose was. When she opened the splintery lid, she saw that her loving husband had placed some covers and a soft pillow inside in an attempt to make her comfortable. With rusty nails protruding through the sides, the vampire was careful not to hurt herself as she climbed inside.

Five days passed and the absent-minded doctor still hadn't found the time to buy a coffin for his petite vampire bride. That evening, the frizzy-headed doctor noticed that his wife's ears were considerably larger than they were the night before. In fact, they were growing at an alarming rate. She was starting to look like a wide-eared elf. Fabian pointed this out to her and when Patricia gazed into the mirror to look at herself she screamed.

"Calm down," the doctor said. "There's got to be something in the *Vampire's Bible* regarding this."

"I wish the myth was true that vampires can't see their reflections," she moaned. "I look like a fanged scarecrow with elephant ears."

The vampire and her husband combed through the pages of the book *"Wisdom of the Dead"* trying to find an explanation for her weird appearance. Chester and Marsha couldn't remember reading anything that gave reference to her strange condition either. The group finally found their answer in Chapter 7: Were-vampires. Beginning in verse 12, the definitions were given describing the rare affliction.

"*When the extremities become exaggerated then the immortal must fast and abstain from blood for three days to cleanse their body, mind and soul. If the condition is ignored, the affected body parts will continue to grow until the infected vampire goes insane becoming a*

Were-creature. If the vampire has intimate contact with anyone while the virus is active, then the curse will be exchanged."

In a panic, Doctor Rubenstein jumped to his feet and ran to the bathroom as fast as he could, yelling incoherently. Chester went in behind him to see what was wrong and the worried man conceded that his sexy vampire wife had seduced him into having a kinky sex party the night before using feather props and scuba equipment.

"We made love like we were newlyweds. It was hard to breathe through the snorkel, but the flippers made up for things, giving me extra traction."

The gray vampire ran his hands through his short hair as he stared at the mad scientist in disbelief. *"How did he manage to get excited looking at those pointed ears? To each his own,"* he thought.

Patricia and Marsha entered the cramped bathroom and the younger vampire spoke up. "We didn't read far enough. The next paragraph explains that this affliction can only be transmitted to other vampires. Stop worrying, you're going to be all right, doctor."

Fabian wiped the small beads of sweat from his brow and blew a sigh of relief through his lips, which sounded like a whistle.

The small group funneled out of the washroom single file and Watkins spoke up as they were headed toward the living room. "We had better take the necessary precautions to avoid becoming infected."

Patricia shook her head in agreement. "I'll try to abide by the advice given in the book and begin my fast right now."

Within a few nights, the woman's ears returned to normal and her strength increased dramatically. The ravages of cancer had taken a serious toll on her body and the strange situation was probably brought on as a result of this. Watkins continued searching the pages of the ancient manuscript and found another cross-reference to her condition in Chapter 17. He reassured the worried doctor that his wife wasn't under a curse and her body was repairing itself.

Early the next evening, the vampires were sitting in the living room reading the newspapers and Watkins caught movement out of his peripheral vision. He slowly turned his head and saw the doctor creeping down the hallway towards his bedroom wearing nothing but a red cape and purple boots.

The old vampire laughed under his breath and remembered all of the fun he used to have with his wife Ruby when they were young. The silliness continued into their latter years until she became too ill to play along. He envied his friends, who had a second chance at love, but at the same time he was happy for them. He hoped that someday he would find someone special to fill the emptiness he sometimes felt in his heart.

CHAPTER 13, SOLSTICE SURPRISES

It was the middle of October and Halloween was only two weeks away. The Bear Creek neighborhood where the vampires resided was littered with candle-lit pumpkins, haunted house signs and ghost banners. In two short weeks, trick-or-treaters would be roaming the streets playing pranks, egging houses and soliciting candy. The Rubensteins were making their final preparations in the kitchen to receive the little guests as Patricia carved a thick, lopsided jack-o'-lantern with her razor-sharp butcher knife. The cockeyed Fabian was breathing down her back as he directed her every move. The orange vegetable began taking on the look of a scary hobgoblin while she skillfully whittled away.

Chester and the teenager sat in the living room talking while the doctors worked side by side creating their unusual work of art. Marsha was very proud of herself because she had just finished reading the *Vampire's Bible* in its entirety. Her infatuation with a strange spell and magic potion listed in the final chapter peaked Watkins' curiosity when she reminded him of what she read.

"I remember reading that," the old vampire replied as he licked the tip of a fat, imported cigar. "Maybe we should give it a try."

"Even though it sounds freaky, that's exactly what I was thinking. It might be an interesting experience."

Chapter 20: Illusions of the Flesh made reference to the fact that the human race originated from a single ancestral origin. According to the ancient text, everyone was interrelated. Fear, ignorance, disbelief and closed-mindedness were crippling stumbling blocks in relation to the advancement of mankind. The last chapter debunked nationalistic myths of racial superiority or inferiority. "*The soul has no color and the spirit knows no boundaries. Racial association, allegiance and alliance contribute to the separation of humanity as a whole.*"

The instructions were specific. The special potion was to be mixed in a steaming cauldron and, after the water boiled away, the smoking fumes were to be inhaled as the enchantment was recited verbatim. The spell could only be performed once every two years and the closer to the Winter Solstice the longer lasting the effects would be—depending on the variables of the individual's DNA, between 48 to 72 hours. The vampire's latent racial genetics would become dominant and within 12 hours they would undergo a physical alteration and awaken the following evening as another color and race. The possibilities of reverting to Neanderthal men, dwarves or other genetic abnormalities were remote, but they did exist. If repeated, the spell would never yield the same results twice in a row.

The purpose of the incantation was to allow the immortals to experience life from the other end and gain a deeper insight into the brotherhood of mankind. The *Vampire's Bible* encouraged everyone who underwent this special transformation to intermingle with their racial counterparts and closely observe their ignorance or wisdom. Within all nationalities there are the chosen few who see their existence for what it really is. Unfortunately, the masses are blinded by the color of their skin. Only the wise develop the mental fortitude to break through these barriers and ascend to a higher level of consciousness.

By interacting with a different culture cloaked as one of their brothers, the enchanted vampire would be privy to their peculiar racial slurs, slogans and certain predispositions that were unique to that race. The vampire's text was careful to remind the readers that their own DNA is what temporarily united them with these people and to be humbled by the experience. *"Prejudice is ignorance and pride is the downfall of fools."*

Marsha and Chester continued discussing at length all the possibilities that this spell could teach them if they decided to use it.

"Maybe Patricia would like to participate?" the dark-haired girl inquisitively asked.

"The more the merrier," Watkins mumbled through the side of his mouth as he withdrew the unlit cigar he was gumming.

The pretty teenager stood up and raised her arms toward the ceiling to stretch. "When is the Winter Solstice?"

"It's in December. We'll try the spell then so we can benefit from its full powers."

When the doctors finished working on their pumpkin, they came out of the kitchen and walked into the front room to show off their handiwork to Chester and Marsha.

"What do you think?" asked Patricia.

"Scary," replied Watkins. "That candle might burn the house down."

Chuckling, the lady vampire rephrased her question. "No, really, do you think we did a good job?"

"I like it," the teenager said with a smile. "I think it looks wicked."

"Yeah," added Chester. "His crooked head makes him look like a mad scientist with a warped brain."

Rolling her eyes, Patricia walked to the front door and stepped outside to find a good place to display their ghoulish decoration. Fabian was close behind and pointed to a spot, saying, "Put him over there next to that holly bush."

"Yes, dear."

When the loving couple returned to the family room, the old vampire told them about their plans of testing the cloaking spell and trying to acquire all the special ingredients listed in Chapter 20. Both of the doctors had knowledge of the procedure, but neither one of them had ever seen it practiced by any of the vampires in the underground organization. Everyone knew that concocting the peculiar potion wouldn't be easy because some of the components listed were not commonly found items. Marsha suggested going back to the fortuneteller for advice, but Watkins objected because he didn't want to pay for any more broken windows.

"I think we can find everything on our own."

"Where can you find toad's eyes?" questioned the teenager.

"That's easy, you can catch one behind the swimming pool," Fabian confidently said. "I've got a sharp scalpel in the lab. You can carve both of its eyes out of their sockets."

"Yuck," replied Marsha. "I'm not going to do that."

"If you squeeze him hard enough, his eyes will pop out on their own," the crusty Marine added. "Or, you can try sucking them out."

Interrupting, Patricia blurted out, "OK, you're going to make the poor girl sick."

The teenager knew that the silly men were teasing her, but she still appreciated the lady vampire sticking up for her. After they finished their jokes, Chester asked Marsha to take a pen and pad and scribble down all the items needed for the spell. He knew that they had plenty of time to find everything, but he wanted to be punctual and have everything in place by the appointed season. Little did the old man know, the final chapter in the vampire's manual would be the ultimate test and play a vital role in their survival.

By the time Thursday arrived, the diligent group had already acquired half of the things needed to mix their potion. Finding an alligator's tongue proved to be easy work because Fabian had a French speaking Cajun friend from Louisiana who ate anything that could swim or walk. From skin to guts, this man knew how to cook it. According to this happy-go-lucky guy, road kill was a delicacy if properly prepared. Being careful not to rouse suspicion, the doctor asked the man for a baby alligator, telling him that he wanted it as a pet for his aquarium.

On his way home from work the following day, the frizzy-headed doctor took a detour down old Hempstead Highway to look for a feed store where he remembered seeing a collection of cast iron junk and farm implements. He wasn't sure if they still had it, but he remembered seeing a big cauldron sitting behind the fence in front of the faded metal building.

When he drove his flashy Cadillac into the parking lot, he saw dozens of wagon wheels and an old carriage sitting next to the big shop doors. He found a place to park, got out and started looking around. When he peered inside the store, he saw a western stagecoach and a dark-haired, middle-aged man who was wearing a ball cap carefully dusting the buggy off. When he entered the building, he stepped on a drive-through hose causing a little bell to momentarily ring out. A couple of seconds passed and then he saw a bearded man coming out of the office located to his right.

"Can I help you?" the fellow asked.

"Yes," replied the nicely dressed physician. "I was looking for an old, metal pot."

"Follow me," the curly-haired man replied. "They're over here in the corner."

When the doctor saw the huge pots, he observed that most of them were welded to big metal rings and the finished ones were being sold as yard ornaments.

"Can I buy a pot by itself?"

The man hesitated for a second and scratched his gray beard. When he looked at the doctor's crooked eyes, he wanted to laugh, but he suppressed his feelings. "Well, I can get more for them when they're welded to these rings and sold as decorations."

Gathering his thoughts, Fabian looked around at all of the old, outdated tools, farm implements, cow skulls, metal milk jugs and nostalgic signs hanging on the shop's walls. The aroma of freshly cut hay smelled refreshing and the atmosphere in the store was a friendly reminder of times past. The intelligent doctor knew that he had just met an expert haggler, so out of respect he smiled and offered the hard working man his going price for the finished cast iron products.

"Pull your vehicle inside and my partner and I will load it up for you."

"Thank you."

When the doctor drove inside, the bell sounded again as the heavy Cadillac's wheels ran across the frayed, worn out hose. Fabian focused his attention on the dark-haired man who was waving at him from the opposite end of the store next to the exit. The gentleman began motioning for him to drive straight ahead and when he reached a certain point parallel to a very old-looking cash register, the man signaled for him to stop. With a smile, the brown-eyed guy asked, "I bet you've never seen a drive through feed store before?"

"No, I sure haven't."

The physician pushed the remote control button and opened his trunk as the other man wheeled the cauldron to the back of his vehicle. Working together, the men grabbed the heavy object and carefully placed it inside of the plush trunk.

Because of the man's lazy eye, the feed store owners weren't sure which one of them he was talking to when he looked at them and posed another question. "I was curious, how much for one of those wagon wheels?"

"The prices vary depending on size and condition," replied the darker-haired man. "Anywhere between $50 and $150 dollars."

"OK, thanks for your help. I'll think about that."

When the man drove off, the curly-headed man smiled and jokingly asked his partner, "Was he talking to you or me?"

His co-worker smiled and then adjusted his cap and mumbled something indistinguishable while he walked away.

When Fabian arrived home, it was still daylight and all of the vampires were still sleeping in their coffins. Later that evening when everyone revived, the ambitious doctor told his family that he purchased a sturdy pot for them so they could test their intriguing spell.

Watkins was very pleased with the solid iron pot and complemented the doctor for finding it for them. After some small talk, he excused himself and went to take a shower. When he finished cleaning up, he returned to his private room and, after putting on his boxer shorts and white T-shirt, Marsha knocked on the door.

"Chester, are you decent?"

"Come in," he replied as he began sifting through the closet for a clean pair of slacks.

The teenager expressed her excitement concerning the spell to the old man and the eager girl told him that she couldn't wait to see what would happen. As they were talking about all of the possibilities the incantation could produce, Marsha noticed a big, nasty scar on the man's left thigh.

"What happened to your leg, Chester?"

"It's a long story. It happened during the war."

The inquisitive girl rubbed her little nose. "We've got all night. Tell me."

Thinking back in time, the old Marine rolled his eyes and asked his slender companion to grab a chair and sit down next to the wooden chess table. He pulled his slacks up, fastened the snap and sat down across from her to relate his passionate sea story from the Pacific Isles.

"It happened on the island of Tarawa. We took out a Jap machine gun emplacement and I got hit with a 6.5 millimeter round in my leg."

"You charged a machine gun nest?"

"We had to," replied the sentimental leatherneck. "They were killing my friends."

Scratching his short, gray hair, the bulldog-faced Marine gave step-by-step details of how the events leading up to the firefight unfolded. Their small patrol was chipping their way through the jungle with machetes in hand when they approached a small clearing. Being mindful of booby traps, land mines and enemy snipers armed with Type 97 rifles, the experienced Marines proceeded with caution. The captain ordered the squad to halt, assuming they were a safe distance away from danger. His calculations were wrong and proved to be fatal. Next, he signaled for Watkins and his best friend Mark to flank the opening and scout for Nips. If they spotted anything suspicious, they were ordered to report back and disclose what they saw.

"If my commanding officer wouldn't have sent me on that mission, I would have been killed with the rest of them," the old vampire said, choking back tears.

With M-1 rifles in hand, Chester and his buddy, nicknamed "Scooter," broke away from the patrol and circled through the jungle to do a reconnaissance check. From their vantage point, they spotted an enemy sand bag emplacement with a Type 1, 7.7 millimeter machine gun trained on their exposed American cohorts. It was being manned by four tough-looking, hardened Japanese defenders who were sworn to fight to the death.

"To surrender was dishonorable and they were totally brainwashed. That's why we never took any prisoners," the old Marine recalled as he spoke of times past, remembering every vivid detail like it happened yesterday. "I heard of other units taking prisoners, but the units I served in were never afforded those opportunities. We killed everyone we fought."

With wide eyes, the totally engrossed teenager leaned forward and asked, "What happened next?"

"We couldn't make it back to the exposed patrol without being seen ourselves," Chester replied as he gummed down on his lip. "Next thing I remember, all hell broke loose."

The old Marine told the enthralled listener how he saw one of the Japs raise his right arm and throw it back down again as a signal to the machine gunners to open fire. There was no warning. A torrent of red tracer rounds sliced through the baffled squad, shredding them to ribbons. Their screams and cries echoed through the jungle.

"Without hesitation, Scooter and I charged with fixed bayonets, only to be cut down by an enemy sniper who was hiding in a palm tree overlooking the battlefield. The Japanese were smart and tried to cover all avenues of advance leading to their defensive positions."

Watkins looked down at the floor as he continued his story. He told the girl how Mark never had a chance because he was shot through his helmet and killed instantly. Never looking back and totally unaware that his friend had just fallen, he continued his screaming advance until he felt a searing bolt of fire shoot through his leg, sending him tumbling to the ground. Crawling on his belly, he raised his head and saw that he was within range to take out the murderous assassins. As he was gasping for air, he yanked a hand grenade from his belt, pulled the pin and lobbed the phosphorus pineapple into their wicked nest of blazing fire and thundering lead.

"Tunnel vision," the old man said. "Everything was moving in slow motion. After my grenade exploded, everything went quiet."

Seconds later, the old man recounted how he heard another shot ring out and when he raised his head to see who was shooting, he spotted the Nip sniper being dethroned from his perch. Unknown to Watkins, they were being covered by an American counter-sniper who was armed with a trusty .30-06 caliber Springfield rifle. The skilled rifleman was trailing behind the squad and attempting to cover their advance as they proceeded through the jungle.

When the serviceman came to Watkins' aid, he told Chester that he was having trouble locating thc Japanese rifleman because of all the noise and commotion going on during the intense fighting. Fortunately for the injured sergeant, the determined Marine sniper kept his eye to his scope until he spotted movement in the trees. When the Jap chambered another round to finish off the bleeding man, the Marine Corps serviceman centered the crosshairs of his scope and squeezed off a round, hitting the Nip between the eyes.

After rendering first aid, the Marine corporal assisted Chester out of the jungle and helped him find a medic. Everyone in Watkins' unit was killed except for him and the young sniper, who was from Poteau, Oklahoma.

"I never saw that kid again. He saved my life twice. I would have bled to death if he hadn't carried me out."

"That's some story," the dark-eyed girl said as she intently listened. "Did you have any idea that something like that was going to happen?"

Leaning back in his chair, the gray vampire crossed his legs. "I couldn't put my finger on it, but I knew that something awful was about to go down. Our unit was just too damn lucky."

"Do you remember what you did that morning before everything happened?"

"I sure do."

Chester told her how he recalled having a conversation with Scooter while they were eating a can of C-rations for breakfast that day. They were talking about all of their hopes, dreams and ambitions.

"Mark was showing me a picture of his wife and newborn baby girl, telling me how much he loved his family. His father owned a small grocery store in a little town in West Texas and he planned on going back and helping him expand their business."

"That's sad," Marsha said as she began gaining a deeper insight into Chester's true feelings about life and things concerning the Pacific war.

"Yes, it was pitiful. There were a lot of orphans and widows back in those days."

When they finished talking about that fateful day in 1943, the 17-year-old girl looked at Watkins and realized how much she really loved him. The gray vampire treated her like she was his very own daughter and she knew that he always had her best interests at heart. As pleasant thoughts entered her mind, Chester changed the subject.

"I'm going to kill that son of a bitch who raped and killed you."

Out of love for her friend, Marsha calmly replied, "You don't have to do that. Let's go to Colorado like Fabian suggested."

With a grin, Watkins nodded his head. "If we don't have to

fight then we won't, but I have a gut feeling that vanquishing this evil vampire is our destiny."

The teenager knew that he was right, but her love for the old man quenched the fire of revenge that was burning in her heart. She didn't want to see Watkins risk his life to settle a vengeful score that was becoming meaningless as her new life progressed. Her future looked brighter and she was exceedingly happy. Marsha looked forward to spending many years with her new family and maybe getting married to a handsome vampire who shared her same morals and beliefs, but only if Chester approved of him.

The vampires returned to the living room and noticed that Fabian and Patricia were watching the World News channel.

"Is there anything interesting going on tonight?" Watkins asked.

"There was an earthquake in the Congo," the cockeyed doctor replied, "and they're not certain how many people were killed."

As the family was discussing current events, they heard a soft knock at the door. Immediately, everyone stood up, anticipating danger, because they weren't expecting any visitors. *"How was it possible to defeat the elaborate security systems without triggering the alarm?"* Chester thought as he withdrew the .45 pistol tucked in his belt. *"Only someone possessing supernatural abilities could do this."*

The cagey old man whispered his orders. "Marsha, take a peek through the window and don't let them see you. Doctors, get down on the floor behind the sofa."

Standing in the shadows, the teen-aged vampire cautiously peered through the sides of the curtains and, when she saw who was standing by the door, the girl couldn't believe her eyes. "It's Zelda, the fortuneteller, and she's with a young gypsy man."

"How the heck did she find us?" Watkins silently mouthed as he motioned for Marsha to step away from the window.

"What should we do?"

"Open the door and invite her inside," Chester instructed as he returned the black matte handgun in the small of his back.

Both of the doctors stood up as Marsha walked to the front door. When she invited the blind old woman and her young companion inside, Watkins noticed that her scraggly facial hair was considerable longer than it was a few months ago. She was clutching the arm of the skinny young man who was assisting her and the woman's shoes sounded like sandpaper scuffing the floor as she shuffled her way through the entry.

"Come in and sit down," Fabian said in a hospitable tone. "We were just watching the news and talking about an earthquake that happened this evening in Africa."

Without uttering a word, the young man, who was acting as the blind woman's guide, steered her in the direction of the living room. Everyone noticed that the strange-looking gypsies were dressed like European vagabonds and their sagging, multi-colored clothes reminded them of circus performers.

Finally, the young man broke his silence and spoke to the old crone, pointing her in the direction of a plush chair. "This way, grandmother."

When the clairvoyant sat down, both of her knees made cracking sounds similar to corks popping. The gypsy man crouched down beside her on the floor and then he adjusted himself, crossing his legs and sitting Indian-style. The hairy-faced woman turned her head from side to side and it seemed like she was trying to gain a sense of her surroundings as she sniffed the air with her crooked nose.

A few more minutes passed and everyone was still silent. Chester was beginning to wonder if anyone was going to talk and what this strange visit entailed. Finally, the gray vampire gave up trying to second-guess things and asked, "How did you find us Zelda and why did you come here tonight?"

The old woman turned her body in Watkins' direction and with her raspy voice cried out, "The spirits have warned me that all of you are in great danger!"

"What do you mean?"

"First, the spirits need money for the taxi ride home."

Having proven herself to be reliable, Chester happily obliged and reached into his back pocket for his wallet. Feeling generous, the wise old vampire approached his humble guests and handed the woman two crisp Franklins and said, "I think that 200 dollars will satisfy the spirits. Who knows, they might need to buy some groceries, too."

"Your warmth is eternal," the soothsayer said as she slipped the paper bills inside of her loose bra. "You must leave this place tonight. The Russian's demons rebuked him during his last séance because they know that you are still alive. They will begin searching for you."

The old woman began to explain that her dreams were clouded with visions of opposing warlords donning armor and preparing for battle. Three nights ago, her spirit guides ordered her to find the "Fangless One" and advise him accordingly.

The white spirits warned her of two impending conflicts that were going to be waged between the forces of good and evil. These interconnected battles would take place on Earth and in the spirit realm concurrently and the outcome would forever determine the destiny of mankind. Because of the old man's forgiveness toward the teen-aged vampire who bit him, things that would have never been revealed have been brought into the light. Their loving bond has had an altering impact on time itself and changed the course of things supernatural and universal.

"Forgiveness is divine, but the knowledge of who to trust is even greater," the old psychic said as she scratched the bothersome white scales of psoriasis in her goatee. "The wicked lords of the underworld hate the gray warrior because his growing strength threatens their influence in the physical world. If you heed this warning, all of us stand a chance of surviving."

The strange prophetess explained how wicked spirits gain a direct link to our realm by controlling and possessing their ignorant, misguided subjects like the satanic vampires and the Crusaders of Light. The disembodied spirits are powerless unless they can find willing hosts to carry out their reprehensible plans.

Pooling from his military and police knowledge, Chester posed an interesting question to Zelda. "Experience has always proven to me that timing is one of the most important factors in determining the outcome of any battle. I know it is inevitable, but when do you suggest we attack our enemies?"

Raising her hand and pointing to the heavens with her bent, arthritic fingers, the sincere gypsy answered the old vampire's question. "There is a mystical meteor passing through our solar system this December called Beelzebub's Comet. You must stop him during this heavenly cycle. If our enemies are successful in casting their spells during the ancient sacrificial ritual called 'The Consuming Fire of the Damned' then all hope for humanity will be lost. The vampire of darkness will become the eighth king spoken of by the prophets of old."

"So, you're telling us that the world is coming to an end if we don't stop them."

"Not the world, only this peaceful dispensation we're living in."

Chester raised his eyebrows as his mind raced, pondering these things. He had no plan, he was outnumbered and he was aware that Vladimir and the evil vampires who followed his every command were physically stronger than he was. Plus, he had to contend with the Crusaders of Light, who had the advantage of exploiting the vampire's greatest weakness, the inability to fight back during the day. He knew that if these mortal followers found them where they slept, they would be easy prey.

"Shit," the old Marine said. "I was hoping that you had some good news."

"I do," replied Zelda. "Good eventually triumphs over evil. The spirits have confidence in you and so do I. If they didn't, then they wouldn't have told us how to find you."

After calling for a taxicab, the hunched over prophetess reminded her friends to seek refuge immediately. "My spirits advised me first, so if my calculations are correct, we're only a few hours ahead of the forces of darkness."

While they were waiting, the psychic asked Chester to give her his hands so she could administer another reading. Remembering what happened the last time she did that, the old Marine quickly checked the legs of the chair she was sitting in to ensure that she wouldn't take a spill on the floor again. The old seer traced the palm of Watkins' hand with her bony fingers and she assured him that he was in good standing with the white spirits.

"You have favor, but no guarantees. You must do the right thing at the exact time in order to succeed."

"Do you have any specific suggestions what the right thing might be?" the old vampire asked.

"Yes, you must disrupt the powers of the underworld. In order to do this, you must destroy their vital link to the physical world. The satanic vampire must be neutralized with as many of his followers as possible. You must kill him when the comet passes through the constellation of Orion. At this exact moment, your powers will be equal to his, but only for a few minutes."

"So, I was correct. Timing is the key."

"Yes," the blind hag answered as she reached into her pocket and fumbled around, pulling some small items out. "Take this four leaf clover sealed in plastic, rabbit's foot and this crumpled up picture of Angel Cakes, my special cat. These lucky charms will bring you good fortune and be a constant reminder to you of my visit and how the white spirits guided me to your location."

Reluctantly, the gray vampire took the silly items from the old crone's hands and looked at the cat's picture before placing the little icons in his right front pocket. He feigned a smile when he saw the photo of the cross-eyed Siamese cat and thought to himself, *"His face looks like it's been through a paper shredder from all of the other tomcats he's been fighting with."*

When the gypsies departed, the small group began gathering essential items for their journey as fast as they could. Fabian made a snap decision and suggested to everyone that they relocate to the small cabin that he owned in Cold Springs, Texas.

"From there, we'll make our stand," the doctor said.

Feeling like refugees, the scurrying female vampires grabbed four ice chests and packed them full of dry ice and blood. Chester and the frizzy-headed doctor loaded the family Suburban with all of the weapons, survival gear and ammunition they could pack into its rear compartment.

"I think there's enough blood here to last us a couple of months," Patricia said to Marsha as they were stooping over the boxes trying to make everything fit. "If not, we'll have to make other arrangements."

The Chevy Suburban wasn't large enough to conceal the vampire's coffins, so at the last minute they decided to leave them behind. As they were driving off, Fabian suggested to everyone that they remove some of the floorboards in one of the cabin's bedrooms and sleep inside the crawl space until they could find some new caskets. The cozy retreat had a perimeter foundation and the temperature always stayed cool underneath the house. It would be the perfect environment for sleeping vampires because it stayed dark during daylight hours.

"Maybe I can build us some new coffins," Chester said with confidence. "We don't want a raccoon, opossum or some other kind of varmint to gnaw our faces off while we're asleep."

With grimaces, both of the female vampires squinted their

eyes and gasped, "Yuck, that's sick."

"Nope, it's part of living in the Pineywoods. I call it survival."

A few more minutes passed and then the gray vampire looked at Marsha as they were leaving their familiar neighborhood. Both of them were sitting together in the back seat and he couldn't help but notice the tears that were forming in her eyes.

"Are you all right?"

The dark-haired teenager wiped her watery brown eyes with her shirt sleeve. "I have a feeling that we'll never see this place again."

Chester adjusted his seatbelt and offered the young girl some advice. "We have each other and this is more important than any house or neighborhood in the world. A home is only as good as the people who live there and the pleasant memories they build together.

Marsha smiled and leaned toward the old vampire and kissed his forehead. "I love you."

Chester smiled. "Because of you, and the doctors, my life has a purpose again. I love you, too."

When the heavily loaded Suburban entered the onramp of the Beltway, its tail pipe scratched the cement as the shock absorbers rebounded up and down. Being conscientious, Fabian eased up on the gas-pedal and did his best to drive conservatively. He didn't want to attract any attention or risk being pulled over by the police.

"Careful, darling," Patricia whispered with a yellow-fanged smile.

The one-hour journey to the Cleveland, Texas, turnoff was uneventful and passed quickly. The cautious doctor applied his turn signal and steered the swaying gray Chevy in the direction of the exit ramp. The sluggish vehicle responded like a large tuna boat as he pulled off of Highway 59 and headed west through the Pineywoods. The lights of the small town faded into obscurity revealing a beautiful night sky filled with stars as they slowly traveled away from civilization.

A red clay dirt road leading through the woods and up a small hill marked the entryway to the doctor's property. Twenty-five secluded acres surrounded by a mixture of Texas pines and hardwoods concealed the cabin from the public's eye. Fortunately, Fabian's retreat had never been vandalized or burglarized like some of the other estates in the general vicinity. Left unattended for prolonged durations, many of the unoccupied cabins were often targeted by thieves who would steal everything that wasn't bolted to the floors. In his heart, Fabian believed that his property was protected by a higher power and the lack of criminal activity was proof of this good omen.

After arriving, the family unloaded their belongings, weapons and the precious supply of blood they were carrying. Fabian started up the electric generator which was stored in a small building behind the cabin so they could utilize the refrigerator that night.

"I'm going to request electric service in the morning," the doctor said. "It looks like we're going to be here for awhile."

Chester scratched his chin and inquired, "Do we have any tools around here, like a skill-saw, hammer and screwdrivers?"

"Yes, I've got a whole bunch of things. They're locked up in the storage shed."

"Good," the old vampire responded. "Be sure to stop by the hardware store and pick up 10 sheets of construction-grade plywood, some 12 penny nails and some hinges with screws. Tomorrow night, I'll build our coffins and after that, I'm going to try to do a little handiwork around here. It looks like some things need fixing."

"They sure do, especially the screens and windows."

Chester suggested they make a list of chores and tackle them one at a time. The old cabin appeared to be in excellent shape, but it was in dire need of small repairs.

When the vampires finally bedded down under the house, they were mindful of Chester's earlier warning regarding hungry varmints. In an attempt to protect themselves, they wrapped their bodies and covered their faces with blankets. When Fabian checked on them an hour later, they reminded him of three shrouded mummies.

Feeling tired, the doctor decided to catch a few hours sleep on the couch before heading to town. He had lots of business to conduct, but he also needed some groceries because the cabin's pantry was practically empty. Fortunately, the medical staff didn't expect him back at the hospital until the middle of January because of the leave of absence he'd taken to care for his wife.

Around noon, Rubenstein woke up to the sound of a buzzing chainsaw. He surmised that his closest neighbor, Lewis Decker was cutting some firewood for the winter or possibly clearing brush. The doctor checked his wristwatch and the time read 12:13 p.m. Feeling tired from the unexpected trip, he swung his legs off the sofa and staggered to the front door. When he stepped on the wooden porch, the cool breeze was refreshing and it helped him regain his senses. A few more minutes passed and the humble doctor climbed into his empty Suburban and headed for town. When he reached the paved road, he saw his neighbor with his young grandson loading a utility trailer full of red oak and kindling.

Waving, Decker shouted from across the blacktop, "Howdy, neighbor, I haven't seen you in a coon's age!"

Fabian rolled his window down and drove the large vehicle into the grass beside the friendly man. "I needed some time off and decided to get out of Houston for a while."

"I don't understand why you still live in that place. It's a rat-race. When are you going to retire and move out here for good?"

"Sooner than you think," replied the doctor. "I've got a few errands to run, but after I tidy things up around the cabin I'll pay you a visit in a couple of days."

"Sounds good to me, neighbor. I'll have a warm pot of coffee brewing. See you later."

As Fabian was driving away, he was thankful that Lewis didn't inquire about his wife or ask too many questions. His desire was to remain friendly, but not allow anyone to get close to him.

Things went smoothly in town, except for the fact that the plywood wouldn't fit into the Chevy because the seats didn't fold down. The doctor made arrangements for delivery and paid an extra $75 to have the materials dropped off at the cabin in the afternoon. Fabian was disappointed with the small grocery store because they didn't have imported cigars or any dark beer in their cooler. They did have the essentials, however, and he was grateful for that.

When the doctor visited the electric co-op, he noticed that one of the men working there was wearing a strange-looking ring exactly like the one he had seen in the satanic book *"Abbadon's Priests." "Could this be a coincidence?"* he thought. Fabian maintained a low profile, paid his deposit and got out of there as quickly as he could without drawing any attention to himself.

Rubenstein made it back to the cabin just in time to meet the delivery driver and help him unload all the items that he'd ordered. Feeling generous, the doctor recognized that the employee was a family man and he tipped him an additional $50 for his efforts.

"Thanks, sir," the man gratefully replied. "I'll put this money to good use. My wife needs baby formula and diapers."

Standing on the porch, Fabian waved goodbye as the flatbed truck dove down the dirt road and away from the cabin. A small cloud of dust filled the air from the rotating tires and reminded the doctor that they needed some rain. Things looked dry in the area and several of the trees on their property were starting to look withered.

As soon as the sun set, the three vampires revived and removed the covers that were wrapped around them. Patricia let out a shrilling scream when she felt the little spiders and nasty water bugs that were crawling around by her face and trying to interweave themselves into her blanket.

"We've got to have coffins," she insisted while spitting a

cockroach out of her mouth. "I hope Fabian bought those materials you requested Chester."

Watkins was removing the floorboards and preparing to crawl out when he answered, "I'm sure he did."

Marsha was the last one to climb out of the small opening when Fabian came into the room and asked, "What's all of the commotion in here?"

"There's lots of nasty bugs and creeping things under there," Patricia said sternly. "I want you to spray for bugs tomorrow evening."

"Yes, dear."

The teen-aged vampire was replacing the loose boards in the corner of the room when the doctor told them that he'd purchased everything they needed to build suitable caskets. He even built some sawhorses out of two-by-fours so they'd have something to prop their work on while Chester assembled everything. The old man had the plans for construction figured out in his mind, so he started his project immediately. The droplight hanging on the front porch afforded enough light to work in the dark and the extra power cord was very useful.

The old vampire proved to be a handy carpenter. He took measurements of the ladies and custom fit both their coffins. His work progressed at an even pace and before morning all three boxes were completely finished.

"All we need to do now is paint them," Chester said as he wiped the beads of sweat from his brow.

"I want pink," Marsha said with a crooked-fanged smile.

"Thank God there aren't splinters in mine," added Patricia.

Everyone agreed that Watkins did a good job and the old man assured them that he'd knock out a few more projects in the weeks to come.

When it came time to move the heavy boxes, the gray Marine asked for some assistance. The group opened up the crawl space door from the outside of the cabin and there was just enough room to slide the makeshift coffins through the tight, cramped space. Fabian held a flashlight to illuminate the pitch-black interior as the vampires worked in unison. Once under the house, things opened up a bit and they had a little more room to move around. Chester figured it would be easier arranging the caskets this way than trying to go through the bedroom and tearing up additional flooring. One concern that bothered the cautious old vampire was the fact that the small access door had no lock.

"We need to secure the opening," Chester said.

With a smile, Doctor Rubenstein replied, "I thought about that when I went to the hardware store and bought a hasp and reinforced padlock."

The frizzy-headed man handed Chester a small paper bag and inside of it was everything he needed, including a shiny new screwdriver to mount the hardware.

"You did good," Watkins said as he returned to the opening to install everything. "You never cease to amaze me."

After everyone finished working, they sat down on the lawn chairs situated on the front porch and took a break. The sounds of crickets, whippoorwills and a distant pack of coyotes howling in the background were a welcomed reminder to everyone that they were far away from the city of Houston and hopefully the danger that Zelda had warned them about.

"How long do you think we can hold out here before they find us?" Chester asked everyone.

"I don't know," answered Marsha. "We're vulnerable during the day because Fabian is by himself."

"She's right," the doctor interjected as his creaky lawn chair squeaked when he shifted his weight and crossed his legs. "I wish we knew a couple of folks around here who we could trust to help us stand watch."

Interrupting her husband, Patricia reminded him, "You know

that that's too dangerous. Secrecy is our best defense."

"I agree with you," added the gray vampire. "But, we could sure use some help."

The group agreed to keep an open mind and hopefully fate would bring someone trustworthy into their lives to assist them in their continual struggle for survival.

Watkins suggested that they try to catch Vladimir by himself because vanquishing him would be a lot easier that way, but how could they do this? The only way to win the battle was to stack the odds in their favor.

"We need someone else on our side," the old Marine concluded. "Not a novice, but someone who has as much to lose as we do."

There's no risk of contracting lung cancer when you're already dead.

CHAPTER 14, LOVE THY NEIGHBOR

Halloween night arrived with a squalling howl as the windy weather was turning wet and nasty. The vampires were just getting situated in the front room when Patricia spotted the headlights of an approaching vehicle driving up the muddy dirt road. Leaves were swirling around in the front yard from the gusts of wind and their exaggerated movements in the lights caught everyone's attention when they looked out of the windows.

"Quick," shouted Chester, "everyone back under the house."

"Wait," replied Fabian, "that's Decker's pickup truck. Let's see what he wants."

As usual, the old vampire had his Colt .45 pistol tucked in the small of his back. He tried to restrain his fight or flight emotions as he cautiously peered through the curtains at the rusty, Ford that was pulling alongside of the shiny Suburban. A few seconds elapsed and, to their surprise, Decker's little grandson jumped out of the truck wearing a green lizard costume. The excited boy was clutching a colorful trick-or-treat bag and it was swinging back and forth as he ran toward the porch. The big man slowly got out of the truck and laughed as he watched the energetic child trying to open the heavy screen door of the cabin.

The doctor turned and looked at the vampires, assuring them that Decker meant them no harm.

"Yeah, that's obvious," replied Watkins. "Ask them in. That's a cute little boy."

Shouting "trick or treat" with a high-pitched voice, the harmless little child brought a smile to everyone's face, and for an instant they forgot about their plight and why they were there hiding out in the woods.

"May we come in?" asked Decker. "It's starting to rain out here."

"Sure," replied Fabian, who extended his right hand toward

the husky gentleman. When Lewis shook the doctor's hand, he grinned and looked him in the eyes with a genuine sincerity that only comes from an honest heart.

"How's it going tonight?"

"Fine," replied the doctor. "I've got some fresh coffee, would you like a cup?"

"Thanks, I sure would."

Decker told Rubenstein that he hated to drop in unannounced, but he thought that it was necessary because he had some very important information that he wanted to share with everyone. Little Danny wanted to go out for Halloween, so he figured it would be an opportune time to pay them a visit.

Patricia tossed a couple of chocolate candy bars into the youngster's bag while Fabian introduced Watkins to his friendly neighbor. "This is my older buddy Chester and his niece Marsha. They're visiting us for a few weeks."

When the two men shook hands, the old vampire felt the same warmth radiating from this kind individual that the doctor had instinctively sensed.

"It's nice to meet you," the gray Marine said. "So, you live across the road?"

"Yes," replied Decker. "I retired from the Sheriff's Department two years ago and I wouldn't go back to that environment if they offered me a million bucks."

The old vampire raised his eyebrows as they pulled up chairs and sat down at the kitchen table. Patricia and Marsha were entertaining the little boy on the other side of the room and complementing him for picking out such an interesting outfit.

"Are you a lizard king?" the teen-aged vampire asked. "That's a cool suit."

The cute little boy shook his head up and down and pretended to growl at the ladies as they poked fun at him. Marsha made herself comfortable on the couch and placed the small child on her knee while Patricia got him a pencil and paper and asked him if he knew how to draw a picture of a dinosaur.

Once he was certain that the youngster couldn't overhear his conversation, Decker got to the point quickly and warned the men that there was a satanic cult operating in the area and that strange things were happening. He imparted his suspicions of coven members infiltrating local law enforcement and various governmental positions of power. The friendly man conceded that he was practically forced into retirement because of an investigation he was working on. Churches were being burned down and forensic evidence pointed to human remains inside of some of these buildings.

"Hitchhikers, homeless folks and undesirables just disappear around here," the blue-eyed man said as he removed his cowboy hat and swept his big hand through his blondish, graying hair. "My wife and I don't trust very many people around here and, I have to admit, at first I didn't want to warn you guys either, but my intuitions compelled me to."

Watkins and Fabian made brief eye contact as Decker continued expounding on his theories of mayhem and murder. The old vampire knew that the doctor was thinking the same thoughts he was, but at the same time both of the men were still reluctant to include anyone in their plans.

Chester wanted to hear more, but not until he discussed everything with the group. Being cordial, he made an intelligent offer. "It looks like little Danny is growing impatient over there. I think he wants to visit a few more houses and collect some goodies. Why don't you come over tomorrow evening by yourself around eight o'clock and we'll continue our discussion then."

"That sounds like a good plan to me," replied Lewis. "I could spend all night telling you guys about some of the things I know."

Fabian thanked his neighbor for warning them and he promised him that his advice would be taken into strict confidence. "I believe what you're telling us, thanks for the tip."

The three men nodded their heads in agreement while the big man raised his coffee mug to his lips and gulped down the warm cup of java. When he finished, he scooted his chair out and with a smile he thanked everyone for their hospitality.

As the old Ford was chugging down the driveway, everyone pulled up chairs and gathered around the table to discuss what they had just heard. Was it a coincidence or was it fate that brought Decker to their doorstep? Could he really be trusted or would they jeopardize their safety by talking to him? These were some of the doubts and questions that immediately came to their minds.

Marsha surprised everyone when she made a statement that was beyond her teenage years. "If we confide in him, we need to disclose our true intentions. This entails revealing to him the secrets of our vampirism and everything we know up to this point. Before we do this, we need to devise a test for this individual to make sure we can trust him."

"She's right," interjected the gray Marine. "It sounds like we're on the same side, but we need to make sure."

"I've got an idea," the yellow-fanged Patricia said. "Why don't we use some of the knowledge that we've learned from the book of wisdom and quiz him with some parables?"

"Yes, my wife is right," agreed Fabian. "We need to find out what he has to gain or lose. By probing him with lots of questions, if he's a fool, he'll lose his cool and become agitated.

Interrupting, Marsha added, "Traitors hate questions according to the *Vampire's Bible*. Let's gang up on him and really put him to the test."

Laughing, Chester agreed. "If this guy is full of bullshit, then he's in for the surprise of his life tomorrow night."

Everyone consented to being friendly, polite and playing the role of stupidity to its fullest until this man's patience was tested beyond normal limits. "I think we'll have some fun," Fabian concluded.

After they finished their conversation, Marsha and Chester walked outside to get some fresh air while the doctors tidied up the living room and did a little dusting. Standing on the front porch, the old vampire got another idea. He told his teen-aged companion that he was going to do some reconnaissance and fly over to the neighbor's house to check things out.

"They'll never notice a little bat flying around in the dark," he said.

It was still drizzling outside, but the wind seemed to be dying down and that was the break that he was looking for. "Bat of the night, take flight," he intoned.

The tiny mammal fluttered out of sight as Marsha laughed under her breath at her silly friend. She knew that if anything suspicious was going on next door, Chester would notice it. She trusted his wisdom, and instincts, because they usually panned out. If Decker proved to be a Judas-conspirator, the old man would peg him for exactly that.

Over an hour passed, and the gray vampire still hadn't returned. The teenager was starting to get concerned when she saw a silver wolf trotting up the driveway. As he got closer, she saw a puff of smoke and, when the white mist cleared, Watkins was still bent over on the ground advancing towards her on all fours.

Giggling, Marsha spoke up. "Hey, you're getting muddy down there."

"I know," the old man replied as he stood up and brushed his hands off on his trousers legs. "I forgot to stand up right away. They call it Alzheimer's disease of the dead."

"Did you see anything out of the ordinary?" the inquisitive girl asked.

"Yes, something very interesting, but nothing fishy."

The sneaky Marine told the girl that he couldn't see very much from the air because of the thick cloud cover and precipitation, so he decided to land in the woods next to Decker's property and investigate. As soon as he transformed into a wolf, he began snooping around the property boundaries and, shortly thereafter, he saw Decker returning home with his grandson. Approximately 20 minutes elapsed and the creepy vampire noticed that all of the lights went off inside of the old farmhouse, so he assumed that the family had gone to bed.

The bristly-haired, silver wolf slipped under the barbed-wire fence and maintained a low profile as he silently crept in the direction of the residence. When he reached the barn, he saw two ferocious Rottweilers that were guarding the estate and still unaware of his presence. Trying to be cautious, he stepped backwards and unintentionally placed his paw on a twig causing it to snap. Upon hearing that, the watchdogs were immediately alerted that their territory had been violated. A fiery chase ensued with the vicious canines breathing down his back. The slick old wolf ran around the house and lured the dogs inside of the barn. As soon as they entered, he made a quick exit and closed the door behind him, trapping both of them inside. The agitated animals feverishly clawed and gnawed at the entryway, but to no avail. The cagey trickster took off running in the opposite direction, and when he rounded the corner, he spotted Decker coming out of his back door armed with a pump shotgun.

"I didn't stick around for long after that," Chester said, "but I noticed that our neighbor had three expensive telescopes under his porch awning. Either our friend is an avid astronomer or he's looking for the same thing that Zelda warned us about.

The two vampires chatted for another half hour about Decker's optical gear and the probability of him knowing more than they first suspected. Marsha suggested to Chester that they go back inside and tell the doctors about everything he saw. She wanted to hear their opinions because they were very analytical and might be able to piece things together.

It didn't take Fabian long to come up with a hypothesis regarding the costly equipment. He agreed that what Watkins observed sounded strange, but he was certain that it was a good sign that Lewis could be trusted. "If this man was an enemy operative, he wouldn't be searching for Beelzebub's Comet with such tenacity."

"I agree," Chester said. "He's not a typical stargazer, he's looking for something out of the ordinary like we are."

The anticipation regarding the following evening's meeting grew as some of these details were discussed. The group had some extra information to work with and this would figure into their strategy of barraging Decker with multiple questions.

After they finished their conversation, Patricia suggested to her husband that they clean the kitchen the following evening. The floor was covered with tiny mouse droppings and she was embarrassed because she was sure that Lewis had noticed.

Abiding in complete secrecy only 10 miles away, the stealthy Vladimir and his wicked servants were performing the required Halloween sacrificial rites. Standing in a circle wearing brown hooded robes, the evil coven hovered over their next victim as he cried out and pleaded for mercy.

"Please don't kill me," he begged.

"I promise you we won't," replied the handsome vampire. "You're going to die from natural causes."

Upon hearing that, the chained man started crying and cursing at the witches while they taunted him with insults and ridicule.

"You filthy vagabond! You low-life moron!" the intoxicated Miller yelled as he extinguished his red-hot marijuana cigarette on the prisoner's arm. "You're the scourge of society."

The evil vampire praised all of the witches as they spit on the doomed man and belted him with their clinched fists. Laughing like a hideous demon, he ordered them not to strike him too hard because this would numb his senses and he wouldn't be able to languish in agony during his torture. The wicked master derived immense gratification by seeing his victims suffer, and he believed that he could draw satanic powers from their pain. Vladimir boasted to his followers that he was the greatest sadist who had ever lived.

Holding a black candle in her left hand, one of the female witches began fanning the man's bare feet with the flames as he fought in vain to free himself from the splintery alter. The rattling, clanking chains sounded like cheap jewelry as the man arched his back and screamed.

The abandoned cottage the Satanists invaded was located deep in the woods and was totally isolated from society. Their sinister voices dissipated into oblivion as their devilish party raged on.

"Tonight is a special night!" the insane vampire yelled. "On with the show."

Halloween was a sacred night of celebration according to the satanic book *"Abbadon's Priests."* Sexual rituals consecrated with the sacrificial blood of the innocent were the only ways to appease the evil spirits of the underworld. Obedience was paramount.

Vladimir needed all of the supernatural strength he could muster because next week would be his prime opportunity to sabotage the Dynasty of Immortals and wrest power from the governing body. He was angry because the toothless vampire was still alive, but his pride and arrogance blinded his eyes to the truth that Watkins was not an ordinary individual. *"How could a gray old vampire contend with his great eminence?"* he deduced.

Although he was confident, the Russian was also frustrated because the vampires he'd sent to spy on the Rubenstein mansion in Bear Creek came up empty-handed. Vladimir's emissaries were clueless as to where the occupants of the house had escaped to. If they couldn't find them, then they couldn't murder them.

The prideful liar underestimated Chester's resolve. If necessary, the old man would sacrifice his own life to see the Russian destroyed and this was something that Vladimir had never encountered in the many centuries that he'd been alive. Self-preservation during war was a weakness and the old Marine learned this when he was on the battlefields of the South Pacific. During this phase of his life, he always believed that he would never live to see another day, so he committed himself to fighting with the heart of a lion. These memories were locked deep inside of his spirit and they would soon be rekindled as the appointed time approached.

When the sacrificial torture ended, the helpless man was suffocated to death by one of the warlocks who wrapped duct tape and cellophane around his head. As the dying man's face turned blue, the Russian looked at him with an emotionless expression.

"I told you we wouldn't kill you. You're just having a hard time breathing."

When the victim succumbed, the murderous vampire took the sacrificial athame and slit the man's throat. Like a thirsty child at a water fountain, he locked his mouth to the gaping wound and raised his right hand into the air, flashing the symbol of Satan with his index and little finger extended.

"Hail Vladimir," the witches cried out. "Master of darkness."

Before the conclusion of every ritual, the cunning vampire always made it a point to show everyone the weaknesses of his tortured victims as they writhed in agony. The Russian promised the loyalists that he could free them from all physical pain and suffering by turning them into gods like himself, but only if they proved themselves worthy through strict obedience.

At the break of dawn, Fabian was awakened by the sounds of passing fire engines. With sirens blaring, the speeding vehicles drove past his driveway and continued westward on the blacktop road toward the abandoned building that the arsonists had vandalized and set ablaze. Curious as to what was going on, the groggy doctor stepped outside on the rustic wooden porch to listen. A few minutes passed and then the high-pitched sounds faded into the distance until they were no longer audible. Scratching his frizzy hair, the sleepy-eyed doctor retuned inside and went back to bed.

Around 2:10 p.m., the doctor woke up again and staggered to

the kitchen counter to make a fresh pot of coffee. As his eyes cleared, he looked at the calendar hanging on the wall. When he flipped the page to the month of November, he saw that it was Saturday. The Sabbath was always a special day to him because of his Jewish heritage and he thought to himself, *"Tonight's meeting will be perfect because it's on the Lord's Day."*

The afternoon was pretty uneventful as Rubenstein worked around his property and repaired a damaged barbed-wire fence. A large tree limb fell on a section of wires and snapped a corner post during the passing storm. The backside of his acreage bordered the National Forest and he was very conscientious about maintaining his property boundaries and keeping trespassers out.

Some of Chester's firearm habits were beginning to rub off on the doctor and he made it a point to carry a .357 Magnum revolver with him while performing all of his chores. Trying not to become too preoccupied, he occasionally looked over his shoulder and checked for danger while he labored.

Feeling like he'd accomplished something important, the hungry, sweating man picked up his work tools and walked back to the cabin. *"The meal that I placed in the oven two hours ago should be done by now,"* he thought.

Nightfall was approaching and the colorful sky reminded him of a beautiful painting he'd seen the year before at the Houston art museum. Before he reached the cabin, he saw a magnificent whitetail buck standing in the woods about 50 yards away and to his right. The startled deer raised his tail, cocked his ears forward and looked in the direction where he perceived danger. After a couple of seconds, the animal snorted and bounded out of sight as Fabian continued walking up the gentle slope.

The doctor had grown accustom to eating alone, but he wasn't very fond of it. Sharing meals with another person seemed to make things taste better. Maybe it was the conversation.

Because it was an inconvenience, Rubenstein seldom

purchased, or bothered eating, kosher foods. His deceased father, who was a devout rabbi, would have been ashamed and disowned him if he only knew how much pork sausage his son had secretly consumed during his lifetime. Fabian tried to hide his addiction from his Jewish friends, but to no avail. One of his colleagues at work, who shared his religion, was aware of his weakness and he was constantly kidding him about it. His clever friend nicknamed him "The Great Pork Connoisseur."

Fabian opened the raspy, hinged door of the oven and removed the rack of smothered barbecue spareribs. His mouth watered as he saw the sizzling beads of grease dripping off the piping hot meat. The pleasant aroma filled the kitchenette and drifted into the front room. Acting like a professional chef, the man took great pride as he dished up his cuisine. Collard greens and sweet potatoes were heaped on a plate next to the piece of pork that the doctor carefully sliced off with a butcher knife. Just as he was sitting down in his chair to eat, the roller wheels slid backwards unexpectedly causing him to lose his balance and tumble to the floor. Attempting to break his fall, he grabbed the table with both hands, tipping it over and spilling everything that was on it, including his delicious plate of food.

With his head still spinning, the frustrated man looked at the dirty floor and all of the food that was covered with particles of dirt, hair and rodent droppings. In an angry rage, he stood up and kicked the plate, sending it sailing into the kitchen cabinets. The delicate china broke into dozens of tiny pieces as the doctor cursed at his jinxed chair.

"You son of a bitch, I'll break your wheels off."

The mad scientist grabbed the inanimate object and headed for the front porch to exact his revenge. Just as he was opening the screen door and preparing to smash the chair's pedestal off, Patricia hollered from under the house, "Hey, what's going on up there? What's all of that noise about?"

"Nothing, dear," the man replied through gritted teeth. "Just adjusting the wheels on this chair."

The doctor regained his composure and growled as he turned around and went back to the kitchen. "I'll fix you later, you cursed piece of furniture."

When Patricia saw the mess in the kitchen, she said, "Serves you right for sneaking pork again, you hypocrite."

Defiantly, Fabian's eyebrows slanted down and he answered back, "Now wait a minute, what side of the coffin did you wake up on?"

I'm sorry, honey," the humble woman answered. "I'll get a mop and help you straighten up."

Chester and Marsha exchanged glances and smiled at one another as they quietly slipped out the front door and onto the porch. Once they were outside, they started laughing until both of their faces turned red.

"Who needs a television for entertainment when we've got both of the doctors to watch every evening?" whispered Watkins.

While the two vampires were joking, they saw Decker's truck coming up the driveway. Chester waved as the vehicle pulled alongside of Rubenstein's Chevy.

"Howdy," the big man said as the door swung open. "You two doing OK this evening?"

"We sure are," answered the gray vampire. "I can't answer for the doctor though."

"What do you mean?"

Laughing, Chester replied, "He accidentally knocked the kitchen table over and spilled his dinner on the floor."

"Did you guys want me to come back another time?"

"No, we're looking forward to visiting with you tonight."

While they were talking, Patricia came to the front door and invited everyone to come inside. Fabian dished up another plate and was making a second attempt to eat dinner.

With a mouth full of food, the doctor said, “Come in, sit down. Would you like a plate of oven-baked barbecue?”

“No thanks, my wife made some fried chicken and taters. I’m stuffed.”

The doctor asked everyone to pull up chairs and sit down while he finished eating. Decker inquired as to why no one else was having dinner and the incognito vampires made up excuses that they had their meals earlier. The four people made small talk until Fabian finished and then they got down to business.

Decker advised his neighbors that he wanted to reiterate regarding the things he had warned them about the night before. “There’s a satanic cult operating around here and I’m concerned.”

Playing the devil’s advocate, the intellectual Patricia asked, “Why are you so worried about these people? Have they threatened your family?”

Before Lewis could answer her, Chester jumped in with the question, “Could you go into detail regarding the criminal evidence you were talking about last night?”

The big guy slowly turned his head to look at the gray old man when Marsha suddenly interjected, “Satanism happens all over the place. What makes Cold Springs any different? Are you on a crusade?”

Not knowing who to answer first, and wondering if they were being sarcastic, Decker smiled and said, “I hope I’m not offending anyone.”

“No,” replied Fabian, “we just have a lot of questions, that’s all.”

Decker smiled and leaned back in his chair. “I’ve got all night. I wish that the police and Sheriff's Departments had been this inquisitive.”

Sticking to their plan, the vampires kept the questions coming for several hours while Lewis patiently maintained his cool, answering each and every one to their satisfaction. The clock on the kitchen wall read 11:43 p.m. and the group was still engaged in conversation.

To everyone's surprise, Decker leaned forward and said, "When I was 10 years old, my grandfather warned me about a cosmic event that would occur in the heavens. He even predicted the year."

Acting like she didn't know anything, Marsha inquired, "Is a meteor going to decimate the planet?"

"No, it's not going to crash into the Earth. This event is very significant however. When a certain comet passes through our solar system, it has the potential to open the gates of the underworld. If this happens, a disembodied spirit will empower the most wicked ruler who's ever lived. If this tyrant successfully casts his spells, he'll rule for a thousand years until the comet returns. Millions of people will die as a result of his atrocities. "

The kind neighbor confided that he'd recently purchased three expensive telescopes and, on clear nights, he would search the heavens for the appearance of this celestial body. He invited everyone to come over and help him stargaze when the conditions were right.

Fabian inquired, "If you find it, what are you suppose to do?"

"Grandpa Ed told me when the Devil's comet appears in the sky, a gray warrior would assemble a small force and face insurmountable odds trying to stop these things from happening. He told me to unite myself with him and fight against the forces of darkness."

"Can these people be stopped and did he tell you who would win?" the teen-aged vampire asked.

"I don't know and neither did grandpa. All he told me to do was fight."

Watkins looked the man squarely in the eyes and asked, "How did your grandfather know all of these things and who told him?"

Leaning back in his chair, Decker took a deep breath and

sighed. "I don't know how to tell you this, so I'm just going to come out and say it. My grandfather was a vampire."

"Prove it!" Chester emphatically ordered.

Decker smiled, nodded his head and reached into his coat pocket. To their amazement, he laid a book on the table titled *"Wisdom of the Dead."*

"He gave this to me before he was killed and I made a vow that I would avenge his death."

The five of them sat there in silence for a few minutes as their eyes focused on the fascinating book. The old Marine was convinced that Lewis was an ally. The passionate tone of his voice and the fact that he possessed a copy of the sacred manuscript was evidence enough. Marsha looked at Chester and he winked signaling that it was OK to speak freely. The teenager turned toward Decker and smiled, showing him both of her pearly white fangs.

Startled, the husky man jerked back from the table, "I hope you're not hungry."

Chester gently placed his hand on Lewis' shoulder and assured him that he was in the company of friends.

"You've shared your heart with us," the old vampire said. "Your wisdom and honesty was not in vain."

Decker scratched his chin. "Are you the gray warrior?"

"Yes, I am."

Watkins and Patricia confided in their new friend that they were vampires also. They told him about the fortuneteller, Zelda, and how her information coincided with his late grandfather's warnings.

"After 45 years, the pieces of the puzzle are finally coming together," Decker stated. "This is confirmation. Pops also said that the Satanist would be a vampire."

Patricia spoke up, posing another question. "There's a lot of secret covens in the United States, how do we know that the creature we're looking for is even operating in this area?"

The big man took his best guess at answering her question.

"We don't, but from the body count, I'm willing to wager that he is. A lot of folks have been murdered around here and the police keep turning a blind eye."

"I agree," added Chester. "I have a feeling he's closer than we think. Our weakness to sunlight limits the distance we can travel. It would be ludicrous for a vampire to try to run a coven in a distant region. The logistics would be too complicated."

Decker went on to explain that his deceased relative also told him the last stand would occur in Texas.

"Being a vampire has changed my perspectives." the old Marine said. "I don't believe in coincidences like I used to. I bet if we drive over to your place right now, we'd spot that comet with one of your telescopes."

"It wouldn't surprise me," the scientific-minded doctor interjected, "but let's talk some more. Zelda told us not to fight until late December."

Three more hours passed and the men were still chatting. Lewis couldn't believe that he'd found others who were willing to fight for the same cause. Watkins and Decker had many things in common. Both men were former law enforcement officers and combat veterans. Lewis joined the Marine Corps when he was 18 years old and, in 1969, he was sent to Vietnam. Wounded in action, he was returned stateside to finish out his enlistment.

Fabian brought up the incident at the electric company where he saw one of the employees wearing a strange ring. Chester reached into his shirt pocket and handed the doctor the ring he'd taken from the trooper several months before.

"Did it look like this?"

With his mouth hanging open, Fabian couldn't believe it and asked, "Where did you get one of these?"

Chester didn't go into all the details of his nightly excursion that sultry evening, but he did tell them that the ring's picture was in the satanic book *"Abbadon's Priests."*

"My grandfather told me about that wicked manuscript," Decker said. "He tried to find a copy before he was murdered so he could gain a better insight of how his enemies operated."

"Sounds like your gramps was a smart old dude," the gray vampire said as he stretched his arms. "Marsha and I were lucky enough to find one."

"Would you mind if I borrowed it?" Decker asked.

Getting up from the table, Chester excused himself as he went into the back bedroom to retrieve the book from his duffle bag. When he returned to the kitchen, Marsha hissed when she saw the wicked hardback in his hand.

"I hate that evil thing," the teenager stated. "Why don't you burn it?"

"Not yet," the old Marine answered as he handed the ugly thing to Decker.

The husky man ran his fingers over the book's front cover and inquired about the strange leathery texture. Watkins frowned, shaking his head, and told him it was bound with human skin— most likely from a sacrificed victim. The shocked man jerked, dropping the nasty book on the table. The object made a loud thud when it landed, and a dusty cloud shot out of the pages.

"You weren't ready for that surprise, were you?" Chester asked.

"Hell no!"

Decker carefully picked the ancient book back up and opened it to one of the chapters in the middle, titled Valiant Servants of Darkness. Torture methods, ritualistic practices and unholy Sabbits were listed throughout the entire section. As Lewis turned the pages, he envisioned many of the crime scenes he'd investigated years ago and some of the bizarre details began to make sense.

Was it true that there was a dark underground theocratic society governed by satanic followers who were dedicated to secretly promoting their cause by controlling governments, police departments, religious organizations and ultimately a ruling world body?

"Can I borrow this for a couple of weeks?" Lewis asked. "I want to study it."

"Yes," answered the gray vampire. "I'm finished looking through it, but a word of advice. After you're done reading it, burn it."

"I will," the husky man responded. "Evil attaches itself to objects like this."

Decker suggested to everyone that they begin a surveillance vigil and start tailing as many individuals as possible so they could find out exactly how many people were affiliated with the cult. He thought it would be a good idea to start with the man Fabian saw working at the light company and go from there.

Lewis seemed very optimistic. "At least we've got a lead. By following this chump, we might be able to find out the identity of the other coven members."

Decker and Watkins knew that their success revolved around one thing: If they could locate the exact spot where the sadistic vampire was going to perform his ritual in December, then this would be their chance to destroy him.

"It sounds like the Russian likes to play with matches," the old leatherneck growled. "If I could get my hands on a flamethrower, I'd teach him a lesson he'd never forget. "

The group decided to meet again the next evening. Unraveling all the pieces of the puzzle wouldn't be easy, but they were certain about one thing— some of these mysteries surrounding the evil cult would soon be brought into the light for everyone to see. Lewis was confident that he'd tag every last one of them who lived in the county and expose them for what they were— criminals.

Two days later, as the sun was coming up, Miller and his family were gathering around the breakfast table and preparing to say grace. His 9-year-old daughter and 7-year-old son sat quietly in front of their plates as their mother asked them to bow their heads.

With eyes closed, Lucious said a quick, mumbled prayer that no one at the table could understand and when he was finished rambling he shouted, "Hallelujah, let's dig in."

"Daddy, is there a God?" the young boy asked.

"Yes," the wicked father blurted out as he shoveled a large portion of scrambled eggs into his mouth. "We're all gods at this table. I'm a god, you're a god and our dog Rex over there is a little god. Now shut up and eat before I send you to your room."

The young boy began to cower as the sarcastic man stared at him with piercing eyes and a scowling, red face. The wicked parents were always sending mixed messages of confusion to their young children regarding religion. This was an intricate part of their generational satanic training. Confusion teaches frustration, and the doubt associated with it brings about rejection. If the concept of religion is too complicated to understand, then the children won't devote their time trying to learn its virtues. The ultimate goal of the devil-worshipping parents was to guide their children down a path of self-interest. A true follower of Satan will always be self-serving and place their own ambitions above others.

According to Miller's philosophy, friendships were based on selfishness. There was no need to befriend anyone who was incapable of reciprocating beneficial deeds to one's self. To do so was a waste of time.

In the work place, Lucious was a masterful tactician of gossip. He was instrumental in spreading the lies that forced the honorable Decker to resign. As he climbed the ladder of success, he ruined many people's careers in the process. His wickedness destroyed the financial stability of numerous families causing some of them to lose their homes and file bankruptcy. When divorces occurred, the sexually immoral man always pretended to be a comforting friend. After gaining a grieving wife's confidence, he always made it a point to try to sleep with her.

Miller's lavish lifestyle and aspirations of becoming a millionaire were achieved because he always recognized the opportunity to capitalize on a shady deal. Dishonesty was OK, if you never got caught and it made you rich.

The wicked warlock was basking in the spotlight of prosperity as the newspaper reporter interviewed him that morning. His recent promotion to chief deputy meant that the only one who commanded more authority in the county than he did was the sheriff. Miller knew that his friend was grooming him for the highly coveted position because he made it known that he wasn't going to run for re-election. An honest man, the sheriff was certain that his understudy would do a good job, or so he thought.

With pen and paper in hand, the reporter inquired, "What do you think about all of the arson that's going on in the county?"

Subconsciously, the warlock projected an air of importance through non-verbal communication and body language. The subtle mind control techniques Miller used during his press release made the young man nervous. The arrogant deputy leaned back in his reclining chair and propped his dusty boots up on top of his desk. A few second passed as he thought up a lie.

"Aw, it's just a bunch of juveniles. Nothing to worry about. Eventually, we'll catch them or they'll just quit because they got tired of starting fires."

With trembling hands, the perspiring reporter wrote down the officer's lackadaisical response and brought another detail to his attention. With a cracking voice, he could hardly ask his next question. "A couple of bowhunters were camping out in the woods and both of them claimed that they heard some cult screaming and chanting inside of an abandoned farmhouse. Any comments?"

"What they probably heard was a pack of coyotes howling or some teenagers drinking beer. We've got lots of varmints and kids around here who make quite a ruckus at night."

Miller faked a smile as he tried to hide his growing contempt toward the curious reporter. He knew that the young man was only doing his job, but he was starting to piss him off. When Miller got angry, bad things happened. Folks mysteriously disappeared or they lost their jobs.

The officer began daydreaming about killing the ambitious columnist as the interview progressed. He envisioned everyone in the coven torturing the reporter with cattle prods while he sliced his ears off with a dull, rusty knife. Another fantasy popped into his demented mind as he continued to drift off into dreamland. In his next vision, he saw the man crying out in excruciating pain while he placed his hand over his mouth and stabbed him in the stomach. As the knife plunged deeply, he yanked the sacrificial blade upward, eviscerating his intestines from his midsection.

"Did you hear me, sir?" the man questioned as he made his third attempt to gain the chief's attention. "Are you going to run for sheriff in the next election and, if so, what are your plans?"

"Yes, I've got big plans for our county. Our outgoing sheriff did an excellent job and we plan to continually build our administration on the foundation that he laid. We'd also like to see additional funding for a larger jail facility, but that issue will be left up to our taxpayers. I believe in democracy, so we'll let them decide."

The reporter loosened his tight collar, handed Miller his business card and thanked him for his time. The wicked man thought to himself as he looked at the information on the tiny laminated piece of paper, "*This writer had better pen an article worthy of the Pulitzer Prize or he'll wind up spread eagle on the alter of pain.*"

Miller put in for some vacation days the following week so he could carry out the lewd vampire's directives. His seniority practically guaranteed that he could take any day off that he needed. The dedicated Satanist and five of his warlocks would be traveling to Memphis, Tennessee, to capture Count Marius and the two faithful council members who would be accompanying the chancellor during his business trip. Vladimir ordered his ruthless followers to murder all of the mortals who were associated with the safe house and to set fire to all the buildings so there wouldn't be any evidence. All the other estates were destroyed in this fashion and it seemed to be working good for them, so they decided to keep it up.

The witches made arrangements to rent an enclosed moving van so they could easily transport the three coffins back to Texas without anyone seeing what they were hauling. Daytime travel would ensure that there was no chance of the vampires escaping.

A concise strategy, weapons and backstabbing traitors with an appetite for cash would make this mission successful.

After all of the arrangements were in place, the coven leader called his Russian spiritual advisor and confirmed to him that everything was ready.

Before ending the telephone conversation, the wicked master boasted, "Next week, we seize power. Next year, we conquer the world."

Vladimir was extremely proud of the Crusaders of Light. Their blind allegiance and unquestionable stupidity were unsurpassed. A master of psychology, the cunning vampire was able to manipulate everyone in the group. His relentless devotion to studying the evil book *"Abbadon's Priests"* empowered him with this special magic.

The fire ritual in December would be his grand finale and he would prove to all of his followers that he was the greatest ruler of all time. Everything was going according to plan.

CHAPTER 15, SURVEILLANCE TEAM

Decker and the doctor sat patiently across the street from the light company waiting for the suspected coven member to leave work. The idling Suburban looked inconspicuous sitting in the grocery store parking lot next to the other customers' vehicles.

At 5 p.m., the man they were waiting for walked outside and held the door open for the two ladies who were following him. As soon as the secretaries came out, he turned and locked the door behind them.

Fabian spoke up. "That's our man. The skinny dude with the red hair and beard."

The employees spoke briefly for a couple of minutes and then waved goodbye to one another as they strolled toward their personal vehicles.

Decker, who fancied using the best equipment he could afford, watched the individual through a pair of expensive German binoculars. From his vantage point, he could easily read the Texas license plate of the car the fellow climbed into. A few seconds later, they were leaving the parking lot and following the Toyota as it proceeded through town.

The former investigator advised Fabian to lag behind, and not to follow too closely. Keeping a low profile, they tailed the man for approximately 25 minutes until he pulled into a tavern that was situated right next to a colorful tattoo parlor. The purple neon sign on the saloon's roof read "The Feline Palace."

Lewis told the doctor to drive past the two buildings and maintain a steady speed. "When we get to the end of the block, circle back and we'll park across the street next to the truck stop."

Moving slow and deliberate, the husky man turned his head just in time to see the bearded warlock entering the tavern. "Good. If he gets drunk, he'll be a lot easier to follow when he comes back out."

The dusty, trash-littered parking lot across the highway afforded a good view of both establishments. The frizzy-headed doctor parked behind a dumpster and the vehicle melted in perfectly with the environment. The men watched and rotated the binoculars in 15-minute intervals. According to the seasoned retiree, this was the best method to employ because eye fatigue was reduced to a minimum. Decker adjusted his reclining seat to get comfortable as he watched the suspect through the big bay window in front of the saloon. The bearded man pulled up a stool next to a couple of other patrons and ordered a beer.

Two hours and 11 bottles later, the man staggered out of the front doors, and began weaving his way in the direction of the tattoo parlor. Fabian started laughing as he watched the foolish guy trying to walk straight.

"Take a look," he said, passing the eyeglasses to Lewis. "He just went inside the needle-joint to get painted."

Sitting down in a comfortable-looking leather chair, the redheaded warlock removed his shirt and leaned back. A longhaired, burly-looking guy with a cigarette pressed between his lips, stood over him and prepared to go to work with an electric ink gun.

Decker handed the binoculars back to the doctor, reached into his tactical bag and pulled out a spotting scope.

"I want to take a closer look," he said. "This is interesting and kind of funny at the same time."

After a couple minutes of adjustments, he increased the power setting to 24x and zoomed in on his subject. The image of the redheaded man's grimacing face filled the scope. Decker watched and lightheartedly snickered. "What a wimp."

"Can you see what kind of design they're tattooing on his stomach?" the doctor asked.

"Not yet, but from the look in his eyes, he's not having a very good experience."

Lewis had been on dozens of stakeouts when he was on the

force and because of the long hours involved, he always came prepared. "I've got a thermos full of coffee in that black bag of mine and two plastic cups. I've also got some crackers, beef jerky and candy bars. Would you like something?"

"Thank you," the doctor replied. "I could use a cup of coffee and a few crackers right now."

The men ate their snacks as they watched the scene unfold. It became obvious that the tattoo session was really hurting the red-faced recipient. The artist abruptly stopped his work and went over to one of the cabinets to fetch a bottle. Decker's eye was pressed to the scope's ocular lens as he observed the burly guy pouring a double shot of bourbon whiskey. When he finished, he handed the client the drink. The skinny man lifted the tiny glass and quickly gulped it down. The artist resumed his work and occasionally he'd pause so the pain-sensitive warlock could have another belt.

When they were finished, the intoxicated fellow stood up and looked down to admire the design that was tattooed on his stomach. With a smirk on his face, he nodded his head in approval.

Decker focused in on his midsection and when he saw the ugly, 12-inch-tall devil's face above the man's navel, he grumbled something that prompted the doctor to ask a question.

"Did you say something?"

"Yes," the investigator replied. "I never could understand why someone would want to abuse their body like that."

Lewis refocused his eyepiece until he could clearly read the inscription written above the hideous demon's head. The words "Lucifer's Child" were tattooed in red just above the crooked-looking goat horns.

Demanding that his services be paid for in cash, the tattoo artist took the wad of bills from the customer's hand and stuck them in his front pocket. When the man walked out of the door, a trashy-looking woman with rose-flower-tattoos, stringy hair and large breasts entered the studio from one of the rooms in the back. Both of them started pointing and laughing at the warlock as he staggered away toward his vehicle.

"They must really think that dude's a sucker," Fabian said as he turned the key and started up the Chevy. "I hope he drives better than he walks."

Surprisingly, the liquored up man was able to keep his Toyota between the lines of the highway as he traveled home. The short journey lasted about 15 minutes and took them to a small, wood frame house located several miles out of town. Decker was shocked when he discovered that the fellow lived with his mother. Being acquainted with lots of people in the county, he recognized the residence and the yellow Chrysler parked in the driveway. Keeping their heads and eyes straight forward, the men drove past the residence as the guy parked.

Lewis shrugged his shoulders before speaking. "Old Lady Hawkins is a sweet Christian lady. It's a shame that her only son turned out to be such a lowlife scumbag."

The men traveled another mile and took the detour leading them back to their side of the county. The night sky was clear and the trip home went pleasantly as the men discussed their work.

"Now we know where he lives, what he drives and who he's related to. We'll come back this weekend and follow him again. He's bound to lead us to some of the others."

Fabian turned his blinker on and spoke up. "I don't think he'll be entertaining any company at home, at least not with the old lady living there. What do you think?"

"Not hardly. She's a Sunday school teacher. Mrs. Hawkins is one of the few people I know who practices what she preaches."

When the Suburban drove up the dirt road leading to the cabin, the vampires met them outside in the driveway. Greeting them like they were secret spies returning from a reconnaissance mission, they started bombarding them with questions. The two men looked at one another and didn't know whom to answer first.

"One at a time," Decker pleaded. "You first Chester."

"What happened? Did he lead you to anyone else?"

"No, but I'm sure he will."

Both of the men slowly climbed out of the vehicle and started stretching to loosen up their stiff muscles. Fabian methodically rolled his head from side to side and his neck made an audible cracking sound as he worked out the kinks.

Grasping the black bag that contained his tactical gear, Lewis closed the vehicle's door behind him. "We watched him get drunk, then the numb-nuts went and got a silly tattoo."

Looking disappointed, Patricia squinted her eyes, frowned and asked, "Is that all? He didn't meet with anyone else?"

Responding with confidence, Lewis patted her on the shoulder with his free hand. "Work like this takes lots of patience. Give it time. He'll lead us to someone important. After that, it gets easier."

"The good news is, we found out where he lives and we're going to follow him again this weekend," Fabian told his wife. "This guy's an alcoholic and he looks careless."

"Where's his house, and how far away is it?" the teen-aged vampire inquired.

Decker stepped up on the porch steps, grinned, and then chuckled. "20 miles from here, and get this— he lives with his mommy."

The group went inside the cabin and sat down in the living room to discuss what they needed to do next. The doctors situated themselves together on the sofa beside Marsha, while Decker and Chester pulled up chairs. The gray vampire brought up something that was weighing heavily on his mind. They needed to find a safe way of retrieving more of their belongings from the house in Bear Creek, without getting caught. Everyone agreed that returning would be extremely dangerous, but it was a chance worth taking if they could do it during the day. The vampires' blood supply was dwindling faster than planned, and they needed more.

Watkins pointed out another important fact. All of the ingredients they'd gathered for the magic potion were still in his bedroom. Trying to reacquire everything would be too time consuming, and they needed to concentrate on tracking the coven members. He insisted that the solstice spell would play a vital role, because it would disguise their identities. If they were going to kill the Russian, they needed to get close to him.

While they were brainstorming, the investigator came up with the answer. He and Fabian would catch a couple of hours of sleep and leave first thing in the morning. If they arrived at the house around noon, the chances of a confrontation would be slim. Decker figured that they wouldn't encounter anyone, but if they did, they'd be contending with mortals instead of vampires.

At 10:30 a.m., the men drove to the city and arrived in Fabian's neighborhood shortly before noon. Packing concealed, snub-nosed .38 special revolvers under their jackets, they wanted to look as inconspicuous as possible. If one of the neighbors happened to see them, they didn't want to rouse any suspicions. The men drove around the block a couple of times as a precautionary measure and, to their satisfaction, it appeared that no one was watching the house. When the doctor pulled into the driveway and up to the security gate, things looked normal. After entering the property, he circled around the water fountain and parked the big Chevy right next to the front door.

Before the frizzy-headed man could get out of the vehicle, Decker grabbed his arm and said, "Not too fast doctor. We need to check for booby traps."

"You're right. I wasn't thinking."

Lewis was conscious of the fact that they were both tired from last night's stakeout and he knew that this could affect their judgment. Acting hastily could cost them their lives. Proceeding slowly, methodically and with purpose was the only way to ensure their safety.

"Don't open or touch anything without me looking at it first," the wary officer instructed. "Doors, cabinets, drawers, anything that has hinges could be rigged to explode."

Rubenstein advised his friend that his security alarms looked normal. There were no signs of tampering, intrusion, or activation. The wise doctor trusted his friend's experience, however, and conceded that Lewis was the expert regarding these matters and not himself.

Decker's instincts kept telling him that something wasn't right. He was certain that they would be entering a death trap if they tried to unlock any of the mansion's doors or windows. Experts in espionage were capable of foiling the most elaborate security systems known to exist. He needed to find another means to gain access to the house, but how?

"Have you got a step ladder around here?"

The sleepy-eyed doctor rubbed his forehead and thought for a few seconds. "Yes, we've got one inside the pump house."

When the men rounded the corner of the mansion, the tired, absentminded doctor remembered the secret passageway leading to the house. It had been several months since he'd used it, and he almost forgot it existed.

"Hey, there's another way inside."

Fortunately, there were no curtains hanging on the windows of the utility-room. With ease, the officer was able to peek inside and look at the door without endangering himself. Decker's eyes scanned in all directions looking for suspicious wires, dynamite, plastic explosives or anything else that could be attached to the entryway. Satisfied that no risks existed, he slowly made his way toward the door and turned the knob. Once inside, Rubenstein showed him the concealed entryway leading to the underground corridor.

Lewis opened the hatch and signaled for the physician to disarm the security alarm. A cool, refreshing draft blew into the men's faces as they descended into the darkened tunnel. With mini-flashlight in hand, the husky man led the way, ever mindful of tripwires and killing devices. When they reached a solid looking panel, Rubenstein showed the detective how to unlock the rotating bookcase leading into Chester's room. Marsha's coffin partially obstructed the entry, so they stepped around before proceeding.

"Stay behind, while I check this room out," Lewis ordered. "There's no telling what we're going to find."

Decker walked over to Watkins' coffin to inspect it. The savvy investigator took out his pocketknife and carefully slid it into the gap where the lid joined the lower section. "Just what I thought."

"What?" inquired the curious doctor. "I don't see anything."

"This thing is set with a hair-trigger detonator. It's rigged to blow."

Lewis advised his friend to stay back, because the slightest nudge could set it off. The big man went over to the bedroom door and carefully checked it from top to bottom before opening it. When they stepped into the hallway, Fabian made it a point to walk single file behind Decker. As they looked around, they could see that most of the windows and doors were wired with plastic explosives and detonators.

"Good thing we didn't try to come through the main foyer," Fabian mumbled.

The retired officer was impressed with the handiwork of his enemies and he knew that he couldn't let his guard down for a second. During his extensive career, he'd seen quite a few explosive devices, but he never encountered anything as elaborate as the setup that he saw that afternoon. The villains who pulled this job were experts in pyrotechnics and they definitely wanted the occupants of the mansion terminated.

"I've got a bad feeling," Lewis blurted out. "Let's gather all of the ingredients for the Solstice spell, get some blood for our vampires, and get the hell out of here."

"I'm with you," Fabian replied as he pointed in the direction they needed to go. "The research room is that way."

When they reached the laboratory, Lewis had to defuse another bomb that was attached inside of the refrigerator door. After clipping the suspect wires, he carefully opened the icebox and started handing the bags of blood to the doctor who packed them into some plastic garbage bags.

Looking like a Jewish Saint Nicholas, the white-haired man slung both bags over his shoulder and followed Decker back to Chester's room. Inside of the cauldron they found all of the ingredients the vampires had collected for the spell.

"How are we going to get that heavy thing out of here?" Rubenstein asked.

"Like this," Lewis grunted as he hoisted the metal pot with both hands, cradling it next to his stomach. "Follow me."

The big man waddled duck-footed toward the secret bookcase and set the pot down when he reached the obscure opening. After exhaling a sigh of relief, the investigator carefully opened the door. He ordered the doctor to go inside and close the case behind them. Stepping around Marsha's coffin proved to be a difficult task for both of the men because of the unruly loads each were toting. Once they cleared the obstacle, things went a little smoother. When they reached the midway point, they set their goods down and paused momentarily to take a break.

"Ten years ago, this would have been a cake walk," Decker mentioned, implying he was getting older. "When I was in my 40s, I could have carried this cast iron pot all the way to downtown Houston."

"I know what you mean," the out of breath physician responded. "If we could just tap into the vampires' secrets of immortality and find out how to defeat their weakness to sunlight, we'd have it made."

After the men emerged from the tunnel, Lewis set the black

cauldron down and unsnapped his revolver's holster with his right hand. After withdrawing his sidearm, he peered out of the pump house window to check for danger. His instincts were strong and his gut was telling him that the house was possibly bugged with high-tech listening devices. The seasoned officer was certain that a contract killer was on the way to dispatch any unsuspecting intruders. He whispered to the doctor telling him to get ready for some action.

Within seconds, Decker's instincts proved true. He spotted a man dressed in a utility worker's uniform creeping around the corner of the house, armed with a 9 mm semi-automatic pistol with a silencer attached to the barrel. Hiding in the shadows of the outbuilding, Lewis pointed the assassin out to the surprised doctor.

Keeping his voice down, the husky officer turned and whispered to Fabian a second time. "Do any of the kids in this neighborhood set firecrackers off?"

"All the time, Why do you want to know?"

"I'm fixing to cap this dude, and I don't want to draw any attention, that's why. Hopefully I can take him out with a single shot."

When the hit-man turned his back to peek inside one of the windows of the mansion, this was the opportunity Decker was waiting for. Knowing that he only needed a few inches of clearance, he quietly cracked the pump house door just enough to stick his .38 special's muzzle out of the opening. The sneaky cop wedged his hand against the door jam, assuring a solid rest. Drawing a deep breath, he took aim for the center of the man's back. Fighting the adrenaline rush and steadying his nerves took a considerable amount of self-discipline. Decker's heart fluttered inside of his chest, because he knew that he had to make this bullet count. If he missed, he was certain the assassin would return fire and things would get nasty.

The big man hated being in this position. It was one thing shooting targets at the pistol range, but another feeling altogether when you were forced to take a human being's life.

Inside of the cramped utility room, the blast was almost deafening as the revolver rang out. Fortunately, most of the noise was confined inside of the little room. With ringing ears, Fabian raised his head, and looked outside of the window. He saw the lifeless body of the hit-man lying motionless in the grass next to the brick wall. He turned and glanced at Decker and noticed the remorseful look in his eyes.

"Are you all right?"

"It's never easy. I don't care how many times I've done it," Lewis replied, as he stood up. "It was either him or us."

"Better him," Rubenstein added. "Now, what's next?"

Being cautious of a secondary assailant, the veteran quickly regained his composure and reassessed the situation. He knew if another individual was dispatched to kill them, he'd be on the scene within minutes. Lewis ordered the doctor to cover him as he sprinted to the side of the mansion to investigate. Seven minutes passed as he cautiously roamed the perimeter of the mansion looking for troublemakers. When he was confident that they were completely alone, he returned to the utility house and told Fabian that they had another problem to contend with. How were they going to dispose of the dead body?

"That's what coffins are made for," the frizzy-headed scientist said with an impassive expression. "We'll stick his sorry, no good carcass inside of Marsha's casket."

The secluded backyard, with its high fences bordering the swimming pool, afforded absolute privacy from the outside world as the men went about their business. Before moving the body, Decker retrieved the assassin's pistol and stuck it in his belt. Working as a team, the two men moved the corpse with impunity into the pump house.

"Boy, are we getting a workout today," the panting doctor sighed.

As they were dragging the limp body through the tunnel,

Fabian apologized to Lewis for sounding like an emotionless grump. He explained to his friend that he didn't want his feelings to interfere with everything that was happening, because he might not be able to cope with all the stress.

"I understand," Decker replied. "There's no need to say you're sorry."

Before placing the dead man's body inside of the teenager's casket, Fabian removed the pink, cuddly teddy bear that he found laying next to her pillow. Seeing the fuzzy object reminded him that she was still vulnerable because of her adolescence. Conflicting thoughts entered his mind as he tucked the little bear under his arm for safekeeping. He knew she'd be happy to see her stuffed animal again, but at the same time he worried for her safety because their enemies were such ruthless murderers.

Placing the hit man's corpse inside of the coffin was easy work for the two men. Standing on opposite ends and grabbing hold of his flopping arms and legs, they flung him inside like a rubbery mannequin. As soon as they finished, they slammed the lid shut and returned to the utility room.

Only 25 minutes elapsed since the shooting and Lewis was satisfied that they were making good time. Before loading their goods into the Suburban, the investigator checked the vehicle to ensure that the assassin hadn't planted any bugs, or explosives to its frame. The husky man could see the fatigued look on the doctor's face and he asked him if it would be all right if he drove home.

"Certainly," replied the physician. "I'm worn out."

When they left the estate, Fabian gave Decker a hand-full of quarters, and told him to turn right on Clay Road. "Take the toll-way, it's faster."

During the trip back to Cold Springs, the men hardly spoke. The doctor dozed off a couple of times and when they reached the Farm Road exit, he suggested to Lewis that they take the rest of the evening off. The big guy agreed because he knew that he was pushing himself to the limit.

Later that evening after the vampires revived, they found the worn out doctor sleeping on the couch cradling Marsha's teddy bear in his arms.

"Look how cute he looks," Patricia said as she gently caressed her husband's frizzy, white head.

When Chester opened the refrigerator door, he saw that it was packed with fresh blood. The ice chest sitting next to it was also full of red bags. The old vampire was grateful that he had friends like this whom he could count on when times were bad. He hadn't experienced this type of camaraderie since his tenure in the Marine Corps.

Watkins sat down at the kitchen table and noticed the unloaded 9 mm pistol that was lying next to the sugar bowl. The slide was locked to the rear and the high capacity magazine was laying next to the weapon. The silencer attached to the barrel intrigued the curious Marine, so he picked it up to examine it. He wondered how the strange weapon got there because he'd never seen it before in Fabian's collection.

Patricia and Marsha came into the kitchen and when they saw Chester they asked him where he got the fancy pistol.

"I found it here on the kitchen table," he replied, laying it back down next to the salt and pepper shakers.

"We've got good news," the bright-eyed, teen-aged vampire said bearing a white-fanged smile from ear to ear. "They brought back the cauldron with all of our special ingredients."

"Great," replied Chester as he stood up and pushed the chair back under the table. "All we need to do now is mark the date on our calendar."

The slender girl grabbed a pencil from the table, walked over to the calendar hanging on the wall, and turned the page to the month of December. While everyone was staring at her, she scribbled the note "Solstice" inside of the box dated December 22.

"Is that the correct date?"

"Yes," they answered, nodding their heads in agreement.

In the northern hemisphere, the Winter Solstice marks the longest night of the calendar year when the sun looms at its farthest point in the southern sky. During this particular phase, vampires living north of the equator enjoy extraordinary powers. The declination of the sun is often referred to as the Tropic of Capricorn. The farther north an immortal lives, the more powerful they become, but the effects are only temporary. When the Summer Solstice occurs and the days are longer in duration, physical capabilities are minimized.

Taking all of these facts into consideration, Chester surmised that he would be facing Vladimir on Christmas Eve, a day that he dreaded the most, because of all the painful memories associated with it.

While the vampires were nonchalantly discussing the weather in the other room, Fabian started moaning and crying out in his sleep.

"No, you can't have the teddy bear!" he shouted as he swung his fist into the air fighting off an imaginary villain. The struggling doctor took defensive measures and turned on his side, pinning the bear underneath himself. "I'll kill you if you touch it."

The three vampires came into the front room to investigate and when they saw the animated-looking man tossing and turning, they realized he was dreaming.

"Fabian must have had a rough day," his sophisticated wife deduced. "He used to do this whenever he lost a patient on the operating table. Let him sleep it off, and he'll be OK tomorrow."

Trying to be considerate, Watkins put his index finger to his mouth and motioned for them to go outside with his other hand. Marsha led the way, opening the front door as the elders followed her outside. The chilly night air was refreshing, and the stars were glistening. The blissful setting washed away all of the negative thoughts that were lingering in their minds.

"It's beautiful tonight" Patricia said, looking up to the heavens. "I'm grateful to be alive."

"I agree," Watkins responded. "Let's sit a spell."

The rickety aluminum lawn chairs that the vampires sat down on squeaked every time one of them moved or tried to adjust their positions. Squirming about, the rambunctious teenager asked a pivotal question. She wanted to know if they believed in life after death.

"Yes, I do," Chester stated. "All of us died, and now we're alive because we've turned into vampires."

Shaking her head back and forth, the wide-eyed youngster tried to reconfigure her question. "Do you believe in heaven or hell?"

"I sure do," Watkins answered with a gummy smile. "We sure gave those Japs hell in the Pacific. When we got back to Hawaii, it was heaven to drink a cold beer and dance with the foxy dolls in the enlisted men's club."

Patricia started laughing when she realized what Watkins was doing.

"Can we be serious?" the frustrated girl asked. "Do you believe there's more to life than all of this?"

Taking a serious posture, the old man leaned back in his creaky chair and responded in wisdom. "Can your finite mind fathom eons of eternity? Life is a continuum and so time. There is no beginning or end. When this world ceases to exist, another one takes its place. The law of opposites is also an absolute. You have good, evil, right and wrong. There's also a physical world and a spiritual realm. A sun to govern the day and a moon to rule the night. Leaders, followers, and people who care, and others who don't. Yes, there's more to life than we'll ever be able to understand, but somehow we all fit in somewhere."

When Chester finished speaking, Marsha looked at him with her mouth hanging open and said, "Wow, I didn't know all of that was bottled up inside of you. Leaning over to kiss the gray-headed man, she added, “You sure have a way of making someone think.”

“The only thing that matters in life is the truth,” Patricia interjected, “Misguided souls will never be enlightened because of preconceived ideas. Fools hate being wrong, so they tune out what’s right. A closed minded know-it-all can never learn anything, because they believe they have all of the answers. Touchy subjects like politics, religion, and science are what make the world go around, yet some people refuse to discuss these topics. Intellectual strength should be our number-one priority in life. Knowledge comes with a price.”

“And what’s the cost?” queried the slender girl. ’What should I do?”

“Sacrifice— invest your time, and study everything you can get your hands on. Keep an open mind, admit when you’re wrong, and always listen to another person’s point of view.”

“That makes sense. I’ll try to do that.”

Acting philosophical, Watkins expounded on his theories of love. “When the United States went to war against the Axis powers, they did it because they were drawn into the conflict intentionally. The Germans and Japanese knew that we were secretly supplying weapons to their enemies and Japan plotted to attack us at Pearl Harbor. Many of us who fought for our country in those days sacrificed our lives because we loved our families and ultimately our country. Love drives us to do extraordinary things. I’m going to fight the satanic vampire because of the love I have for my friends. If I’m successful, we might be able to live in peace. If I fail, then it’s going to be up to someone else to set things right.”

Like an absorbent sponge, the teenager drew strength from her elder’s wisdom. She hoped that someday she could measure up to their standards and be in a position to give advice to those who were less fortunate than herself. Marsha’s respect and admiration for her eternal family exceeded the former relationship that she had with her biological parents. Although she still cared for them, and loved them dearly, she knew they were narrow-minded and set in their ways. According to Watkins, people like that never achieve much in life.

While the vampires in East Texas were discussing politics and religion, the wicked Vladimir, who was still hanging out in Northwest Arkansas, decided he wanted to feast on a living meal that night. He despised drinking from a chalice all of the time and in his opinion, some of the Red Cross blood they had in storage was tainted. Warm meals taken directly from living human beings always tasted better, especially when he had the discretion of selecting one.

The immortal's mouth started salivating as he thought about the little nursing home located in Bentonville that he planned on raiding. A superb strategist, the wicked creature concocted a sinister plan. He would select two convalescent residents, slowly feast on them and take special precautions not to kill them immediately. By alternating victims, he could return on consecutive nights to enjoy himself. Patients who suffered from retardation, senile dementia, or Alzheimer's disease would be perfect candidates for his immoral plan. By chance, if one of them remembered anything, it would be attributed to delusions. None of the nursing staff would take them seriously or believe their vain ramblings.

Shortly after arriving, the creepy vampire snuck around the building a couple of times, being careful to stay hidden in the shadows. The neatly pruned bushes that surrounded the brick-covered, long-term care facility offered perfect cover as he quietly tiptoed around each wing. Dressed in a black ninja-suit with a matching hood, the demented Russian looked like a prancing cat burglar. His head darted back and forth as he peered through the windows trying to select helpless patients.

Gaining entrance into the building would be easy work for the experienced crook because he'd burglarized hundreds of places in the past. With lock-picks in hand, he worked like a professional and within a couple of seconds he easily breached the West-wing door.

Once inside, he sprinted to the mop closet and hid himself

behind a rack of towels. When all of the nurses finished their hourly rounds, he slowly opened the door and stuck his head out to investigate. Confident that the staff was attending to patients in the next wing, he made his way into one of the rooms he'd selected.

When he entered the dimly lit quarters, he saw a little old lady sitting in a wheelchair watching late night television. She was rocking from side to side and babbling incoherently to herself.

"Is that you George?" the white-haired woman blurted out when she spotted the approaching dark figure.

Thinking up a lie as quickly as he could, the deceptive creature replied, "Yes, dear, it's me."

Acting disgruntled, the patient's eyebrows slanted down and her shriveled face turned red. In a blind-rage, she quickly snatched the nasty bedpan that was lying at the foot of her bed and flung it in the direction of the advancing vampire. Before he could duck out of the way, the filthy little toilet smashed into the side of his face, halting his forward momentum. The seemingly helpless woman became increasingly violent as she lashed out at what she believed to be her deceased husband. "George, you rotten bastard, why in the world did you put me in this god-forsaken nursing home?"

With feces dribbling down his neck, Vladimir growled as he used both hands to wipe the nasty mess off of his hooded head. When he looked back up, he saw the cantankerous woman picking up a lamp from her nightstand and preparing to hurl it. Jumping backwards, the man dodged out of the way just in time to see the porcelain object smash into the wall.

"Hey, wait a minute lady, I'm not George."

Ceasing her attack momentarily, the confused lady asked, "Who the hell are you then, you lying dog?"

"I'm the janitor."

"I hate the cleaning people around here. They're always going through my drawers and taking things that don't belong to them."

The vicious woman leaned over and picked up the cane that was lying next to her dresser. Like an African rhinoceros on wheels, she steered her chair in the direction of the disoriented intruder and hooked him between the legs with her heavy walking stick.

Doubling over and clutching his testicles with both hands, the Russian shrieked like a soprano singer. “Stop hitting me, you crazy bitch.”

With a stabbing motion, the woman began thrusting the cane against his abdomen as she reached for the emergency buzzer that was lying in her lap. “You’re the one who’s been sniffing my panties, and stealing my bras. I’m calling the nurses.”

Ripping the electrical cord out of the wall and bearing his fangs, the powerful vampire slapped the lady with a backhanded blow, knocking her out of the motorized chair and onto the floor.

“Enough of your antics,” he snarled while removing his facemask. “It’s dinner time.”

Gasping and wheezing, the dizzy-headed patient fainted when Vladimir clamped down on her throat with his sharp fangs. The psychotically deranged carnivore fed with the ferocity of a starving wolf. When he realized that his prey was at the brink of death, he ceased his gluttonous frenzy and licked his lips. Gathering the woman up, he placed her unconscious body back into the hospital bed.

After tucking her in, he whispered, “Good night, you mean old hag. I’ll see you tomorrow evening.”

The menacing creature walked into the bathroom, stuck his soiled mask in the sink, grabbed a bar of soap, and washed the slimy mess off. With a scowl on his face, he squinted his eyes, hissed and placed the stinky hood back over his head.

“These feeble senior citizens aren’t as defenseless as they look,” he thought. *“Next time I’ll be more aggressive.”*

Before opening the door, the pretentious vampire stuck his ear to the cool, wooden surface and listened for suspicious sounds. Confident that the coast was clear, he peeked across the hall at the second room he'd selected. In a mad dash, he crossed the passageway and entered without being noticed.

Tied to her bedrails, the drooling vampire observed his next victim trying to free herself from a pair of leather restraints. "Doctor, can you please loosen these straps? They're cutting off my circulation."

Refusing to take any more chances, the master of deceitfulness rushed to her bedside and cinched the buckles as tightly as he could while placing his hand over her mouth. The struggling woman tried gumming at his hand and the tickling sensations caused the Russian to quietly laugh.

"Stop tickling me, I need to check your pulse," he whispered while placing his fingers next to her pulsating carotid artery. "Now, hold still."

Vladimir's feeding session proceeded quickly because he'd already indulged himself in the first room. The adrenalin rush from fighting with the tough old lady caused him to drink more than he'd initially planned.

Removing his blood-soaked mouth, the glutton belched, squinted his eyes and farted. As he glared at his second victim, another idea came to mind. Before leaving, the mischievous man removed the patient's restraints in hopes that she'd wander off and be blamed for the nasty mess the nurses were going to find across the hall.

Reciting the bat incantation under his breath while simultaneously opening the window, Vladimir flew through the crack to escape. Monitoring his retreat, the distracted creature crashed into an electrical bug-zapper that was hanging under the eaves of the building. As he fought to disentangle himself, the power surge caused all of the lights to flicker inside of the nursing home. When he finally broke loose, the breakers tripped blacking everything out.

Back in Texas, Chester and his friends were getting hungry themselves. Content with drinking their meals from a glass, they went inside and prepared their cups. When they finished, they returned to the porch and toasted together. Searching the starlit sky as he tipped his glass, Watkins looked for the celestial object that everyone was anticipating.

The vampires chatted into the wee hours of the morning and speculated on things to come. In his spirit, Chester sensed a strange atmosphere in the air, but he couldn't put his finger on it. Somehow, he knew things were about to change. He wondered where these strange premonitions were coming from, so he decided to search for his answers in the, *"Wisdom of the Dead."*

CHAPTER 16, LORD OF TYRANTS

Germantown was a nice urban community located on the outskirts of Memphis, Tennessee. Vampire dignitaries who traveled to the East Coast were afforded the leisure of stopping for a day's rest at a wonderful safe-haven located there. The proprietors who managed this facility were members of the medical community and their lavish estate had the capabilities of accommodating 10 immortals. The doctors were generational servants and their families had faithfully served Count Marius since the reconstruction days following the Civil War.

It was business as usual for the noble Count as he discussed investment strategies and complemented his hosts for their wonderful hospitality. Marius was accompanied by two cabinet members who served in the dynasty for nearly 300 years. These entrusted politicians played a vital role in helping him make decisions. Whenever there was a disagreement, they always found a suitable compromise to the benefit of everyone involved.

Four bodyguards were constantly on staff at the gated mansion and their rotating presence was a deterrent to thieves and the criminally minded who were interested in penetrating the fortress-like walls.

The security personnel had never encountered any problems, and over the course of time they grew complacent in their duties. After the dayshift relieved their counterparts, they settled in for another routine day, or so they thought.

It was Sunday and two of the guards were searching through the sports section of the newspaper in hopes of finding an exciting football game. At 8 a.m., an ambulance drove to the security gate and activated the intercom. "We've got some important supplies," a voice squelched through the speakers.

The subordinate guard turned to his supervisor and inquired if they were scheduled for any deliveries. Thumbing through the pages of his log book, the captain answered, "I'm not sure. They must have forgotten to tell us. Go ahead and let them in."

The red and white vehicle drove through the electrically activated gates and proceeded to the back of the building. When it rounded the corner, the garage doors were already opening. The van slowly backed inside the building and was greeted by the two officers who were armed with revolvers. The ambulance parked in the delivery slot and when the employees opened the back doors, they were ambushed by masked gunmen packing submachine guns.

"Oh, my God!" one of the guys screamed, as he unsnapped his holster and drew his weapon.

Two rapid bursts of automatic gunfire made quick work of the ill-equipped officers. Their bleeding, bullet-riddled bodies quivered in death-gripped spasms as they floundered like fish on the icy cement floor.

Dressed in black fatigues with matching combat boots, the six gunmen jumped from the van's doors and began their murderous rampage of terror. The tinkling noises of ejecting cartridge cases being littered throughout the estate were mixed with the muffled rat-a-tat sounds of suppressed blasts. When the assassins were finished with their merciless house-clearing project, the trio of sleeping vampires were the only one's left alive.

At the predetermined time of 8:15, a moving van containing the garlic-laced coffins arrived at the estate's gates. Within seconds, the iron doors swung open and the rented vehicle drove straight to the back. The two warlocks sitting in the cab were laughing at the thought of placing the sleeping Count and his associates inside the boxes filled with allergens. "I can't wait to hear their voices when they wake up and discover the nasty surprise that we've prepared for them."

"Me either," snickered the driver with a devious-grin.

The special caskets were thicker than ordinary models and each one had padlocks and chains wrapped around the exteriors to prevent the immortals from escaping. Transferring the hibernating creatures went a lot quicker than the ecstatic coven members had calculated. Twenty-three minutes elapsed before the vehicles left the property. When the wicked caravan was approximately a mile away, an explosion and consuming fireball engulfed the mansion, destroying everything in its wake.

Because of the distances they were traveling, Miller knew that the trip would carry over into the late afternoon hours. A prearranged layover outside of Linden, Texas would be their first stop. A mini-storage unit located off of Highway 59 would be used to conceal the van for the night and the following morning the group would drive the final leg to Cold Springs.

As soon as the sun dipped below the horizon, the vampires started writhing like serpents tossed into a fiery-bed of coals. The garlic fumes were so repulsive that the immortals could hardly breath. Their agonizing cries were barely audible as they gasped for air. Like panting dogs, they feverishly clawed at their entombing lids.

The four-walled storage unit offered a degree of privacy from the outside world and suspicious ears. With a smirk on his face, Lucious walked around to the back of the truck, opened the door and checked on his prisoners. With his police flashlight in hand, he tapped on the sides of the caskets and taunted his hosts. "Stop all of that damn scratching in there, you sound like a bunch of flea-bitten varmints."

"Who are you?" the Count croaked with a gravelly voice. "Why have you taken us prisoner?"

"My friends call me Garlic-breath and my enemies know me as the vampire extortionist. Money makes the world go-round, and you're worth more than all the gold in Texas."

"Tell me what they're paying you and I'll double it. Name your price."

"I'll think about it," Miller responded in a patronizing tone. "Now shut up, before I change my mind and build a bonfire out of these coffins"

When the cult leader returned to the truck's cab, he grabbed his cell-phone and called the Russian to advise him of their success. "Mission accomplished, Master."

"Fantastic," Vladimir gleefully responded. "I'm proud of you. As a gesture of my appreciation, I'm going to let you sacrifice all three of the council members, but first you must prove yourself worthy by making them beg for mercy."

"Thank you, my Lord. I won't let you down."

"Think nothing of it my faithful servant. I have the utmost confidence in your abilities."

The twisted Satanists conversed for 15 minutes, discussing how they were going to extort the Count and his cabinet members out of their financial holdings before slowly torturing them to death. Trickery was one of the cornerstones of darkness according to the ancient book *"Abbadon's Priests."* Although Miller wasn't privy to this secret manuscript, he was a dedicated student of black magic. Having memorized most of the passages in the Satanic-Bible, the perverted man understood exactly what they were going to do to their captives. The love of money was indeed the root of all evil.

Every man for himself and never give anything unless you can receive something in return. Sincere practitioners of Satanism create their own reality through the manipulation of others. Miller lived by this credo.

According to Vladimir, if you want to become a god, then you must exercise superiority by torturing people. The more people you murder, the more powerful you become. Sacrificing the three immortals at the appointed time would be the crucial key to unlocking the gates of the underworld and unleashing the powers of hell. If Vladimir and his servants succeeded, then no one on Earth would be able to stand against them.

Unknown to Chester and his loyal entourage, when the coven finished their dirty work, they would be targeting them next. The witches were determined to accomplish their ultimate goal of placing Vladimir in his coveted position of power. Achieving global domination would be easy once the dynasty was reorganized. All resistance would be ferreted out and eradicated. His government would rule for a thousand years while his followers reaped the benefits of fame and fortune, or so they were led to believe.

The following morning, the devil worshippers drove the final leg to Cold Springs, while their helpless hostages slipped into unconsciousness. Spending 48 hours inside of a sealed coffin was torturous, especially for the undead who needed to use the restroom.

When the tormentors reached the secluded warehouse, they backed the ambulance and van inside of the double bay doors and quickly turned the ignitions off. The smoky exhaust caused a couple of the witches to cough as they exited their vehicles. The men were awestruck when they saw the stout cages resting on the cement deck. To ensure the immortals wouldn't transform into bats and escape, the prison cell bars were covered with thick wire mesh., and supercharged with 220 pulsating volts.

"These suckers aren't going anywhere." Miller barked as he motioned for his men to unload their cargo and transfer it to the cubicles. Echoes resounded through the partially empty building as the men worked. "When these creatures wake up, avoid eye contact with them. They might try to hypnotize you."

"Yes, sir," the Crusaders replied as they hoisted the heavy boxes out of the truck and began moving them down the loading ramp.

Everything was carefully orchestrated and planned out. Once the three caskets were in place, Miller ascended a stairwell and opened a sunroof on top of the building. Using a large mirror, he reflected the bright rays of sunlight in the direction of the cells. The group had traveled too far to take unnecessary chances. The warlocks worked feverishly to disengage the padlocks and chains that encircled the coffins. When they finished, the men stepped outside and bolted the metal doors shut. Waiting for the signal from Miller, one of the warlocks threw an electrical switch energizing the cages. A sizzling noise could be heard as power surged through the bars. In case of electrical failure, a backup generator was stationed outside of the building as added insurance.

Confident the immortals were trapped, Lucious closed the window and calmly walked down the stairs. "I can't wait to see the expressions on their faces when they wake up."

"Are we going to feed them?" one of the sweating Satanists asked.

"We'll give them a small supplement," Miller jokingly responded. "Slaughter a pig and drain the blood into a bucket."

After the wicked group finished having a laugh, the coven leader told his cadre that arrangements had already been made to accommodate their prisoners' eccentric habits. A chest-freezer in the corner of the warehouse contained enough blood to sustain them during their confinement. Lucious emphasized the fact that food depravation was one of the torture methods they were going to employ to extort information. "When we're finished with these chumps, they'll tell us anything we want."

At dusk, all three coffin lids sprang open and the vampires erupted like jack-in-the-boxes. "Ugh!" they groaned, coughing and spitting.

Sitting in an office chair behind a small desk in front of the three cages was Miller, who was eating a greasy hamburger and French fries.

"Where are we?" one of the scratchy throat immortals grunted. "Why are you holding us?"

With his mouth stuffed full of food, Lucious introduced himself. "Howdy, fellows, I'm your concierge. I bet you guys are hungry." The cocky warlock leaned back in his leather seat, propped his feet up and looked down at the floor as he waited for a reply.

Hissing with phlegm in his throat, Count Marius rebuked his

captors. "I'll rip your throat out and feed your carcass to the vultures if you don't release us immediately!"

"Tough talk from a baboon trapped in a cage," the defiant warlock chuckled as he interlaced his fingers together and popped his knuckles. "But first, you might want to check those bars. I think you'll be SHOCKED when you find out what we did."

The Romanian leaned forward, extended his hand and touched the metal bars with the tips of his fingers. Like a venomous snakebite, a sizzling jolt shot through his hand, causing him to jerk backwards. Standing there like a rigid-looking statue, the Count gritted his teeth and made a fist.

"See the wire mesh? If you're thinking about flying off, it's charged too. You better kick back and relax because you're here for the long haul. Who knows, maybe we'll start a dialogue and become better acquainted."

"You arrogant fool. My vice chancellor and the Dynasty of Immortals will serve your head to me on a golden platter when they find out what you've done."

Acting like a television game show host, Miller pretended to make a consolation buzzer sound. "AAAAAANT, wrong answer snaggle fangs."

The Count shrugged his shoulders, turned and looked at his caged companions who appeared just as bewildered as he was. "What do you mean by this?"

"You stupid idiots, you'll find out soon enough."

"We demand answers now."

"People in cages don't make demands, now shut up."

Lucious slid his heels across the tabletop. The rubber bottoms of his cowboy boots made a screeching noise as he pulled his legs back and removed his feet from the desk. When he stood up, he stretched his arms and belched. "Yep, dinner was sure good. I bet you dudes could use a bite yourselves. Did you hear the black-market price of blood just went up to $5,000 a pint? Yes, I'm an investor of sorts and I've got a small stockpile in that icebox over there in the corner. I'm willing to wager— after a couple of dry nights, you and your stuck-up buddies will begin seeing things from a totally different perspective."

The hostages exchanged glances as they tried to hide their hunger pains.

"Think of me as a bartender," the wicked deputy said choking back laughter. "You guys are going to rack up the biggest bar tab in history."

When the Count reached into his back pocket to retrieve his wallet, Lucious spoke up again. "We had to frisk you guys. Are you looking for these?" The warlock opened the top drawer of his little desk, pulled out three leather billfolds and held them up. Each wallet was bulging with greenbacks and credit cards.

Scolding his tormentor, Marius lunged at the bars, "You're nothing but a petty thief!"

"Hey, man, I had to charge you guys room and board. Those cages are expensive, top of the line. Plus, I work for tips."

The glaring captives began hissing as they saw the crook rummaging through their personal belongings.

Sporting a devious smile, the slick deputy pulled all of the money and plastic debit cards out of the vampires' wallets and shoved them into his pockets. When he was finished, he tossed the empty objects into the trash pail next to his desk. "You won't be needing these anymore."

The dim florescent lights inside the warehouse blinked intermittently from the surging electricity that was circulating through the cells. "Look at those flashing bulbs. They remind me of a Disco-hall. Now, I'm warning you spooks to be on your best behavior while I'm gone. Please enjoy your stay at this luxurious hotel. I'll put the do-not-disturb sign on the door."

"What about bathroom accommodations? We haven't gone in two days."

"Piss in your coffins, we don't care— but please don't urinate through the bars, because you know what that'll do."

"Wait a minute. Aren't you going to feed us?" inquired the Romanian with a cracking voice.

"Nope, because you didn't remember your manners. I'm a very sensitive man. I want you to think about all of the rude things you said to me and, if you work up a good apology, we might just open up that icebox."

Pretending to be meek, the hoarse chancellor spoke up again. "Please forgive us. Maybe a proper introduction is in store. I am Count Marius, to my right is Count Rufus and to my left is Prince Vitas."

"Now, that's a lot better," the unsympathetic warlock replied as he slowly strolled to the front door. "Just hold those thoughts until tomorrow evening and maybe we'll get somewhere."

Standing outside of the building were two cult members who eagerly awaited for Miller to fill them in. The coven leader gave explicit orders, telling his men to stay put and monitor the vampires' conversations through the bugging devices he'd planted in the walls. He handed the men electronic headphones and ordered them to take notes and record everything they heard.

Patting his pals on the back, Lucious congratulated them for everything they'd done. "I'll check back with you guys tomorrow morning. Keep up the good work."

Back at the council hall in northwest Arkansas, Vladimir was calling an emergency session of the Dynasty of Immortals to order. Everyone noticed that the vice chancellor was dressed in one of his flashiest outfits. Like a barnyard rooster, he strutted to the podium to address the audience.

"Count Marius, Rufus and Prince Vitas will be in Europe for several months as special envoys representing the superlative interests of our highly esteemed organization. They've entrusted me with the honorable position of interim chancellor until they return. As a precautionary measure against dissidents who might be conspiring with the Crusaders of Light, our ruling king has advised me to place everyone on restriction until he returns. Yes— I've been informed there are traitors in our ranks. All immortals will be confined to the premises until further notice. Thank you and good evening."

While the Russian was leaving the stage, Destiny, who was sitting in the back, looked at Nakata. When their eyes met, their souls connected. Like a lethargic reptile, the wise Sensei nodded his head so slowly that no one noticed except for the blue-eyed girl.

Late that night, the loyal vampires met privately in Katsumi's dojo to discuss what they feared was happening. "Did anyone see you enter?" Nakata quietly asked.

"No," whispered Destiny, "but we better make it brief."

The instructor spoke candidly with the beautiful woman and told her that he knew in his heart Marius and the other vampires would never return. His intuition told him the cunning Russian was telling a lie and he couldn't be trusted. Over the centuries, he'd seen the same thing happen in different countries, including Japan. He recalled how the Emperor became so powerful and arrogant that he made himself a god. When this happened, his political opposition started disappearing.

"How do we survive?"

"We play along until we can figure out what's happening. We wait, watch and see what our instincts tell us to do."

"Do you think anyone else can be trusted?"

"Only time will tell," the humble man answered as he leaned forward and kissed the sweet vampire on her forehead "Be silent and patient my child. Our enemies will reveal themselves and so shall our allies."

When Destiny left the dojo, she was met in the corridor by Vladimir and the pompous Lloyd Buckles, who was accompanying him. The pair joined arms and blocked the beautiful woman's path as she tried to slip past them. "What were you doing in there with that chink?" the Russian sternly inquired. "Were you learning how to do the splits?"

Before the startled girl could answer, Katsumi stepped into the hallway, closed the door behind him and locked it. The quick-witted man's perception was unparalleled as he pretended to thank Destiny for helping him straighten up the gymnasium and organize the laundry. In his next breath, he feigned a promise of teaching her martial arts and meditation techniques.

The tyrannical Russian sneered at the innocent-looking girl until she began to tremble. "I forgot to mention to everyone at the meeting tonight— Count Marius ordered us to close the dojo until he returns. He doesn't want our enemies conspiring against us."

The peppy Japanese man smiled, bowed and tossed Vladimir the keys to the martial arts room. "Yes, your excellency. I understand."

Clutching the key-ring in his left hand, the vice chancellor and his fiendish-looking friend turned and briskly walked away. When they were out of sight, Destiny looked at her dark-haired comrade with tears in her eyes. "I'm so sorry."

Katsumi smiled and replied with a soothingly kind voice, "Karate is in the heart, mind and soul. This is one of Vladimir's weaknesses. He fails to comprehend this mystery. I will still be practicing, but not in the confines of a physical room."

Exchanging smiles, the two walked their separate ways and returned to their quarters. Destiny thought about the words of wisdom the Sensei told her. She made a mental note of the powerful-looking vampire who joined ranks with Vladimir. It was apparent that Buckles was jockeying for position also.

The nights that followed were filled with additional restrictions imposed by the crafty Russian and his satanic vampire supporters. All of the blame was cunningly shifted to the deposed Count and his righteous cabinet members who were being held hostage in Texas. The wizard-of-deception was creating an atmosphere of dissention against the former ruler, while pretending to carry out his orders. One of Vladimir's prime objectives was to see the mansion filled with bickering, and gossip. By creating this kind of culture, he could easily manipulate the angry hoards by restoring a certain degree of freedoms in the future.

CHAPTER 17, DEVIL'S DEATH SQUAD

December 7 was the anniversary of the Japanese sneak attack of Pearl Harbor, a day forever etched in the Marine's mind. When he revived that evening, his thoughts caused him to travel back in time. He remembered exactly where he was that fateful day when he heard the breaking news. His next-door neighbors lost their only son who was an Ensign aboard the USS. Arizona.

Chester had a strange feeling and sensed that something was terribly wrong. *"Maybe I'm being superstitious,"* he thought. The vampire eased out of his coffin and stuck his trusty Colt .45 in his belt. Crawling on his belly in the dirt underneath the cabin, he slowly made his way to the small opening leading into the bedroom. Marsha and Patricia were just waking up as he carefully removed the boards that concealed the entryway.

"Good evening, ladies. I trust you slept well."

"Like the dead," Patricia answered. "I think I've got termites inside of my coffin. Can you please check?"

"Me too," the teen-aged vampire added. "I can hear crunching sounds coming from both sides."

"Sure," replied Watkins as he reversed direction and crawled back toward them. "I'll take a look."

A quick inspection by the experienced handyman revealed substantial damage to both of the women's boxes. The sawdust-eating insects were steadily munching away while Watkins shook his head in disgust. "We'll have to remind Fabian to pick up some bug spray. If we don't, these insects will eat their way to China."

"I asked him to do that several weeks ago," Patricia complained. "I hope it's not too late."

Chester dusted the hungry termites off with his hands before crawling away. When the vampires came out from under the house, Patricia went straight into the kitchen and started scolding her forgetful husband. "You should see my bed, it's infested with nasty bugs!"

"What are you talking about?" the surprised doctor inquired as he was finishing up the dirty dishes in the sink.

"Remember when I asked you to spray under the house last month? Well, you didn't and my bed is full of termites."

"Oh, no," Fabian sighed. "I promise, I'll go to the feed store first thing in the morning and buy the strongest ingredients they sell."

Watkins butted in and told the doctor he didn't see any structural damage to the floor joists. He added that it wouldn't be long before the feisty bugs worked their way up. "In a couple of months, they'll chew their way into the walls."

After drinking their chalices of blood, the reenergized vampires went outside to join the lonesome physician who was sitting by himself on the porch swing. Patricia sat down beside him, apologized for her angry outburst and kissed the white-haired man on the cheek. "I love you, darling."

"I know," replied Fabian, "and I'm awful sorry about forgetting the bug spray. I've got so many things on my mind, it's hard to think straight."

"I didn't mean to snap at you like that," his wife replied, kissing him repeatedly with little pecks. "You're the best husband in the whole world and don't forget it."

While the lovers nestled together on the swing reconciling, Watkins noticed someone driving up the dirt road. As the vehicle approached, he recognized that it was Decker. After parking, the friendly neighbor got out and told everyone he had some very exciting news. Enthusiastically he pointed to the sky and proclaimed, "I can see Beelzebub's Comet."

"Where?" asked the surprised group of onlookers.

"With my telescope. You can't see it with the naked eye, but believe me, it's there."

The gray vampire jumped up from his chair and told Lewis that he wanted to come over to his house and take a look. Marsha asked if she could tag along because she'd never seen a real comet, except on television documentaries and in science books from school. "I want to see it, too."

"Sure," laughed Decker. "I think you'll be amazed when you see the bright tail."

Fabian winked at Chester as he put his arm around his wife's shoulders and casually said, "I think me and the little lady will catch up on some private time, if you know what I mean."

"Gotcha," the slick old vampire replied. "We'll hang out next door for a while."

Before leaving, Watkins suggested to Marsha that they bring the special ingredients with them that they'd gathered for the cloaking spell and lay them out in Decker's barn. Without hesitating, Lewis agreed, because he knew the appointed time was drawing closer. This strange potion might give them the edge they were looking for.

Decker assisted the vampires while they loaded everything into the dusty bed of his pickup. Working together, they placed the heavy cauldron next to the tailgate and Chester lashed it down tightly with some rope he found next to a sack of feed. When they finished, they climbed inside of the cab and drove away, never looking back at the lovebirds who were nestling on the swing.

When they reached the dark, blacktop, Lewis instinctively turned his head and checked both ways before crossing. The bumpy cattle guard on the other side of the road jolted the passengers as Lewis piloted the sluggish rig through the gate in the direction of his barn. The vampires could see the obscure figures of cows meandering in the hay meadow and grazing under the stars. Both of the sharp-eyed canines that Chester encountered weeks before seemed to come out of nowhere as they trotted alongside the truck. Without uttering a word, Decker smiled at his passengers as if to imply that his faithful sentries kept an eye on things while he was away.

"Don't worry, Marsha, they won't bite you if you don't make

any sudden moves."

The slender girl slowly opened the truck door and climbed out. The muscular Rottweilers stood poised to react to the potentially dangerous strangers. With bristly hair raised on the backs of their necks, one of the trained dogs snarled at the girl as she knelt down and attempted to befriend him. "Come on boy— good doggy."

To everyone's surprise, the stout animal approached the girl and sniffed the palm of her extended hand. Sensing her gentleness, the Rottweiler allowed her to scratch his backside as she tried to coax the other one to come closer. Within minutes, she was petting both dogs and it appeared to everyone that she was bonding with them.

The husky man shook his head. "I can't believe it. The last time someone tried that, Flavius bit him on the backside and Romulus chased him up a tree."

Marsha confided that she always wanted to work with animals. Before her death, she had aspirations of going to Texas A&M University and earning a degree in veterinary medicine.

Chester looked at the cute girl with admiration and a sad thought entered his mind. He wondered what would have become of such an ambitious person, had she been afforded the opportunity of living a normal life. Marriage, children and a meaningful career were just a few of the things that were stolen from her.

A light pole situated next to the barn illuminated the immediate area as the group stood and chatted for several more minutes. When they started unloading the ingredients from the truck, the dogs sniffed each item investigating the strange odors coming from the boxes.

A gentle breeze drifted through the open barn doors while Watkins inspected all of the contents. The pleasant aroma of freshly cut hay stacked in the loft reminded Chester of a feed store that he'd worked at while attending high school. Knowing they were going to need a fire in a couple of weeks to heat everything up, Chester glanced up at the tall ceiling and felt confident that there was plenty of clearance to safely perform the spell. He figured the cauldron would emit a considerable amount of heat and he didn't want to risk burning the place to the ground.

As soon as they finished their last-minute calculations, Lewis suggested to Watkins that they take a peek at the comet. Marsha eagerly agreed and followed the men to the back of the porch where the telescopes where located. Flavius and Romulus flanked the group on both sides as they casually strolled through the ankle-high grass in the direction of the wooden deck.

Pressing his eye to the ocular lens of the center telescope, Decker said, "Let me readjust everything because it's been a couple of hours since I checked the settings. The Earth has rotated a bit since then and I need to reacquire the comet."

When he found it, Lewis invited Marsha to take a look. He adjusted the two neighboring optical devices while carrying on a conversation with the fascinated astronomers. Chester stood behind the young girl sporting a gummy smile and when Decker finished focusing the second scope he invited the old vampire to take a look.

"Where's Orion 'The Hunter?'" Watkins asked.

"To the left of the comet," replied Lewis. "It looks like they'll intersect in a couple more weeks."

Before Chester could ask another question, a fast succession of gunfire erupted from across the road. The trio turned their heads in the direction of the thunderous noise and they intuitively knew that the doctors were fighting for their lives.

Decker and Watkins exchanged glances momentarily and it was evident that they were thinking the same thing. *"To charge in would be suicidal."*

"What do we do?" screamed Marsha, "They need us."

"I know," the gray Marine said as he pulled the trusty Colt .45 from his belt and racked the slide. "Decker, fetch your shotgun and stay here. Protect your family while Marsha and I slip through the woods to investigate."

Like Olympic sprinters, the immortals dashed across the field at a phenomenal speed. When they reached the barbed-wire fence bordering the farm road, Chester grabbed Marsha's shoulder and tugged, motioning for her to stop. The echoing gunfire dissipated into silence while the wise man collected his thoughts and came up with a plan.

"Recite the bat incantation," he whispered. "We'll glide in and check things out. Whatever you do, don't expose yourself to any danger. Follow my lead and don't let anyone see you."

The gray and black bats took flight together and ascended high into the air. As they flew in the direction of the heavily wooded thicket across the road, their eyes scanned for movement. Clearing the tops of the tall pine trees, Chester led the young girl in a swooping circle toward the cabin. As they descended and approached the night light that was mounted next to the storage shed, they could see Fabian's naked, bullet-riddled body laying face down in a pool of blood on the front porch. Clutched tightly in his hand was the stainless 686 Smith & Wesson .357 Magnum revolver. Both bats kept their momentum and soared into the shadowy woods behind the cabin.

After touching down and reversing their spells, Marsha collapsed into the old vampire's arms. With her face pressed tightly against Chester's chest. she whispered in a muffled voice, "He's dead, isn't he?"

"Yes, but at least he went down fighting."

The combat veteran ordered the teenager to stay hidden in the woods while he slipped in to investigate. With .45 pistol in hand, Chester quictly made his way to the side of the house. When he peered inside the kitchen window, he saw that the rollaway bed was pulled out and was positioned in the center of the front room. On top of the sheets, he saw a big, dusty pile of ashes with a splintery stake driven through the middle and embedded into the mattress. "*Patricia's vanquished remains,*" he surmised. A large, wooden mallet was lying on the floor and its broken handle was a testimonial to the violence that had occurred.

Proceeding with caution, Watkins squatted down, and looked around the side of the house before stepping up on the porch. When he reached the doctor's body, he noticed that he was wearing his kinky purple boots. *"At least he died like a real cowboy,"* Chester thought to himself as he removed his jacket and covered his friend's nude corpse.

As he knelt down, he could smell Fabian's favorite aftershave lotion. Watkins was certain that the couple was frolicking when they were caught off-guard. He gently removed the revolver from his friend's hand and opened the cylinder. All six rounds were spent as he examined the weapon. After tucking it in his belt, he continued looking around.

A quick inspection of the crime scene revealed several clues to the former policeman. Chester recognized that the perpetrators knew exactly what they were up against because of all the physical evidence. The only mistake they made was attacking while he and Marsha were away. As he studied the situation, another thought came to mind. *It was obvious that they didn't link their relationship to Decker. If they had, they would have tried to murder him also.*

Lack of additional vehicle tracks revealed to Watkins that the killers were nearby. *"They must have hiked through the National Forest on foot."* he pondered. When he realized this, his attention was turned to Marsha who was alone in the woods. In a flash, the agile vampire leaped from the porch and ran back into the shadows. When he reached the girl, she was crouched close to the pine tree where he ordered her to hide. To his surprise, she was armed with the trooper's pistol.

"Let's get out of here. The creeps who did this are still in the area."

"Is Patricia dead, too?"

The old man looked down at the ground, gummed his lip and

solemnly shook his head. "I'm afraid so."

"You're not going to let those bastards get away, are you?" the teary-eyed vampire contested. "Let's find them and make them pay for what they did."

"We'll take revenge, but on our terms— when the time is right."

Marsha was furious with the decision, but she realized she was acting irrationally, To be lured into a confrontation before the appointed time would be foolishness on their part. Chester's wisdom was the pivotal factor that rescued her from the streets and she'd gone too far to disregard his advice now. Fighting her emotions, she stomped her foot on the ground. "Damn-it you're right, Chester, let's get out of here."

When the bats flew off, they headed straight for Decker's farmhouse to relay the tragedy. After imparting the gruesome details, Lewis saw the situation for what it was. He realized it was only a matter of time until the Crusaders of Light linked his involvement with the Rubensteins. *My family could be next,* he feared.

"I'll understand if you want to back out," Chester said, "but I think it's too late."

"I'm going to see this thing through until the end," answered the husky guy. "I've got a score to settle."

Decker reminded the vampires that he knew exactly where one of the warlocks lived and he suggested that they pay this character a visit, capture him and make him talk.

"We might be acting prematurely," Watkins replied. "If we catch this dude, then we're going to have to snuff him. His friends are going to wonder who did it and why."

"Not if it's an accident." Marsha added. "Maybe we can make it look like a suicide."

"She's got an idea," Lewis answered as he placed his hand on the girl's arm. "It's time to do something. Let's beat a confession out of this guy. When we're finished, we'll stage his death."

"From the way everyone is talking, I'd be willing to wager that you two are proponents of assisted suicide."

"We are."

"I am."

After the group finished discussing possible scenarios, they went inside Decker's house and his wife introduced herself. "Hello, I'm Linda. My husband's told me all about you. Please forgive the way the living room looks. It's just an old, rundown farmhouse and keeping up with the dust is impossible."

Speaking softly, Chester replied, "Don't worry, madam, the place looks just fine."

Lewis explained to his wife that their neighbors had been murdered and the vampires were going to need a new place to hide out. The friendly lady suggested the immortals sleep in the root cellar because it was cool, dark and underground.

Decker made plans to return to the Rubenstein's cabin at daybreak, bury Fabian's body and retrieve the vampire's caskets. "I'll gather Patricia's ashes and sprinkle them inside of his grave. I think that's what they would have wanted."

"Yes," replied Watkins. "The two were inseparable in life, and now in death."

The Deckers knew the vampires were going to need something to eat and hopefully the murderous perpetrators hadn't sabotaged the blood supplies that were stored in the refrigerator.

Chester brought up the fact that the assassins attacked so quickly that they probably overlooked this crucial detail. "Their mission was to kill and vacate the premises as quickly as possible," the old man interjected. "Hit and move, we called it in the Marines."

Settling into the root cellar for the day seemed strange to the vampires who'd grown accustom to sleeping in their boxes under the house. Once they closed their eyes however, they didn't seem to care.

The morning sky was red and lowering as clouds loomed over the horizon. Lewis was careful to observe his surroundings as he drove across the farm road and made his way to the crime scene. The husky man took care of business in short order, burying the Rubensteins in a common grave. Before he left, he saw something that Chester had overlooked. A blood-trail leading away from the house and into the woods indicated that Fabian had wounded one of his attackers.

Nightfall in December comes quickly as the days grow shorter in length and winter closes in. Both vampires noticed a slight change in their energy levels that came with the changing of the seasons.

"Let's go catch our man," were the first words out of Chester's mouth when he revived that night.

"I can't wait," replied the wide-eyed, girl with a serious intensity in her face that Chester had never seen before. "It's payback time."

When the vampires came out of the underground storage shelter, they proceeded with caution before entering the farmhouse. Acting like it was a war zone, Chester wasn't taking any chances. Decker and his wife were sitting at the kitchen table sipping a cup of coffee when the vampires entered through the back door.

"Good evening," the gray vampire said as he greeted his new hosts. "Are we ready to take care of business tonight?"

Quick to answer, Lewis snapped back, "You bet."

Watkins pulled up a chair and sat down. "I've got a plan I think everyone is going to like— so hear me out."

Chester looked at Lewis and told him that he was going to use Fabian's Suburban to capture the warlock. Locating him would be the hardest part of the plot. Pretending to be senile, he was going to crash into the back of the man's car. "When he gets out to check the damage, I'll lower the boom. You and Marsha tie him up, gag him and load him into the back. I'll steal his vehicle because we're going to use it to finish him off. We'll return to Fabian's cabin and beat the truth out of him. When we're finished, we'll knock him out again and drive him to mommy's house. We'll leave his car running and slip a garden hose from the exhaust pipe into the backseat."

"Do you think it's safe to go back to the cabin?" interrupted the young vampire. "What if the killers come back?"

"I don't think they'll make the stupid mistake of returning two nights in a row. If they do, we'll be ready for them."

Decker agreed with the old man. "It's too risky for the witches to venture there again."

Watkins scratched his head. "Any thoughts where our friend might be tonight?"

Lewis suggested to Watkins that they drive to "The Feline Palace" and maybe they'd get lucky and find him there. Hopefully, he'd be intoxicated and apprehending him would be easy.

Two hours later, the unsuspecting man was in the vigilantes' custody. When he regained consciousness, he found himself hanging by his wrists in Fabian's storage shed. A single light bulb was positioned overhead and the eroding filament caused it to dim intermittently, making it hard for the man to identify his captors.

The former Marine smiled, showing his gums as he ripped the prisoner's flannel shirt from his chest and tossed it aside. "There's one advantage the Japanese had that you don't, you pitiful piss-ant. They were willing to die with honor for their cause, but you're nothing but a coward who lives with his mother."

All three of the interrogators noticed the bandaged wound on the man's left side and wondered if he was the perpetrator who Fabian shot the night before.

Disregarding the painful look on the man's face, Decker reached down and brutally yanked the taped gauze from his body.

"Just what I thought. Who shot you?"

"It was a hunting accident."

"Really?" answered Watkins in a sarcastic tone. "Were you hunting vampires and doctors?"

"I don't know what you're talking about."

The senior reached into his shirt pocket, pulled a fat cigar and lit it with his butane lighter. Marsha and Lewis looked at one another, wondering what he was going to do next. Chester continued to puff on his stogie until a glowing red ember was dangling off of the tip. When he removed the smoldering thing from his lips, he slowly guided it in the direction of the man's right nipple.

With bulging eyes, the bearded warlock screamed as he saw the fiery red tip just inches away from his chest. "Stop it! I was here last night, but I wasn't the one who shot your friends."

Chester turned his head and winked at Decker as he barked another question at the skinny man. "How many of you were there?"

Looking around, the man started hesitating and responding in a vague manner, "I didn't count, I don't know."

To everyone's surprise, Marsha snatched the smoky cigar from Chester's hand and planted the hot tip into the warlock's left ear. A sizzling sound, coupled with the man's screams, filled the cramped little building.

"You evil Satanist!" she hollered. "I'm going to rip your balls off and feed them to the rats if you don't tell us everything we want to hear."

"You heard the young lady," Watkins interjected as he reached into his trousers and handed Marsha his pocketknife. Stepping away, he motioned for Decker to follow him outside so the young girl could antagonize the man by herself. "She needs to release her anger. I guarantee you, she'll make him talk. This kind of stuff always worked in the Orient. She'll probably threaten to emasculate him again."

"Yep," replied Lewis. "In Southeast Asia, the Vietcong used tactics like this and it worked every time. Woman interrogators are the worst. They have a way of humiliating people psychologically."

The men closed the door behind them and listened intently as Marsha threatened to kill the warlock's mother. "I'm going to turn your mommy into a vampire."

"No," the redheaded man blurted out. "Please, don't do that. She's innocent."

Seeing that this topic obviously bothered the man, she played it for everything it was worth. "I was innocent once and no one gave a damn about my welfare. Are you familiar with the fairy tale about Pinocchio?"

"Yes," answered the man. "Why?"

"Remember what happened every time he told a lie, how his nose grew?"

"Yes."

The emotional girl slowly opened the pocketknife and placed it under the struggling man's nose until its razor-sharp edge drew blood. Without batting an eye, she hissed at her prisoner and said, "I'm going to ask you a question and if I don't believe your answer I'm going to whittle on your nose until I cut it off. After I'm done carving you to pieces, I'm heading straight to you mom's house and she's getting the same medicine."

"Who murdered my friends?"

"The coven did. We were ordered to."

"By who?"

"I can't tell you, he'll kill me."

Marsha's eyebrows slanted downward as she moved the sharp blade into one of the man's nostrils and with a flicking motion sliced it open, drawing blood.

"Vladimir," he screamed, closing his eyes and gritting his teeth in pain. "You're hurting me."

Hearing the name struck fear into the young vampire because she knew that this was the creature who killed her and caused her so much turmoil. Memories of her rape and murder flooded into her mind as she stood there in momentary silence. Concealing her emotions, the young girl pretended to be a lot tougher than she actually was. Proceeding with her next question, she asked, "Where's the next ritual going to take place?"

"In an abandoned warehouse."

"Tell us where it is."

When Chester heard the information that he was waiting for, he burst into the dimly lit room and cut the prisoner down. With a thud, the man fell face-first onto the floor. "Handcuff and gag him, Decker."

The husky guy placed his big knee in the center of the warlock's back and pinned him face down as he secured the cuffs and double-locked them. Jerking him to his feet, he warned the man to cooperate.

Guiding the prisoner from the rear, Lewis escorted him to the Suburban and shoved him into the back seat. Climbing in beside him, the big man pulled his snub-nosed revolver and brandished it next to the man's face, reminding him of who was in charge. When Marsha jumped in behind the driver's seat, she tossed the man's flannel shirt into the back so Decker could cover him up.

Driving the warlock's Toyota, Chester followed close behind as they traveled east. Before arriving at their destination, it became obvious the skinny thug was starting to balk on his promises and suddenly his directions became sketchy.

Lewis grabbed a handful of the man's red hair, jerked his head back, shoved the compact revolver into his mouth and cocked the hammer. "You're wasting our time. You better hope that she doesn't hit a bump because one jolt and this hair-trigger is fixing to go off."

When Decker withdrew the .38 special, the warlock knew the big man meant what he said. He began cooperating again and told them to turn around and go back to the farm road they passed.

"You just ran out of second chances. You better not be bullshitting. If this turns out to be another wild-goose-chase, I'll blow your brains out. When we get there— if there's no warehouse, you can kiss your ass goodbye."

Marsha checked her mirrors, made a quick U-turn and

wheeled the Suburban around. Chester followed suit, whipped the steering-wheel and accelerated quickly, trying to stay close behind.

"Turn right at the next road," the prisoner mumbled. "Then, you go another half mile until you see a dirt road on your left. The warehouse is back in the woods, you can't see it from the road."

"It better be there," Marsha added, "or the rats are having mountain oysters for dinner."

"I swear to God, I'm telling you the truth this time."

"You don't believe in God," the teen-aged vampire responded, "so you better swear on your mother's grave that you're telling the truth because after my friend shoots you, we're going to make the old lady pay for all of your sins."

"I promise you, I'm not lying."

"We'll see in just a minute," the agitated girl growled. "I wonder how your mother's blood is going to taste as I drain the life from her frail little body?"

Using her turn signal, Marsha exited the blacktop. Next to a National Forest sign was the dirt road that the warlock described. The tall Texas pines bordering the highway made it impossible to see more than a few yards into the woods. The vampire drove approximately a mile past the turnoff and pulled into the first secluded spot she could find, which happened to be an old abandoned Methodist church with graffiti spray painted all over the sides of the peeling, whitewashed walls. Every window in the antiquated building appeared to be broken and the shiny cross on top of the steeple looked like someone peppered it with double .00 buckshot.

While Decker guarded the prisoner, Marsha got out and asked Chester what he wanted to do next. The two talked for a few minutes before coming up with a plan.

"I'll recite the wolf incantation and slip through the woods to check things out."

"Be careful and howl if you need me. "

As the gray canine trotted off into the darkness, Marsha

returned to the vehicle and fixed the prisoner a Jack Daniels cocktail laced with a dozen sleeping pills. She made a conscious effort to conceal her actions as she stirred the drink with a straw. Pretending to be kind, she climbed into the back seat and offered the warlock his drink. When he refused, she shouted at Decker, "Hold his nose while I pour this booze down his throat!"

Decker started laughing while tugging on the man's bearded chin, gouging his eyes and forcing his mouth open. "Bottoms up," he said as the teenager slowly trickled the plastic cup's contents into his mouth.

Sputtering and coughing, the redheaded man was compelled to swallow every drop because Marsha started threatening his mother again. When the cup was empty, the girl tossed it onto the floorboard, climbed back into the driver's seat and waited for the gray vampire to return.

When Watkins reported back, he advised his friends that the warehouse was heavily guarded and there appeared to be an elaborate security system installed around the perimeter. "I'm certain that no one saw me, but I'm not taking any chances. Let's get out of here, quick."

Unknown to Chester, the honorable vampire who rescued him from the morgue's crematorium the previous year was being held hostage inside of the secured compound.

Decker and Marsha loaded the unconscious warlock into the passenger's side of the Toyota and replaced the frayed shirt on his skinny torso. Working like a mastermind, Chester rigged the garden hose up to the exhaust pipe. When he slipped it into the trunk, he used the slotted tip of the tire-iron to punch a hole into the back seat so he could funnel the hose through the opening. When he finished his premeditated act, he turned the ignition on to make sure that he had a tight seal. As he watched the noxious smoke puff through the small opening, he told everyone it was time to go.

Having knowledge that vampires were immune to carbon

monoxide fumes, the old codger played chauffer and drove the sleeping man to his mother's house to ensure his death. The gray Marine hated fighting dirty, but he had no choice. He knew that the warlock's demise was a necessary part of ending this wicked ordeal.

Twenty-five minutes later when he pulled into the driveway, Chester noticed that the redheaded man's face was turning bright-red and his breathing was shallow and wheezy. When he climbed out, he pulled the limp man over into the driver's seat, removed the handcuffs and gently closed the door behind him.

Never looking back, he slowly walked across the lawn and waited for Marsha and Decker to circle around and pick him up. When they drove off, Watkins reassured his friends that the overdose and fumes would take their toll shortly. "If he makes it two more minutes, it'll be a miracle."

CHAPTER 18, THE BEGINNING OF THE END

The little fire that Chester and Marsha built in the middle of the barn's dirt floor broke the frigid chill that was in the air that evening. The sound of howling wind gusts whistled through the loft as the vampires waited for the water in the cauldron to start boiling. All of the special ingredients were systematically laid out on an old Army blanket beside the small pile of wood that the vampires had stacked in preparation for the genetic transformation spell.

Using a metal fireplace poker, Watkins raked the red coals underneath the pot and stoked the flames before adding another piece of red oak. A few minutes passed and a steamy mist began to rise from the charcoal-blackened object.

Scratching his gray, stubbly chin, Chester pointed to the edge of the pile and said, "Hand me that alligator's tongue."

"Do I have to touch it? That thing looks nasty."

Watkins shook his head from side to side and rolled his eyes. "Sometimes I forget that you're still a lady. Never mind, I'll fetch it myself."

When he tossed it into the pot, the splash of water made a sizzling sound when the waves hit the sides. Marsha smiled as she handed her friend the next item he was pointing to, which looked like a shriveled reptile skin.

"Do you really think this silly spell is going to work?"

The old man carefully unwrapped the cellophane that contained the coral snake shedding and meticulously sprinkled it into the center of the cauldron. "Yes, it has to."

When they were finished adding all of the strange ingredients, they stood in front of their brew and waited for it to simmer down. As the water began to evaporate, the smell of burning flesh mingled with hair reminded Chester of a fortified Japanese cave the Marines attacked with a flamethrower. The stench of singed bodies was something forever etched in his mind.

Invoking the spell, they began inhaling the repulsive fumes as the thick green, nasty cloud rose into the air and enveloped them. A few minutes passed and both of Decker's dogs began growling because of the suspicious odors coming from the barn.

After the cloud dissipated, Chester's eyes seemed to be playing tricks on him. As he tried to focus on Marsha, he noticed that she was changing colors. Shaking his head, he asked, "Are you all right?"

"No, I feel kind of dizzy."

Without warning, both of the immortals fainted, and fell to the ground. When Watkins regained consciousness, he was so dazed and confused that he believed he was on a Japanese island. When he noticed the young Oriental woman lying next to him, he was almost convinced. As his mind began to clear, he came to his senses and slowly began to reorient himself. A few minutes passed before Marsha slowly opened her eyes and began laughing when she saw the strange-looking red man glaring at her.

"What's so funny?"

"Nothing, chief."

"Why did you call me that?"

"Because you look like an American Indian."

Chester rubbed his forehead briskly and stood up. "It must have worked. You look like Tokyo Rose and I'm Chief Charging Buffalo. Why did we change so fast, we weren't suppose to?"

"I don't know, we followed the instructions, what now?"

The old man extended his hand and helped the young girl to her feet. "Let's go inside and show Decker."

As they were walking toward the house, both guard dogs stood at attention and cocked their heads from side to side. Their sensitive black snouts were working overtime sniffing the air trying to figure out why the vampires looked different yet smelled the same.

When they entered the kitchen, the husky man was astonished when he saw them. His friends looked totally different.

The only similarities he recognized were their corresponding ages. Watkins still looked old and the slender girl was still young. Other than that, he would have been clueless as to their identities.

As he poured a fresh cup of coffee, Decker's eyes seemed to lock on the mug as if transfixed in deep, soul-searching thoughts. "This might be the break that we're looking for."

"I know it is," Chester replied. "I've got a plan, but first I'm going to need some authentic-looking Indian clothes and a full headdress with turkey feathers."

"You've got to be kidding me."

"No, I'm dead serious."

Lewis told the gray vampire that he would have to drive to Houston to find a costume store because he was certain that no one in the general vicinity would carry anything that exotic. With one day to spare, everyone knew they didn't have any time to waste. Although he was skeptical, the big man trusted his friend's instincts and agreed to carry out his strange request.

The group spent the waning hours talking of strategies and what they would do if their plans failed. Although the situation seemed hopeless, there was still a glimmer of optimism because Beelzebub's Comet was now visible to the naked eye. It was approaching the constellation of Orion "The Hunter" just as the fortuneteller had predicted.

The following evening when the vampires returned to the kitchen to feed, Chester saw a complete Indian War Chief costume with matching headdress and a decorative set of bear tooth beads draped across one of the kitchen chairs. Lying on the table in front of the outfit was some grease paint and a small compact mirror. When he looked down, he noticed a pair of calf high leather moccasins neatly positioned between the table's legs.

"All I need now is a peace pipe packed full of wacky tobacco."

"Did the natives smoke marijuana back then?"

"Yes, Marsha, they did and it was perfectly legal and morally acceptable."

"If weed is suppose to mellow you out, why did the Indians scalp and kill so many people?"

"Maybe because the white man was stealing their cash crops," the gray vampire added, chuckling under his breath "I'm just kidding. They were infringing on their territorial boundaries and kept breaking treaties—all the time demanding more concessions. Eventually, the Native Americans decided they'd had enough and declared war against the Union."

"You should have been a history teacher, Chester. When I asked that question in school, the only answer I got was, 'Read your classroom book.' I did and after sifting through all of the bullshit, I still couldn't find the answer. Thanks."

"Sure, don't mention it."

A few minutes later, Lewis and his wife entered the kitchen and sat down at the table to join the vampires. A solemn atmosphere gripped the room that evening as the group rehashed their seemingly futile plans of attacking the warehouse and dispatching their foes.

The former Marine's mind began to slowly drift away as he remembered the night before the massive invasion of Tarawa. Some of the men in his unit suffered from insomnia, while others tossed and turned in their bunks with anxiety. The ship's berthing area reeked from the putrid smell of vomit. Some of the men instinctively knew they were doomed and in their minds they were already casualties of war. Mentally defeated, dozens of these men went through the physical motions of combat until meeting their fates.

Watkins looked at Marsha and the Decker family and wished there was another way to achieve their objectives. Who would live and who would die was now in the hands of a power much greater than anyone could comprehend.

When the vampires retired to the root cellar that morning, there was still a feeling of uneasiness that followed them to their graves. Regardless of their apprehensiveness, Watkins knew that nothing could interfere with their ability to sleep soundly. Being a vampire had its advantages, especially when all bodily functions shut down, including a restless mind. The only thing capable of responding to stimuli during daylight hours was a vampire's spirit and it was seldom aroused unless channeled into the vortex of another dimension.

Christmas Eve arrived with the twinkling of an eye for the immortals. When the breath of life reentered the old man's body, he punched a hole through the top of his makeshift coffin and violently yanked the plywood lid off, throwing it to the side.

With squeaky hinges, Marsha carefully opened up her box and sat straight up. "Hey, is everything all right?"

"It will be after tonight."

"Why did you bust your top like that?"

Watkins explained that when he regained consciousness, he envisioned the Russian's face right in front of him and reacted involuntarily. "I lashed out in anger and that was stupid."

The young girl knew that tonight would be an emotional experience for both of them. Success would only be achieved by playing it cool. Clutching the trooper's pistol and a hand-carved, ebony stake, the girl slid them under her dress. "I want you to know something Chester. Whatever happens tonight, I love you."

"I love you too Marsha— now let's get ready. I'm going inside to put on my Indian war paint. After that, our tribe is declaring war on the witches."

Marsha laughed as she climbed out of her coffin. Chester always had a way of adding some humor to a serious situation. "I'll be right behind you."

When the vampires reached the back porch, they saw Lewis looking through one of the telescopes and studying the comet's path. He was dressed in black fatigues and armed with an M-14 rifle, topped with a starlight scope. "This is what I carried in Vietnam and

I'll stake my life on it again."

Watkins understood his sentiment and nodded before going inside the house to change clothes. A few minutes later, he returned to the porch dressed in his Indian garb. Marsha and Lewis tried to contain their laughter, but to no avail. The gray warrior started acting silly by jumping around and pretending like he was performing a ritualistic rain dance.

"If our weapons don't kill them, they'll probably die laughing," Decker said. "I hope this plays out like Custer's last stand."

"Me too," replied the old vampire. "I like it when the Indians kick ass."

Their plan was simple. Decker's wife would drop the trio off a mile away at the abandoned church. From there the group would hike through the woods to the secluded warehouse. Linda would travel with their grandson to her sister-in-law's house in Dallas and wait for her husband's call signaling the final outcome. If the situation played out faster than planned, then she'd double-back and return to the rendezvous point.

Four hours later they arrived at their final staging area. As the married couple kissed goodbye, the woman's fears overtook her and she pleaded with everyone to get back into the truck and flee with her to safety.

"We've come too far to give up now," Chester said as he looked at the husky man embracing his wife. "If you want to turn around and go with your family, I won't hold it against you."

The big man glanced at his watch and the time read 1:29 a.m. With a determined look on his face, Lewis responded, "Let's get moving."

The group estimated that it would take them at least 30 minutes to make their stealthy trek to the metal building. When Linda drove away, Decker feared that it would be the last time he would ever see her again. "They might kill us, but let's take as many of them with us as we can."

"We'll put a hurting on their sorry asses, that's for sure."

With .40-caliber pistol in hand, the teen-aged vampire followed orders and stayed close behind the experienced veterans. Making certain to cover their backs as they picked their way through the thick underbrush, the young girl constantly looked behind them as a precaution. Thorns, briar patches and small saplings impeded their advance, but the determined allies slowly pushed forward maintaining a level of silence rivaling the most specialized recon forces known to exist.

2 a.m. signaled the beginning of the witching hour. It was Vladimir's final opportunity of the millennium to unleash the Cockatrice spirit from the depths of the abyss. A spiritual hybrid, part serpent and rooster, this wicked creature was renowned for its fearlessness. Historical legends recounted tales of these demons possessing the power to kill their victims by merely looking into their eyes. If the Russian succeeded in channeling the supernatural strength of this devil, all the inhabitants of the world would bow to him and become his slaves.

The witches took their rightful places in preparation of the Consuming Fire ritual of the Damned. The stage was set, everything was in place and nothing could stop Vladimir except an act of divine intervention. The emaciated vampires were helplessly subdued inside their electrical prisons and awaited their fate of being burned alive. Their sacrifices were the necessary key to opening the gates of the underworld and uniting hell with humanity.

Decker and the two vampires got on their bellies and low-crawled the final 20 yards to the edge of the wood-line to scope out the seemingly abandoned warehouse. Chester looked up at the clear night sky and took one final glance at the comet and the constellation of Orion "The Hunter." When he looked back at the warehouse, he noticed two sentries posted on either side of the building dressed in hooded robes and touting submachine guns.

Suddenly, the muffled noise of a raspy-sounding horn bellowed from inside the building signaling the beginning of the satanic séance. Screams and drum beats soon followed and during all of the commotion, Watkins instinctively knew it was time for him to make his move. "Stay here and cover me, I've got an idea."

Marsha objected as she pointed to the sky and whispered, "Look, the comet isn't where it's suppose to be, wait."

"Trust me, I'm going in."

The cagey Marine slowly crawled away from his two counterparts, stood up and circled approximately 50 yards away from their position. When he emerged from the edge of the forest, he started walking in the direction of the two warlocks who were taken by surprise. When the sentries saw him, they were momentarily confused and wondered why an American Indian with a feathered headdress was approaching their secluded site.

Watkins walked right up to them and pointed to the sky. "Me hear drums. Me come to summon Great Spirit."

With their weapon's muzzles trained on the strange-looking native, both warlocks looked back and forth at one other and wondered if he was an unannounced visitor Vladimir had invited. "State your business. Who are you and why are you here?"

"Me Chief Charging Buffalo. You stand on sacred Indian burial site. Ancestors angered. I must appease spirits with sacred dance before too late."

The superstitious men grew more confounded as the old bullshit artist laid it on as thick as he could. Chester pointed to the sky again and started bobbing and weaving from side to side. "Me dance, you meditate— ask spirits for forgiveness."

When the guards lowered their weapons, the cunning vampire spun around and snatched their rifles out of their hands, disarming both of them at the same time. The nimble immortal pulled a Bowie knife from the sheath tethered to his side and quickly subdued his opponents, slitting their throats and stabbing them in the chests. Unable to cry out for help, the gargling sentries faded into unconsciousness quickly expiring.

The former Marine glanced at the wood line and motioned for his comrades to hold their positions and stay hidden. With little regard for his own life, the determined warrior walked over to the front doors of the warehouse, opened them up and stepped inside. Memories of a liberated prisoner of war camp flashed through his mind as he saw the degradation of humanity in its basest form.

Count Marius and his two cabinet members looked like skeletons, barely clinging to life. Their beautiful suits were torn, dirty and hung from their bodies like loose fitting rags. Totally insane, the vampires screamed meaningless, unintelligible words when they saw the Indian Chief standing in the threshold.

Situated in a semi-circle with fiery torches in hand, the coven members stared in disbelief at the motley-dressed man who was blocking the doorway. Watkins noticed the two ritualistic sulfur circles that were drawn on the warehouse floor. His gut feeling told him that one of these objects was the gateway into the physical realm for the demonic entity that Vladimir was conjuring.

"Let the festivities begin," the Russian proclaimed with a boisterous voice. "Time is of the essence. Purify our sacrificial goats while I attend to our uninvited guest."

Three female witches broke ranks and sprinted to the cages that held the immortals captive. With torches in hand, the wicked servants lit them on fire and jumped backwards when they saw the flames totally engulf the screaming occupants. The enraptured coven began laughing as they watched the tortured men squirming in agony and the sparks of electricity shooting from the sizzling bars.

Chester looked through the maze of smoke and inside of the circle to the left he saw a hideous, 12-foot-tall creature beginning to materialize. Swaying back and forth like a mesmerizing genie, the hellish thing had a big-horned head, red feathers and a snake's tail. Like a phoenix rising from the ash pile of a bottomless sewer, the wicked manifestation emitted an odor that smelled worse than anything he'd ever smelled before.

The old Marine's attention was turned to the red-eyed vampire who was walking straight toward him through the billowing smoke. When their eyes met, the Russian knew that this was no ordinary Indian, but an immortal like himself.

"Who are you and why are you interrupting our unholy services?"

Chester capitalized on the element of surprise and Vladimir's inability to recognize him. "You speak with forked tongue. Ancestors say church service over!"

"We'll see who says what when the Cockatrice empowers me with all knowledge, wisdom and power."

Outnumbered and outflanked, Watkins knew that his only chance of surviving was to even the odds and shoot as many coven members as he possibly could before the Russian reached him. Drawing his trusty Colt pistol from the small of his back, he unleashed a barrage of seven rounds, killing three Satanists and wounding two others. In an attempt to save their own lives, two warlocks broke ranks and bailed out of the blackened windows of the warehouse and began running to safety. Chester heard a rapid secession of gunfire ringing out from the exterior of the building and he knew that Decker was picking the enemy off like shooting-gallery-ducks at a carnival. Before he could reload his pistol, the Russian moved with phenomenal speed, closing the gap and striking him with a devastating blow to the side of his temple. Shaking his gray head from the mind numbing punch, the toothless Indian crumpled and fell to the floor.

The spiritual bond between Marsha and the old man was so powerful that she immediately sensed he was in trouble. "Lewis, I'm going in. Watkins needs me. Bat of the night, take flight!"

In a flash, the tiny vampire-bat took off and flew to the top of the building to search for an entry point. When she reached the sunroof, she reversed the spell and yanked the covering from the window and threw it away from the building. Looking down, she saw Vladimir overpowering Chester and beating him to death. Two warlocks and the coven's leader Lucious stood poised with ropes in hand, awaiting their leaders commands to tie the struggling vampire up and place him on the sacrificial alter.

"All power is mine. I'm the apple of the Cockatrice's eye," the Russian boasted. "When you're finished securing him, drag his pathetic ass to the alter and we'll skin him alive."

"Yes master, we'll make him beg for his life."

Pulling the homemade ebony knife from her dress, Marsha jumped through the window feet first and landed on the wicked vampire's back. With all of her might, she thrusts the splintery object through the center of his shoulder blades with such force that it exited through the front of his chest.

Falling to his knees, the Russian turned his head sideways and let out a deafening shriek, "I summon the powers of hell. Help me my wicked master."

Still struggling, Watkins looked up through the hole in the roof and saw Beelzebub's Comet passing through the center of Orion "The Hunter." A serge of energy shot through his entire body revitalizing him with the strength he needed to overpower the warlocks who were binding his arms and legs. Kicking like an angry mule, the fierce looking warrior bucked the three assailants and pulled his Bowie knife from his sheath as they ran through the front doors to escape. Seconds later, he heard another succession of gunfire and he was certain that the men had met their fates.

When he looked at Marsha, he noticed that the affects of the racial spell had worn off and she looked like herself again. Barely clinging to life, the Russian began clawing at the cement floor and dragging himself towards the Cockatrice, crying out for it to enter his body. "I summon you, my beloved master. Empower me."

The young vampire turned to look in the direction of the evil spirit and Chester rushed to her side and placed his free hand over her eyes. "Don't look at his face, my child, he's the epitome of evil. He'll kill you."

Standing at the front door, Decker yelled and pointed at the dying vampire. "We have to sever the link, finish the bastard off."

The gray Marine ran to the prostrate Russian, grabbed a handful of blond hair and yanked his head back. "Remember me you arrogant idiot, checkmate again!"

With his razor sharp Bowie knife, Watkins severed the Russian's head from his body and threw it into the Cockatrice's circle. The vanquished remains disintegrated into a pile of dust and a strange humming sound filled the warehouse, causing everyone to cover their ears. The demonic spirit's pathway to the physical world was blocked, forcing the foul creature to return to his prison in the underworld.

On bended knees, with blood oozing from their wounds, the two gun-shot witches pleaded with their master to take them to hell and release them from their anguishing pain. "Save us, oh Lord."

Before vanishing, the evil creature started flapping his wings and cackling like a Rhode-Island red-rooster. With his forked tongue flicking through the tip of his curved beak, he admonished his adversaries and threatened to kill them in the future. When he was finished with his hollow curses, he turned and faced his pitiful servants and commanded them, "Look into my eyes."

As the manifestation began to slowly fade, Watkins shouted his own insults, "Kiss my ass, you pigeon-toed chicken-snake."

The combining stenches of charred bodies and burnt sulfur swirled through the air causing everyone to wince and spit. As the funky yellow cloud rose to the ceiling, the victorious trio looked at one another and couldn't believe they were still alive. Banished to the barren wastelands of the abyss for an undeterminable season, Watkins hoped that it would be a long time before anyone else tried to summon the Cockatrice again.

After regaining their composure, Chester pointed in the direction of the beseeching witches. Decker rushed to their bodies, knelt down and checked for a pulse. "They're both dead. Is there anyone else?"

"No," replied Watkins. "We got them all. There were 13, counting the Russian."

Thankful that they were still alive, Marsha wrapped her arms around the old vampire and kissed his bleeding forehead. "Last year, I killed you, but this year I saved your life. I hope this squares things up."

"You bet it does sweetheart, now let's cover our tracks and get out of here."

Chester took another look at all of the dead corpses, the three smoldering cages and wondered why fate had brought him to this specific place at this appointed time. Suddenly, another thought came to mind. He was forgetting something. The man walked over to Vladimir's ash pile, stooped down and sifted through the remains until he found the pentagram amulet that Marsha had described. To his surprise, he found something else— another metal object. When he dusted it off, he noticed that it was exactly like the ring he'd taken from the trooper's finger months ago.

At the last minute, the vigilantes decided to forgo burning up all of the evidence. Why not let the authorities discover everything. No skeptic on earth could deny these tangible facts.

Decker knew that the only way the authorities could link his involvement to the incident were the weapons he had in his possession. Dispose of the hardware and he couldn't be held accountable. His wife would provide the perfect alibi and no one would ever question them.

The warriors walked away, never looking back. Lewis called his wife on her cell-phone and asked her to return. "We're OK. Turn around and meet us back at the Methodist church."

When they reached the edge of the woods, Chester stuck his

right-hand into his front pocket, pulled out the lucky charms that the fortuneteller gave him and took another look. He remembered the encouraging words the old crone had spoken. These simple items were a reminder that he had favor with the good spirits. "*Maybe this kind of stuff really does work,*" he thought.

Little did the group know this was only the beginning of the end. Vladimir's followers were more widespread than anyone had ever imagined. Poised to wreak havoc and introduce as much evil into the world as they could, more sinister vampires were lurking in the shadows and awaiting their destiny of facing the toothless vampire.